LAWYERS IN THE FOG

By VINCE AIELLO

Published by SarEth Publishing House
SarEth Publishing House
Carlsbad, California

Cover Art Copyright © 2019 Sarah Rose Aiello
Armorer Advisor: Ethan P. Aiello

Audiobook Narrated by Beth Deehan (bethdehanhanvo.com)

First Edition: November 2019

ISBN 978-0-9883413-9-5

SPHN 18-12250731

SarEth Publishing House

*For **My Qualitas Insurance Family***
– For those that I love and those that have loved me.
For the rest, I hope that God will forgive them for their sins.

Don't ever tell me how strong a plaintiff's case is. That's their job and it implies our case is weak. If we go to trial, I will get a defense verdict. The plaintiff attorney knows it. And he's afraid. His fear is what we need to capitalize on. Regardless of the facts, his fear makes his case weak.

-Roger Legion
Lethal Equity

PROLOGUE

AMERICA'S FINEST CITY BUILDING, 24TH FLOOR
SAN DIEGO, CALIFORNIA
THE LAST THURSDAY IN JUNE

San Diego's reputation for beautiful weather is well-earned. The average daily temperature is 72 degrees. Most days, along the coast, there is no humidity. The sun beams down on the city like a proud parent, whose child is in the spotlight.

There is a weather condition that is rarely known to people who live outside of the county. Low altitude stratus clouds form over the cool Pacific Ocean to create a condition that spreads into the coastal area of San Diego County, bringing with it fog and drizzle. The fog generally burns off between mid-mornings to early afternoon. Residents refer to it as "May Gray," "June Gloom," "No Sky July," and "Fogust." The condition is notable only due to its antithesis to San Diego's bucolic beauty.

Roger Legion was spending this day on conference calls discussing topics from evidence presentation by opposing counsel for upcoming trials to legal maneuvers. He also reviewed strategy with the claims department personnel of various general liability insurance carriers that hired him.

Legion was the emperor of Legion & Associates, an insurance defense law firm located on the twenty-fourth and twenty-third floors of the 30-story America's Finest City Building.

All the lawyers were located on the twenty-fourth floor. There were no female lawyers at the firm. Roger would tell close friends that he had no use for female attorneys. He considered them to be window dressing that served no real purpose, but required high maintenance. The only non-lawyer on that floor was the receptionist, named Nina Larkin, who has worked at the firm for the past 9 years.

Legion and Associates also had some unique rules. All non-lawyers had to refer to the lawyers as "Mister" and the lawyer's last name. Swearing was not allowed. Words were weapons, as far as Legion was concerned. Overuse diminished their power. No one from the twenty-third floor was allowed on the twenty-fourth floor unless they had a reason. Violation of these rules would often result in expulsion from the firm.

Roger Legion was in his mid-60s, six feet tall, 190 pounds, on an athletic frame. If you did not know his age, a person would definitely suspect that he was twenty years younger. He had a full head of black hair, accented with gray throughout. Legion wore a dark, blue custom-made suit of fine Italian fabric, with an executive, white shirt, also custom-made, with a silk, blue and black striped tie.

In the office, he never removed his suitcoat. He considered the suitcoat to be part of a uniform that is worn into battle. And Roger Legion always wanted to be ready for battle.

His office was finely appointed with two walls of floor-to-ceiling mahogany and two walls of floor-to-ceiling glass. His desk was large, also made of mahogany, with burl inlay. It gave off a regal quality: denoting that it was protecting a man of power.

The items on his desk were few: a computer monitor, a landline telephone, his company cell phone, and a single yellow pad that was only on the desk when he needed it.

As his last call of the day was about to conclude, Roger noticed the time in the lower right corner of his computer monitor. It read "3:28 PM."

Legion continued to listen on the phone as he gazed out on his spectacular view of the Pacific Ocean. The marine layer that morning was so thick, it created zero visibility. It did not burn off until the early afternoon.

From outside, the peace and serenity of the air surrounding the twenty-fourth floor was, within a second, destroyed. A high-powered explosive device in Legion's office detonated, which shook the building, and could be heard on the ground. The explosion expelled two hellacious fireballs like rockets that smashed out the windows and continued for at least seventy feet out of the building. Burning debris rained down, including Legion's desk, which continued to burn after it smashed into the ground with ferocious intensity like a runaway train. Something else flew out the window that looked like a body.

Legion's office continued to burn. The sprinklers for his office had been turned off.

Approximately twenty-five miles away, in a palatial mansion, complete with a helicopter landing pad, in Rancho Santa Fe, California, the homeowner's cellular phone came to life. An elderly gentleman, in a wheelchair, rolled over to the phone and picked it up.

"It's done. Legion," a voice declared.

"Are you sure?" the old man inquired.

"He was on his landline when it went off."

"Get me some proof. What about the girl?"

"That's what I was calling you about. Where can I find *La Niña?*"

"She'll be here tonight," the old man said.

"Keep her there," the voice conveyed.

"All right. I'll put it in your good hands."

What the old man didn't know, beyond the topic that was being discussed, was that a much larger criminal plan was about to conclude.

Part 1

CHAPTER 1

SAN DIEGO SUPERIOR COURT
DEPARTMENT 62
6 WEEKS EARLIER

On this Thursday, Roger Legion sat at one of two defendant tables, along with one of the attorneys from his firm, Clinton Eversol. Clint was 6 feet 4 inches tall with a thin, solid frame and well coifed, brown hair. He had an infectious smile and could be often heard singing, or even dancing, in the hallways of the law firm. Clint's effeminate machinations would not seem to make him the kind of lawyer that you would find at Legion and Associates. Roger once saw him go head-to-head in a shouting match with a Judge and opposing counsel when he worked at another law firm. His actions left an impression with Legion.

At the other defendant table sat Linda Green. She was a newly-divorced, 32-year-old lawyer from the law firm of Rayne, Lindstrom, & Avici. As hard as she tried to wear finely-tailored, conservative clothing, her 120-pound body radiated sexuality. Everyone in the courtroom noticed, except Clint.

The lawyers had been advised that a verdict was reached in a case that they had tried over the past three days. The case involved a thief, who while trying to break into a second floor window of a machine shop, fell to the ground and landed on a broken pipe that pierced his spine. The accident left the thief paralyzed from the waist down.

Legion was defending the owner of the building and Linda Green was defending the security company that was hired to patrol the area around the building.

The nervousness of Linda and Clint was noticeable. Linda fidgeted in her chair, while Clint lightly chewed on his fingernails.

The bark of the bailiff caused everyone in the courtroom to re-focus.

"All rise," the bailiff commanded. "Department 62 of the San Diego Superior Court is now in session. Judge Eduardo Pedrero presiding."

Judge Pedrero moved swiftly from a door on the right side of the courtroom bench. He rapidly ascended the two stairs and took his seat. Judge Pedrero was in his mid-60s with a regal look, a chiseled chin, black hair with just a slight touch of gray, and a piercing appearance of seriousness on his face.

"Bring the jury in," he told the bailiff.

In less than sixty seconds, the jury entered and took their places in the jury box.

"You may be seated," the Judge advised the crowd, including the lawyers. As they did, the plaintiff attorney entered and the Judge sent him a darting glance.

"I'm sorry, your Honor," he replied in a somewhat meek manner.

Judge Pedrero turned his attention to the jury.

"Ladies and Gentlemen of the jury, have you reached a verdict?"

An elderly, African-American man in the second row of the jury box stood.

"We have, your Honor."

"Will you please give the verdict form to the bailiff."

The bailiff walked over to the jury foreman and was handed several pieces of paper. The bailiff provided them directly to Judge Pedrero. The Judge raised his tortoise shell reading glasses to his face and perused the pages. He then handed them to the Court Clerk, a 58-year-old, heavyset woman with gray hair.

"Would you please read the verdict," he directed the clerk. "Will the plaintiff and defense lawyers please rise."

The three defense lawyers and plaintiff lawyer obeyed the command.

"In the matter of *Nastasi versus Hemsworth Property Holdings, LLP and Swordpoint Security, Inc.*, San Diego Superior Court number 27-2016-00018067-CU-RC-CTL, we, the jury, find as follows:"

"Number one – Were any of the following parties found negligent? Plaintiff, Howard Nastasi – Yes; Defendant, Hemsworth Property Holdings, LLC – No; Defendant, Swordpoint Security, Inc. – Yes."

Legion had taught his lawyers to never react to a verdict. They should remain stoic and let the loss sink in for their adversaries, like a cancer that grows.

Linda was becoming so nervous that she started to tremble and felt like she was about to pass out. Legion moved over to her and took her arm. He then bent over to speak into her ear.

"Don't worry about anything," he told her in a tranquil tone. "It'll be all right."

"Can you stand with me for a second?" she asked.

Legion nodded affirmatively.

"Can you hand me my water?"

Legion picked her cup up off the table and handed it to her. Her shaky hand raised it to her mouth and she took a slight sip. Legion helped her return the cup to the table.

Before the clerk finished reading the verdict, the audience in the courtroom was told that the jury had awarded the plaintiff $9 million in damages. Linda's client was responsible for 49% of the damages or approximately $4.4 million. The plaintiff was found to be responsible for 51% of his injuries.

Legion's history of never losing a case that he took to trial remained intact.

Legion could see from Linda's eyes that were reddening, that she was fighting back tears. Legion quickly spoke into her ear.

"Make a motion to poll the jury. We'll join. Now!"

"Your Honor, I would like to make a motion to poll the jury."

"We would like to join that motion," Legion added.

Legion pulled Clint over and spoke to both of them.

"See if you can talk to some of the Jurors. Find out how they arrived at the percentages and the dollar amount."

Both attorneys nodded in agreement.

"Take her to lunch," Legion told Clinton. "And make sure she gets back to her office. Escort her right to the door."

Legion left the courtroom, not relishing his victory, but feeling like he had just euthanized a dog that was in good health.

CHAPTER 2

Situated less than two miles from the courthouse and the America's Finest City building was the Little Italy section of the city. It was situated on forty-eight square blocks and it was the largest "Little Italy" settlement in the United States. It has an abundant quantity of restaurants, patio cafés, art galleries and shops.

The main street running through Little Italy is India Street. Just off India Street, on West Grape Street sat the Bagheria Bedda restaurant. The title meant "Beautiful Bagheria" in the Sicilian dialect. Bagheria is a small town located adjacent to the City of Palermo in Sicily. Since the end of the nineteenth century, it has developed a reputation for producing some of the most dangerous men to ever walk the planet.

The Bagheria Bedda was a very non-assuming restaurant with black and white checkered tile on the floor, linen covered tables, and large photos of Sicily decorated the walls.

In the back of the restaurant was an office where basically only two topics were discussed: food and crime. Less of the former and more of the latter.

The restaurant was owned by Vincenzo Fiorito. He claimed to be a "simple businessman." But in reality, he was the boss of the

San Diego crime underworld, who went by the moniker "Jimmy Flowers." Hardly anyone in the County of San Diego knew that name and that was exactly how Jimmy wanted it to be.

He was in his early 60s, full head of gray hair, 235 pounds with a barrel chest. He wore a long-sleeve, blue Polo shirt that was buttoned to the neck and black, Haggar slacks.

Jimmy's presence was imposing. A glance from him could instill blood-curdling fear. But his smile would provide a welcoming, protective feeling.

He admired education. Jimmy had a Master's in Business Administration from Stanford University and within his organization, he promoted any of his men who pursued an education.

Outside of Jimmy's office, a sentry was always posted. On this day, it was Domenic, a former San Diego State University defensive lineman, who was responsible for announcing any visitors to Jimmy and searching them for weapons.

Jimmy was perusing a Staples catalog, researching the costs for office chairs, when there was a knock at the door.

"Come on in," Jimmy answered.

The door opened slightly; enough for Domenic to stick his head into the office.

"Raul Verdugo is here."

"Let him in," Jim told him. "Don't frisk him."

Jimmy stood from his chair as Raul entered the office.

Raul was 43 years old, 6 feet 2 inches tall, and 180 pounds of solid muscle. He wore a black suit, with a black shirt and black tie. His physique appeared to be forged out of steel. His thick, black hair was cut tight on one side and the hair on the top of his head was gelled back and slightly to the other side. Raul had a goatee that perfectly accented his face. His brown eyes had a mesmerizing quality that hypnotized women.

"Raul, *mi amigo* (my friend)," Jimmy articulated as the two met with big smiles and a strong handshake.

"Jimmy, how are you?" Raul asked with a slight Spanish accent.

"*Muy bien* (Very good)," Jimmy answered.

"I only wish my Italian was as good as your Spanish," Raul confessed with a radiant smile.

"We'll stick to English. Sit," Jimmy motioned. "How's work?"

"Busy. Not crazy busy," Raul advised. "But when you call, I drop everything. Your assignments are always quite interesting and challenging."

"I need you for a collection matter," Jimmy imparted with a sinister chagrin. "A pharmacist over in La Jolla, Howard Greenstern, owes me $375,000. I've given him two extensions and now he's ducking me."

"You know where he's located?

"There's a real tall condo on Fay Avenue in downtown La Jolla. He's on the fifth floor. He knows that I'm gonna send somebody. He's got two guys watching the street and the parking garage. He's got two other guys sitting in the vestibule of his condo."

"If he's got the cash, you want me to let him go?" Raul inquired.

"Use your best judgment. I just want you to . . . *finesse* it."

"Understood." Raul nodded affirmatively as he rose from his chair.

"You want something to eat?" Jimmy asked.

"Maybe next time," Raul told him. They again shared a firm handshake.

Jimmy escorted Raul to the front door of the restaurant and they said their goodbyes.

Jimmy considered Raul to be the best *sicario*, or hitman, that he had ever met. Raul's cold-bloodedness, ruthlessness, ability to strategize, and shear strength made him a tsunami of death.

But when you're the best, there is always someone seeking to knock you off the top of the mountain.

CHAPTER 3

Within San Diego County lies the wealthy enclave of Rancho Santa Fe. Known for its huge palatial homes with large lots, this seven square mile community is also well known for its privacy and secrecy.

Off a long stretch of Las Colinas Road, a private driveway led visitors to a gated entrance of a typical Rancho Santa Fe home. It was built in the style of a Spanish colonial home, less than 10 years old, 12,000 square feet of living space, with a movie theater, pool, and casita or guest house. One additional item, which most homes in Rancho Santa Fe did not have, was a helicopter landing pad.

Shortly after 2:00 pm this day, a dark, graphite, late-model BMW 750 drove up to the call-box at the end of the driveway. After the driver pushed the call button, a voice responded.

"Drive up to the house and enter the roundabout to the front door. Please follow the arrows on the driveway. Your car will be met by a valet."

The gate slowly slid to the right and the car was allowed entry into the complex. It traveled nearly one-half mile down the driveway and entered the roundabout that circled right to the front door of the estate. A neatly dressed young man, with a red vest and white gloves, stepped forward and opened the driver's car door.

The leg of a petite, young girl stepped out, followed by the rest of her. She walked directly into the entrance of the home. It was obvious that she had been there before.

Her name was Annabella Romero. She appeared to be in her late 20s to early 30s, but her age would remain as much a mystery as the girl herself. Her body lines and confident strut echoed the clothing runways of Europe. She had brown hair that was lightly tinted with blonde highlights. She was five feet tall and weighed barely 100 pounds. When she entered a room, all eyes gazed upon her. Her beauty was mesmerizing.

This day she wore a blue, Leith ruched long sleeve dress and black, Vince Camuto Kochelda over-the-knee boots. Her outfit was accessorized with a black, Coach Callie Foldover Chain Clutch with deco quilting.

Annabella was met by the home's butler, named Farmington.

"Good day, Miss," he greeted her with a British accent and full tuxedo. He also wore white gloves. "Please follow me to the living room. The Judge will be out shortly."

After a short walk, down a well-lit hallway, they arrived at the living room. It had a twenty foot high ceiling and the walls were adorned with large paintings of bucolic pastoral areas that included the ocean, wooded pastures, and the desert. They were all to serve as reminders of how beautiful San Diego once was before greed poisoned the well.

Annabella sat in a Sofia black, leather armchair. She had not been in the chair for a minute when the sounds of whirling helicopter blades drowned out any other potential sounds. Annabella stood and walked over to one of the windows that looked out onto the northern section of the property.

A Bell 525 Relentless helicopter was landing and Annabella watched it touch down. A side door of the copter opened and off stepped its lone passenger. He nonchalantly strolled toward the house.

His name was Jack Prickett. He was not the owner of the helicopter, but he was summoned, as was Annabella, to a meeting at the home of its owner.

Jack was 43 years old, 6 feet tall, and weighed 175 pounds, with little to no body fat. He wore blue jeans and a gray t-shirt under a yellow, long-sleeve t-shirt. He had short brown hair that had a messy textured top.

His face looked as if he had just come from a barroom fight, but if he did, rest assured, the other combatant or combatants, were either dead or severely injured.

Annabella's eyes followed him as he entered the building. Farmington, the butler, met him and escorted him to the living room. Jack entered the room and surveyed it to make sure no one else was in the room, other than Annabella. She turned and met his eyes.

"Hello," she said rather sheepishly.

"Hey," Jack responded. He had no use for small talk. There was no exchange of handshakes. Jack did not like to be touched.

Jack and Annabella were 'Sicarios' of the highest caliber. A hitman and hitwoman, who had developed reputations for efficiently ending a life for a fee.

In the *sicario* community, Annabella was referred to a "*La Niña*" or 'little girl' in Spanish. Jack's moniker was 'Clipper,' a reference to his beloved New York Yankees, whose logo was tattooed on his right inner forearm.

Jack and Annabella continued to look around the room and out the window at the helicopter to avoid looking at each other. The silence of the room was broken when a single word was uttered by their host who suddenly appeared in the doorway.

"Welcome."

CHAPTER 4

When the elevator doors to the twenty-fourth floor opened, Roger Legion expected to see Nina, the receptionist, sitting at her assigned station in the lobby. Instead, there was a small card on the counter that said "Be Right Back!"

Legion proceeded down the western corridor of the floor and, at approximately the half way point to his office, he heard his name summoned.

"Mr. Legion," Nina called out. She wore an Eliza J, bell sleeve, floral-print dress with black, Tory Burch, Liana ballet flat shoes. Her wavy, brunette hair perfectly accented her china doll complexion.

She slowed her approach as she reached him.

"How did the verdict go?" she wondered.

"Defense," he answered with a smile.

"Congratulations! You have two 'urgent' phone messages regarding the same new case." Legion stopped and she handed him two small pieces of paper from a phone message pad.

"Thank you, Nina," Legion said as he turned to return to his office.

"Mr. Legion." Her voice again stopped him and he turned back to her. "Can I talk to you for a minute?"

"Sure." He looked at her as if he was willing to discuss the matter in the hallway.

"Can we talk in your office?"

"Okay," Legion acknowledged. Nina followed him and closed the door behind her.

Legion rarely closed his door, so he was slightly surprised at her action.

"I just wanted to tell you," she began, "that the reason I keep taking bathroom breaks is because," she paused for a moment and her cheeks reddened, "I'm pregnant."

A wide smile enveloped Legion's face.

"Congratulations, sweetheart!"

Nina's eyes were starting to well up with tears.

"Is it okay to hug?" she timidly asked.

"Absolutely."

They came together for a tight hug. Legion had bent forward to accommodate her 5 foot 1 inch frame. He kissed her on the cheek and she reciprocated. They both stood back and Nina began wiping her eyes.

"I thought you might be mad," she conveyed.

"Why?"

"I don't know. I know other girls who get treated like crap when they tell their bosses they're pregnant."

"Not at all. In fact, this is what we're going to do. We're going to take one of the empty offices and assign it to you. Let's order a name plaque for you to put outside the door. We'll also make sure there is a comfortable couch in there for you to lie down. I do not want you walking the stairs at all. You take the elevator. If you need to go anywhere during the day, like a medical appointment or something for your dog, someone from here will bring you. All right?"

"Yeah. Oh, thank you Mr. Legion."

They exchanged a much quicker hug and Nina turned to exit. Before leaving, she had one last inquiry.

"Do you want me to get anyone on the phone?"

Legion glanced at the two phone messages.

"No. I'll take care of it."

Nina turned and left.

Legion looked out the window of his office and gazed at the fog-shrouded Pacific Ocean without focus. Despite Nina's good news, Legion had a sense of dread. He felt like an earthquake, or something of a massively destructive nature, was about to decimate him and his law firm.

CHAPTER 5

Legion lawyer, Clinton Eversol, escorted attorney, Linda Green, to the lobby of her building, located three blocks from the courthouse. Linda's law firm, Rayne, Lindstrom & Avici, was situated on the seventh floor of the building.

She made a beeline directly to the elevators that serviced the first through twelfth floors. While waiting for an elevator car to arrive, a voice called out.

"Excuse me, Miss."

Linda turned and saw that the voice belonged to a well-dressed, African-American woman in her early 40s. The woman approached.

"Sorry to bother you. I know you're busy. My name is Leticia Harrison. I'm an attorney in the Mission Valley area. But I just wanted to say that I saw you, in action, in the courtroom over the past several days. I was very impressed."

"Well, I'm not impressed," Linda told her. "Did you hear what the verdict was?"

"I did. It wasn't representative of your talent. I run my own law firm, dealing with wrongful termination and workers comp issues. I would like to talk with you regarding potential employment with my firm." Leticia handed Linda a card while she spoke.

"Thank you, but I have a job," Linda told her.

"I don't believe that you will by the end of the day. I'm sorry. Please call me."

One of the elevator doors opened and Linda advanced toward it. She entered the elevator and smiled at Leticia. The elevator doors closed.

The acid in Linda's stomach began to rise. She wondered what awaited her on the seventh floor. She looked at Leticia's card and wondered if she was a guardian angel or a prophet of doom.

CHAPTER 6

On the fifth floor of the Cielo condominiums, located on Fay Avenue in downtown La Jolla, pharmacist, Howard Greenstern, slept in peace, knowing that four executive security officers were guarding him. He also kept a Smith & Wesson .44 caliber handgun with a 4.25-inch barrel on his nightstand, just in case it was needed.

La Jolla is a trendy and affluent area of San Diego, filled with wealthy and prosperous individuals. There were also those 'posers,' who were trying to achieve that status.

Howard Greenstern ran a modest drug store in the Hillcrest area of San Diego. He had grown tired of the daily grind and when he was approached to use his drug store for an elaborate method of illegal drug transfer, he jumped at the opportunity. The profits were great and the risks appeared to be minimal.

The architect of this criminal plan was Jimmy Flowers. Greenstern would receive a guaranteed monthly amount and a percentage of the drugs that were sold. The remaining percentage was paid to Jimmy.

Now, Greenstern owed money to Jimmy and Jimmy sent Raul Verdugo to collect.

All the windows in the condominium were covered by drapes. Slivers of light came into the room. It was just enough to see the outline of objects contained within it.

Howard opened his eyes slightly to see if there was any unnatural movement taking place in the room. He had an uneasiness, which was perhaps just paranoia, about any noise that he heard.

He reached his hand over to retrieve his handgun. Howard scrambled his hand around, but it was not there. He then grabbed his glasses from the night stand and turned on the light, which sat upon it.

Howard jerked his head to look at a chair that was situated across from the foot of his bed. There sat Raul, holding the .44 caliber handgun.

"What do you want?" Howard asked with a rushed voice.

He then sat up and pushed back his white hair on one side of his head. Howard looked much older than his fifty-seven years.

"You know," Raul began, "I like this chair. Where did you get it?"

The chair was a graphite gray armchair. Howard thought for a moment.

"Pier One."

"You know, I've never been there before. I'm going to check it out. How's the pharmacy business?"

"It's tough. The government is on your back, the insurance companies are on your back, and the drug companies are on your back."

Raul shook his head in contemplation.

"What do you want?" Howard begrudgingly demanded.

"Do you know what the greatest challenge is in my profession?

Howard nodded his head negatively.

"Sound suppression. Your gun, even with a suppressor, you know, a silencer, is still loud. There are too many points of sound evacuation on the gun. That's why I like knives with surgical steel. Germany makes the best ones."

"Listen," Howard told him, "you might have gotten in here, but you're not going to get out."

"Oh, do you mean your security people? No need to worry about them anymore. As far as anyone knows, they have disappeared off the face of the earth. Without a trace. Quiet, with minimal blood loss. My people came in, picked up the bodies and cleaned up the blood. No footprint. That's what I specialize in – no footprint.

"I come from a mechanical engineering background," Raul continued, "automation, robotics. I conduct my business using three basic tenets – precision, accuracy, and efficiency."

Howard began to a show a light trace of perspiration on his upper lip.

"The guy who sent me," Raul advised, "says that you owe him $375,000. I've come to collect."

"Jimmy Flowers sent you?"

"Do you owe anybody else $375,000?"

"No," Howard responded sheepishly.

"If you have the cash here, I'll take it and walk out. If we have to go get it, all bets are off."

Howard began to sit up to get off the bed, when Raul stopped him.

"No, no, no," Raul said as he advanced toward him. "You stay there. Keep your hands above the covers. Tell me where it is."

"In the closet, on the left side, there are a couple of suitcases. The brown Samsonite has three hundred grand in it."

Raul went and retrieved the suitcase. He set it on the floor and opened it. It was filled with neatly banded stacks of one-hundred dollar bills.

"Where's the rest of it?" Raul requested seriously.

"I need more time."

"How about I open the rest of those suitcases?"

"Listen, I need that money."

"Which one should I grab?"

Howard realized it was time to pay what was owed.

"The yellow suitcase has a hundred grand in it."

Raul retrieved the smaller yellow suitcase and opened it. It also contained neatly banded stacks of one-hundred dollar bills. He closed the suitcase.

Raul then removed Howard's .44 caliber revolver from behind his back and opened the cylinder on the gun. He pointed the gun to the ceiling and pushed the ejector rod on the cylinder. The six bullets in the gun dropped to the floor. He then placed the gun back on the nightstand.

"I hope that we don't have to meet again."

"Wait," Howard exclaimed with urgency, "I only owe $375,000 and there's $400,000 in the suitcases."

"We'll call it a late fee," Raul responded with a smile. "Stay in the bed for at least ten minutes after I leave. Don't do anything stupid or I'll come back. Have a good day, Mr. Pharmacist."

Raul started to leave, but then pivoted and walked up to the side of the bed.

"Listen, I gave you a break today. Don't make me come back here. Because the next time, will be the last time."

As he spoke the last sentence, Raul pointed his index and middle fingers of his right hand toward his eyes then toward

Howard.   Raul left the condo as quietly as he had entered and disappeared into the night.

CHAPTER 7

When Annabella Romero and Jack Prickett heard the word, "Welcome," they both turned simultaneously to focus on the entrance to the room. Sitting in a wheelchair, was a bald-headed, 72-year-old man. He was enthused to see them both and a wide smile filled his face. He wore a long-sleeve, white, Ralph Lauren Polo shirt. Around his neck was tied the arms of a black sweater.

His name was Caesar Cargyle. He was a retired San Diego County Superior Court Judge. He spent twenty-two years on the bench and the last 8 years in a secluded retirement. He was a man of exceptional mental acumen and gravitated to the darker recesses of the law, where crime could be successfully conducted by those who knew how to bypass it.

"Hello, Annabella; hello, Jack. Don't move. I want to show you something."

Annabella and Jack froze in place and looked at him quizzically. He set the brake on the wheelchair and slowly rose from it. He gained his shaky composure and methodically took a step toward Annabella and Jack. He then took another.

His actions were met with smiles and applause. He motioned Annabella and Jack to come to him.

"Help me back to the chair," he requested. Annabella and Jack each took one of his arms and escorted him back to his chair. He unlocked the brake and wheeled into the living room.

"Very impressive, Caesar," Jack stated.

"It's amazing, your Honor," Annabella added.

"I've spent over forty years in this chair. What you just witnessed is a testament to the power of the mind." He took his right index finger and pointed to his temple. "Set a goal. If you can imagine it, you can achieve it."

Annabella and Jack allowed a moment for his pearl of wisdom to set in.

"Thanks for the chopper ride, Caesar," Jack said.

"Any time. I can't stand traffic. That's what put me in this chair. I have great empathy for anyone stuck in it or fighting it."

The butler, Farmington, appeared in the doorway.

"Would anyone like a beverage?"

All eyes turned to Annabella.

"Sparkling water," she answered.

"I have Pellegrino, Miss."

"That's fine."

"Sir?" He now posed his inquiry to Jack.

"Gin and ginger ale."

"We have Beefeater and Tanqueray gins."

"I don't care. Surprise me."

Farmington turned his final inquiry to Judge Cargyle.

"Would you like a drink, sir?"

"My usual. A martini without the olives."

Farmington recessed out of the room.

"Take a seat." They both complied. They sat at each end of the same couch. The Judge backed carefully to the end of the coffee table that sat before them. "I wanted to go over a few things before lunch."

He gazed upon Annabella.

"Annabella. I heard about your successes in Costa Rica, El Salvador and Peru. Very impressive. Your payments for the various assignments have been wired to your account in the Seychelles. Feel free to verify receipt."

The Republic of Seychelles is a small group of islands off the coast of East Africa. It has developed a reputation for harboring vast amounts of illegal gains for individuals wishing to avoid taxes.

"Thank you, your honor," she told him.

"Three in one week? For real?" Jack exclaimed in astonishment. "Girl, you got somethin' going on."

Jack's comment brought a smile to both Annabella and Judge Cargyle.

"Now Jack, what's the status of the Gibson assignment?"

"It should be done by tomorrow night. That guy's got a lot of security. It's like trying to kill the President. I've got him setup to be poisoned at one of his speaking events. The problem is that you don't want it 'loud.' I want to ask you: If something goes south with my plan, can I just put a bullet in him?"

The Judge thought about it for a moment.

"Get it done."

"Annabella, my dear. I want to ask you a favor. I mentor a group of female attorneys, here at the house, and I help them to navigate the waters of the male-dominated legal community. I would like you to come and speak to them tomorrow night. I would like you to share your story of success."

"You want me to tell them what I do for a living?" she asked astonishingly.

"We'll discuss that a little later in the afternoon. Don't worry about anything. But I ask that you cover up any tattoos you may have. A tattoo is a brand. A symbol of ownership. A symbol of enslavement."

Annabella had extensive tattoos that ran up one of her arms, across her back and down the other arm.

"My tattoos tell a story: a story of those who have harmed me and those that I have harmed," Annabella countered.

"I don't want anyone to form an opinion about you before you open your mouth. Save the story of your tattoos for your boyfriend or husband. For me, just please cover them."

Annabella nodded without emotion.

"Now, for both of you. I have a couple of potential assignments that may be best handled by the both of you. I envision a synergy effect."

"The rate better be doubled," Jack spoke up. "I don't care how good she is, I'm not cutting my rate."

"Money is the last thing you have to worry about, Jack. So, no objections to working together?"

Both shook their head negatively.

"One final thing: Do either of you know a *sicario* named Raul Verdugo?"

"The Executioner?" Jack chimed. "I've heard of him. Never met him."

Annabella was deep in thought.

"Annabella?" the Judge inquired.

"I know him," she answered.

"No emotional connection?" the Judge wondered.

Annabella paused for a moment.

"No."

It pained Annabella to lie to the Judge. But what pained her more was the thought of seeing Raul again.

CHAPTER 8

The elevator arrived at the seventh floor, its doors opened and Linda Green stepped out. She could almost sense the hostility toward her that had charged the atmosphere on the seventh floor. She kept moving forward in spite of her dread. Linda walked down the long corridor to the law office of Rayne, Lindstrom, & Avici.

Linda had worked there for eight years under the supervision of Montgomery Lindstrom, the named partner. For the last four years, she was the top billing associate attorney in the firm.

As soon as she opened the door, the receptionist looked at her in disgust.

"Monty wants to see you – now!" she ordered.

Linda gave her a "go to hell" look, then proceeded to her own office to set down her purse and deposition bag that contained notes that she had taken at trial.

She proceeded directly to Monty's office. There was no point in delaying the inevitable.

When she reached the doorway to Monty's office, Linda could see that he was on the phone. He waved her in and, based on his conversation over the phone, he seemed to be in a jovial mood.

Monty was forty-two years old, 5 feet 10 inches tall. He had a full head of brown hair, with strands of gray within it. He wore a black, 2-button suit, but he was not wearing the suitcoat. He wore a fitted, blue, bold stripe dress shirt (no cufflinks) and a red tie with gray dots on it.

As he returned the handset of the phone to its cradle, his visage molted into severe indignation. He slowly looked up and stared at Linda.

"What was that today?" he asked calmly.

"I know it was bad. We can appeal it."

"No, _we_ can't do anything. Oneonta Mutual called and said they want _you_ pulled off all their files. If Oneonta Mutual wants you out, what do you think that I should do?" he sneered.

Linda looked at him.

"Did he make a deal with you?" Monty asked.

"Who?"

"Legion?"

"No. The only thing we agreed to is that we would not point fingers at each other in regard to liability."

"Are you kidding me?" Monty responded incredulously. "That's a parlor trick that Legion plays. As long as he doesn't have to worry about a co-defendant pointing a finger at him, he can point all of his guns at the plaintiff. And you see the results. I can't believe how stupid you are."

"Well, if I was given a little supervision, maybe I would have known that. Everything around here is later, later, later."

Monty approached her and it looked like he was going to strike her. He stopped.

"The reason I gave you that case is because it was an easy win. It was like a softball game against a school for the blind. You're too nice. Legion took advantage of it. And now my law firm is going to pay the price for it. I should have never let you see the inside of a courtroom. You are a paper pusher, not a lawyer. You are worthless. You fucking idiot."

Linda thought about crying, but held back.

"Now, I've got one piece of advice for you," Monty declared. "Most of your files were Oneonta Mutual, so I don't believe that you have anything to bill. I suggest that you go back to your office and prepare a resignation letter. It's easier to explain to your next employer, whoever that poor bastard may be."

"Everybody knows what an asshole you are," Linda declared. "I spent years defending you. But I always knew they were right."

As she finished her sentence, one of the paralegals passed by the office door.

"RUDY," Monty yelled.

The paralegal returned to the doorway.

"Escort her back to her office," Monty told the paralegal. "Let her get her things and then escort her out of the building. Get her parking pass. Make sure she doesn't steal anything."

Linda and Monty gave each other a deadly gaze.

"GET OUT OF MY SIGHT!" Monty's voice reverberated down the hallway.

Linda did an about-face and walked the hallway of her former employer for the last time.

CHAPTER 9

Roger Legion sat at his desk and reviewed the two phone messages, given to him by the receptionist, Nina, and deemed 'Urgent.'

One of the messages was from an attorney, named Tom Tobin, who Legion knew and considered him to be competent in the courtroom.

The other message was from a man named Alejandro Lopez, who identified himself as the General Counsel for Tecton Insurance.

Both messages referenced the _Zantoff Transportation v. Tecton Insurance_ case. It did not sound familiar to Legion, but he decided to first speak to the insurance company employee.

Legion dialed the number and it was answered on the second ring.

"Alejandro Lopez," he answered.

"Mr. Lopez, this is Roger Legion. I'm returning your call."

"Thank you for calling, Mr. Legion. I got your name from Tom Tobin. Tecton Insurance is in desperate need of a premier insurance defense attorney. It involves a bad faith case that has the potential to destroy our company. I was wondering if you may be willing to meet with us and discuss it."

"Who is the plaintiff attorney?"

"An out-of-town lawyer from Houston, named Ricky Ray Ransom."

"What's the trial date?"

"I don't have the exact date with me, but it's in about six weeks."

"Who is your defense counsel now?"

"Tom Tobin," Lopez told him. Legion now knew the purpose of the other 'Urgent" call.

"He's a good lawyer," Legion advised.

"I agree. But I think he just became overwhelmed. He's the one who recommended you to us."

Legion contemplated the information.

"When do you want to get together?" Legion asked.

"A mediation is set for this Tuesday at 9:00 at Centext Legal Services. The plaintiff has demanded that all employees of the insurance company that have the ability to bind the company in a financial settlement will attend. He specifically wants the CEO, COO (Chief Operating Officer), and CFO (Chief Financial Officer) to attend."

"Let's get together on Monday," Legion told him. He quickly perused his electronic calendar. "Let's do it at my office. Ten o'clock."

"Thank you Mr. Legion." Lopez replied, sounding relieved.

"I haven't agreed to anything yet."

"I know. I'll hope for the best."

"Take care," Legion told him and ended the call.

Legion looked out the window and gazed without focus. What was it about the *Zantoff* case that would cause Tom Tobin to dump it?

CHAPTER 10

Raul Verdugo was again called into Jimmy Flowers office, located in the back of the Bagheria Bedda restaurant. Raul was again dressed in a black suit, but this time he had a white shirt with a black tie that had a gray pinstripe. Jimmy wore a white, long sleeve button-down shirt with the top button opened.

As Raul entered, Jimmy sat at the desk and pointed to the chair across from him with his opened hand. Raul obliged.

"I have something that I need you to pick up," Jimmy advised as he commenced the conversation.

"Where?" Raul inquired.

"You know the house up in Oceanside?"

"I've been by there, I've never been inside."

"In the garage, there's a big gun safe. We've got some guys coming from out-of-town and we are going to swap our cash for their drugs. It's going to be a large suitcase, probably will have wheels at one end."

"All right," Raul replied.

"We will call you to tell you where it goes after you pick it up. The house is wired with sensors for video, audio, and movement. We will also give you an earbud. If you need us, just talk, we can hear you. Any questions, so far?" Jimmy inquired.

"No."

"Just tell us when you are at the front door. Look through the window on the front door and you'll see a keypad straight ahead with a flashing red light. When it turns green, we'll unlock the front door and you can enter. When you get to the garage, we'll tell you the combination. There is also a keypad on the door of the safe, so we will give you that too. The final step is a biometric feature. We will take your thumbprint over here and you place it on the thumb pad over there. Then, the safe should open."

"Heavy duty security. No?" Raul wondered.

"Sorry, it has to be this way. Any questions?"

"What about the neighbors?"

"It's a cul-de-sac. I own all the houses. They're identical. Anything else?"

Raul shook his head negatively.

"All right," Jimmy uttered as he rose from his chair. "See Mickey out here for the thumbprint."

As Raul rose, Jimmy had a final statement.

"Thank you, my friend."

"*De nada* (You are welcome)."

CHAPTER 11

At the home of Judge Cargyle, Annabella Romero and Jack Prickett were settling into their bedrooms on the second floor of the mansion. The Judge allowed each of them to stay at his home between assignments. The butler, Farmington, had the night off and the Judge had dinner plans in downtown San Diego.

Within Jack's small suitcase, he had several 'burner' phones. A burner phone is a cheap, pre-paid cellular phone. He would use one phone for each assignment and then dispose of it. His disposal method included putting the phone in water, then frying it in a microwave oven and finally, tossing the remains in a dumpster.

The phone that began to vibrate was dedicated to the Gibson assignment that was set for the next evening.

"Yeah," Jack answered.

"There's a little glitch. The Rotary Club cancelled the dinner for tomorrow night," the voice advised.

"Shit," Jack uttered with frustrated flare as he sat on the side of the bed. "Did they re-schedule it?"

"A week from tomorrow. Same time, same place."

"Okay. Let's hit the reset button. I'll call you."

"All right. Take care." With that, the call ended.

Meanwhile, Annabella was hanging several articles of clothing in the closet and then just began to look at items on a shelf, which included several books and a small, heart-shaped picture frame that had a black and white photo of a woman with a baby in her lap.

Annabella simply stared at it and began to remember.

It was eight years earlier and she was the receptionist at a company called Skamatics, Inc. The company specialized in providing schematic drawings for different types of mechanical engineering applications. There were two owners of the company, Artie Smith and Eddy Jones. They were probably two of the laziest engineers on the planet, Earth. Their laziness was well hidden behind an extraordinary engineer and employee, named Raul Verdugo.

Raul did all the engineering work and was treated like garbage. They would call him "Raymond" and took every opportunity that they could to make fun of him and his Mexican heritage. They would jokingly ask him to come over to their houses and cut the grass. Many other jokes were profanity-laced. They would call Raul a "beaner" and would tell him that if he didn't like the work at Skamatics, the Home Depot parking lot was right down the street.

Artie and Eddy made the acquaintance of a local drug dealer who put them in touch with a larger supplier. Soon, they were making more money distributing drugs in a month, than they made in a year at the engineering company. Their drug of choice was _La Cocaína_ (Cocaine).

They developed a lavish lifestyle and were soon living too large. They found themselves indebted to a drug cartel for $250,000 and they did not have the money to re-pay it. They conceived an elaborate scheme to re-pay it that involved Raul.

The plan was to send Raul down to Mexicali, Mexico with a bag of one-hundred dollar bills. Only the top bill of each of the banded stacks would be real and the rest of the bills would be counterfeit. If there was any problem or concern they would blame Raul. This would allow Artie and Eddy more time to get the money they owed to the cartel. If Raul was killed, it was no big deal.

The only thing that Annabella appreciated about Artie and Eddy was that her job there caused her to meet Raul Verdugo. When their eyes first locked, it set off a carnal fire within her that only he could extinguish. And when the opportunity arose, she pounced on him with savage, feral passion.

They moved in together and would talk often about their future together. They were going to move to the United States, become U.S. citizens, get good jobs, buy a house, and start a family. That was until Artie and Eddy decided to disrupt their plans.

It was then that a voice disrupted her thoughts.

"You want to go get something to eat?" Jack wondered as he stood in the door to her bedroom.

Annabella glanced toward him.

"Okay," she replied.

"What are you in the mood for?"

"I don't care. Whatever you want."

"I'm a burger and fries guy. You probably like something fancier," Jack opined.

"I like burgers and fries," Annabella retorted.

Jack thought for a moment.

"Do you like Denny's?"

"Sure," she said in a matter-of-fact manner.

"Do you like pancakes?" he wondered.

"Yeah," she answered with a smile.

"I got the place. Let's go."

With that, the evening's journey began.

CHAPTER 12

Judge Caesar Cargyle sat in the back seat of his late-model Cadillac limousine looking out the window. He poured over the sights and sounds of San Diego after dark. He was disgusted by the volume of homeless people that were staining the once beautiful landscape.

"Drive by the new courthouse," he ordered.

"Yes, sir." The driver complied.

The new San Diego Central Courthouse was located at 1100 Union Street and opened in late 2017. The 25-story building is a tower clad in pre-cast concrete and adorned with aluminum panel sections. The top of the soffit has a distinctive crown.

Judge Cargyle nodded in acceptance. This was the palace in which he wanted to be a king.

His cell phone rang, but before he answered it, he gave another command.

"Let's go home."

The driver modified his route and now headed back to Rancho Santa Fe.

"Yes," Cargyle answered.

"Is the line secure?" the voice responded.

"Yes. I invested in a KryptAll phone as you advised."

The KryptAll phone does not allow calls to be traced, intercepted, or recorded. It performs these functions anywhere in the world.

"Did you get the list of assignments?" the voice wondered.

"I did."

"Do you foresee any problems?"

"No. But I do have a question. Why is Jack Prickett on the list?"

"All *sicarios* have an expiration date. His is up."

"He's staying at my house right now. So is Annabella Romero."

"Have her kill him. Let her use her seductive powers to get close, then slit his throat or poison him."

"Maybe," the Judge considered, "but not in my house."

"The one I'm concerned about is Legion. If he gets Jimmy Flowers to protect him, you may have a problem."

"Don't worry about Legion. I have something special planned for him," the Judge replied, with ghoulish satisfaction.

"I'll look forward to it. Have a good evening, Caesar."

With that the call ended. The Judge returned the phone to his inside breast pocket. He needed to plan for his meeting with the members of the Female Optimization Group or 'FOG,' set for the next evening.

After that, the plan would be in full motion.

CHAPTER 13

The marine layer in Oceanside was thick this evening, causing a foggy haze to cover the landscape and reduce visibility to less than one-quarter of a mile. Jimmy Flowers had sent Raul Verdugo to pick up a suitcase filled with prescription drugs that were to be sold through his network of independent pharmacies.

At approximately 10:30 pm, Raul pulled up to the house on Canella Street in Oceanside in his Cadillac Escalade. All of the six homes in this cul-de-sac were single story, light brown stucco with a single car garage. All of the windows and the front door had vertical white bars. All of them had the front porch light switched on.

Raul scanned the area and stepped out of his vehicle. He proceeded directly to the home that was at the farthest distance from the intersection. When he reached the front door, he stared through the glass and saw the security pad with a red blinking light. Raul retrieved his cell phone and pushed a number that he had on speed dial.

"I'm here," Raul advised.

"Please put in your earbud," a voice replied.

As Raul complied, the light on the security keypad went green, the lights in the house turned on, and the front door unlocked. Raul entered. He did a quick perusal of the interior and walked directly through the kitchen to the door that opened to the garage.

He traversed two steps down into the garage. The garage had a concrete floor, painted battleship gray, and a ceiling made of wooden beam rafters built on wooden trusses. The rafters were parallel with a twenty-four inch span between them.

"Ready for the combination," Raul advised.

"Forty-one, three, twenty-six." The voice stopped for a moment. It then moved from calm to a hastened panic.

"Raul, you've got three guys coming up on the west side and two guys coming up on the east side. They look like Hispanic guys, maybe in their twenties. You want me to lock it up?"

"No. When they're in the garage, lock the doors and kill the lights."

Outside, the intruders could see that the door was unlocked. The lead man pulled out a Ruger semi-automatic 9 mm handgun. He gave a silent signal to other men to draw their guns. The four men acceded to his request and followed him into the house.

The men heard something rustling in the garage. They made a slow and cautious trek to the garage and entered it. As the last man traversed the threshold, the door to the kitchen immediately slammed shut and the locking mechanism could be heard.

All five turned to the door as the lights cut out in the entire building. The room was suddenly enveloped in darkness and the last man in was doing whatever he could to open the door by jiggling the doorknob.

"Stop," the leader of the men said.

"Somebody is in here with us," another one of the men professed in fear.

Raul turned on a flashlight that he had placed right by the slide of his semi-automatic. The men quickly turned their attention to the illumination of the flashlight's beacon.

Raul's gun came to life and fired four shots within three seconds. Each shot struck one of the intruder's directly in the eye. The four men dropped down, like lifeless puppets. The body of one of the men continued to twitch after he hit the ground. Raul walked over to him and gave him a 'double tap,' or second shot, directly to the center of his chest. The twitching stopped.

Now Raul aimed the gun directly at the leader. He was a 24-year-old, heavily-tattooed gang member, named Carlos.

Carlos was slightly trembling and he wondered whether or not, he should engage Raul.

"Toss the gun!" Raul ordered with a no-nonsense flare.

Carlos tossed it with a no-energy drop.

"What's your name?"

"Carlos."

"Who sent you to boost this place?"

"Listen, Raul, I had no choice," Carlos pleaded.

Raul was taken aback.

"How did you know my name?"

"You're the Executioner, right?"

Raul gave a slight, affirmative nod.

"We didn't come here to rob this place," he paused. "We came here to kill you."

Raul took a moment to let the comment sink in.

"Who sent you here? What's his name?"

"Herrero," Carlos answered. "Ruben Herrero. He's a cop in San Diego."

"Where can I find Ruben Herrero?"

"I would meet him at either a park or a bar near the corner of Hill and Elm in Oceanside."

"How did you know I was here?"

"We followed you from downtown San Diego, Little Italy."

"How did Herrero find you?"

"My parole officer. He connected us up. He said that if I help this guy, he could make life easy for me. You know, relax the rules."

Raul began to lower his gun and then, in a millisecond, raised his gun, aimed it, and pulled the trigger. Like the others, the bullet struck Carlos directly into his left eye, then into his brain. His head jerked back and then his body slammed to the concrete floor.

Raul turned two of the bodies face up to minimize the blood loss.

"Audio," he said while touching his earbud. "Are you still with me?"

"Still here. What do you need?"

"I need a Drop & Mop team at this location. Occupied five times. Tell Jimmy what happened and tell Jimmy I'm on my way back."

Raul removed the suitcase from the safe and left the house. He would proceed to the drop-off point for the suitcase and then to the Bagheria Bedda restaurant to meet with Jimmy Flowers.

Could Jimmy Flowers be the architect of this failed assassination attempt against Raul?

CHAPTER 14

Linda Green and Leticia Harrison met at the Gordon Biersch Brewery Restaurant located in the Mission Valley area of San Diego. They were sharing a large order of beer-glazed, boneless chicken wings and garlic fries. They each had a Radler beer, which was a summer beer combined with lemonade and soda.

After some routine small talk, the true substance of the meeting began in earnest.

"So, he really blew a gasket?" Leticia asked Linda, looking forward to the answer.

"He called me some terrible names." Linda's tone was somber. "If I had a gun, I would have shot him."

"Well, you've got him for creating a hostile work environment and constructive termination," Leticia advised.

"Even though I told him 'I quit.'"

"I recall that you just said that you resigned at his suggestion."

"Yes, I did."

"You were terminated. Believe me. It happens all the time. Especially to women. If you don't knock the case out of the park, they treat you like dirt under their shoes. Can I ask you a personal question?"

"Sure," Linda answered.

"Did he ever touch you?"

Linda looked at Leticia and contemplated the question.

"He made a pass at me once, but I told him I was married and that was the end of it."

"He's married? Right?"

"Yeah. Over ten years. He's got three little kids."

"Do you know of any other females at the firm that may have had a physical relationship with him?"

"There was one girl who used to give him oral pleasure on a regular basis."

"Does she still work there?"

"No. She left about a year ago."

"Do you know where she is now?"

"Yes. Do you want to contact her?" Linda asked.

"Not right now. I'm here to discuss you. How about I prepare a wrongful termination lawsuit and we send him a copy as a courtesy. We don't file it. We'll see what he wants to pay for a confidentiality clause."

"Can I think about it?" Linda inquired.

"All right. But not too long. Memories fade. And if we get the press involved, he'll fold," Leticia stated adamantly.

"I'll never work in this town again."

"Yes, you will. I'm going to hire you. But we are going to wait a little while. If you have any bills that are due, bring them to me and I'll pay them directly," Leticia spoke with confidence.

"That's so kind of you," Linda told her.

"I would like you to come with me tomorrow night to a meeting of the Female Optimization Group. They call it 'Fog.' It's held at the home of a retired Judge in Rancho Santa Fe. It is a small club, less than ten women, who find themselves in the same situation as you are. The Judge mentors the women in surviving in the 'Old Boy's Club' that dominates the San Diego legal community."

Linda thought for a moment.

"All right," Linda uttered with her first smile of the day.

Leticia extended her hand to Linda and she reciprocated for a quick handshake.

A deal was made, an offer extended, but now, what would Linda have to give up to consummate the deal?

CHAPTER 15

San Marcos is a city located sixteen miles north of Rancho Santa Fe. It is a quiet, urban community. It is also the home of an International House of Pancakes or IHOP.

It was approximately 8:00 pm, when Jack and Annabella arrived at the restaurant. The flooding lights of the parking lot seemed to burn through any potential mist from the marine layer.

Jack and Annabella entered the restaurant, were seated into one of the orange booths, and handed menus.

"Can I get you something to drink," the waitress wondered.

Jack pointed to Annabella to begin the conversation.

"I'd like decaf coffee."

"Do you have Coke products?" Jack inquired.

"No. We have Pepsi."

"I'll take an ice tea."

"Would you like regular or sweetened?"

"Sweeten it up," Jack requested.

The waitress left to obtain the drink order.

"I like this place," Jack told her. "You can get breakfast food, lunch food, or dinner food, any time. I hope you like it."

"Don't worry. I do like it," Annabella acknowledged.

"You're so small and thin, do you ever eat?"

"All the time. I just don't like to eat alone."

"I don't have a problem with that. I usually eat one big meal a day and a lot of water."

As Jack finished his sentence, he noticed an African-American woman with three small children across and catty-corner from them. She was cutting up the pancakes for the children and putting straws in the drinks for them. Jack reached into his back pocket to retrieve his wallet. He removed something from it. At the same time, he winked to Annabella.

The waitress returned with the drinks. Jack took two fingers and motioned the waitress to come closer to him, so he would not have to raise his voice.

"Behind you," he began, "is a lady with three kids. I want to pay for their meal. Don't let her know it's me paying."

Jack had taken a one-hundred dollar bill from his wallet. He folded it and slipped it into one of the front pockets of the waitress's apron.

"Do you want me to include your meal on it?"

"No. You keep the change. But tell them they can get dessert if they want."

The waitress shook her head in acknowledgement.

"Are you ready to order?" the waitress inquired.

"Give us a few more minutes," Jack requested and the waitress scooted away.

"That was very kind of you," Annabella opined.

"When I was a kid, my mother, three sisters and me went to a Howard Johnson's Restaurant in the Long Island area. Someone paid for our meal. I thought it was a miracle. To this day, my mother talks about it. People should realize what a random act of kindness can do. And you've got to give back, especially," Jack paused for a moment, "in our line of work."

They exchanged smiles and then began a serious perusal of the menu.

Later that evening, back at Judge Cargyle's house in Rancho Santa Fe, Jack prepared for the next day. He would brush his teeth, shave, and take a shower at night, so that when he woke up, he was ready to go.

After he completed the preparations, he laid down in the darkened second-floor, bedroom, naked in the bed, under the covers and debated whether or not to watch television. There was a knock at the door.

"Come on in," Jack requested in a slightly raised voice.

Annabella entered, wearing a white, terry cloth bathrobe.

"Is there anything wrong, Annie?"

She shook her head negatively. She undid the belt on the bathrobe and dropped it to the floor. Her naked body shimmered in the moonlight.

Jack's eyes opened wide as he gazed upon her sublime beauty with awe and admiration. She looked stunning and Jack couldn't stop looking at her. She was perfect in every detail.

Annabella locked the bedroom door and proceeded to the side of the bed.

"Request permission to come aboard?"

"Come aboard?" Jack announced with a Cheshire cat smile. "Isn't that one of those double entendres?" he teased.

Jack could not take his eyes off of her. Her body was like the sculpture of a goddess created by a master artisan. He lifted the covers and looked down under them.

"We're at full mast," Jack advised. "Permission to come aboard granted."

Meanwhile, Judge Caesar Cargyle sat in his first floor bedroom with a disapproving scowl on his face. The room was blanketed in darkness, except for a television that was presenting some sort of pornographic film.

Upon closer inspection, it was not a pornographic film. It was Jack and Annabella.

Part 2

CHAPTER 16

At approximately 7:30 pm, a white, Ford Transit van pulled up to the roundabout in Judge Caesar Cargyle's driveway. The marine layer was thick, impairing visibility, even though the sun had not yet set.

Seven women exited the van, led by Leticia Harrison, and followed by Linda Green. The five other women were in their late 20s to early 30s, rather cute, and wearing business casual attire.

They were met at the door by the butler, Farmington, who escorted them into the living room. There, on the coffee table in front of the couch, were various hors d'oeuvres, small plates, and napkins.

All of the women swooped on the food snacks, while Farmington took their drink orders. The Judge rolled into the room and called for their attention.

"Ladies," he bellowed. "Welcome to our meeting of the FOG (Female Optimization Group). Leticia and I will have a short, executive meeting, followed by our general meeting. Please enjoy the food and drink."

The Judge rolled into his office located down a hallway with Leticia in tow. Once inside the office, Leticia closed the door and the Judge trundled his wheelchair behind his massive, cherry desk. Leticia took a seat in one of the two leather chairs located across from the judge. As she settled into the leather chair, she smiled.

"Linda Green," he inquired. "Is she ready?"

"Yes," Leticia answered. "I believe she is."

"Does she have a taste for blood?"

"I think so. Right now, the scars are still fresh."

"What does she think about Legion?"

"I didn't sense any hostility toward him. It's her old boss, Monty Lindstrom that she hates."

"Well then, let's put him on the list. Is your meeting with Legion still going forward?"

"Tomorrow afternoon," Leticia nodded, "at his office."

"I wish I could be there. Please call me as soon as it's over."

"I will. What are we going to do about Legion?" Leticia wondered.

"Legion is a different type of animal. I have a special plan for him." The Judge smiled at her. "Now, let's go talk to the ladies."

The Judge was about to commence a plan to alter the legal landscape of San Diego through retribution by scorned females.

CHAPTER 17

That evening, Jimmy Flowers sat at his desk in the Bagheria Bedda restaurant reviewing various invoices for payment. There was suddenly a knock at his door.

"Yeah?" he answered as he lowered his reading glasses down to the desk.

Domenic, the sentry watching the office, took one step into the room.

"Raul Verdugo is here," he told Jimmy. He wants to talk with you."

"Send him in."

Domenic motioned to Raul and Raul swiftly entered. He did not sit; instead, he stood across the desk from Jimmy, waiting for Domenic to leave.

"Did you hear what happened out there?" Raul asked referring to his interaction with five gangbangers in Oceanside that left them all dead.

"Yeah."

"Did you know anything about it?"

"No," Jimmy answered bluntly. "Do you think I'd send you into an ambush?"

"Do you know this guy, Ruben Herrero?"

"He's a cop. A captain with the San Diego Armory Unit. The SWAT team. He considers himself to be a top-shelf assassin, backed up by the police force. He's smart, but not as smart as he thinks he is. Internal Affairs have been after him for two years with little success."

"I want to know who hired him."

"My suspicion is that it's the Company."

"The same guys that Cargyle works for?"

Raul was amazed by the disclosure. Little was known about the Company, other than it was a shadowy organization, believed to be a part of the Central Intelligence Agency, but that was never confirmed. All that was known was that the Company was a very well financed organization that engaged in various forms of national and international crime activity.

"Where can I find Herrero?" Raul inquired.

"You don't want to kill a cop. Brings down too much heat."

"So, what should I do? Wait around until he tries again?"

"Let me have some of my guys on the street talk to him. They'll tell him that I said to back off. He'll do it. He knows the consequences."

"All right," Raul conceded. "But if I meet him on the street, I'll end it."

"Fair enough," Jimmy conveyed. "Now, I have a different topic to discuss. It involves a couple of *sicarios*. Jack Prickett, they call him 'the Clipper' and Annabella Romero. They call her '*La Niña.*'"

"What about them?"

"There's a contract out on both of them. Are you interested?"

Raul's face soured.

"I don't know Prickett, but why is the girl on a hit list?"

"I'm told that she has some baggage that is rather damning."

Raul gave a slight rub to his left temple.

"So," Jimmy asked. "Interested?"

"Yeah." Raul answered with a deadbeat tone and no inflection.

Raul had no intention of killing Annabella. He planned on saving her.

CHAPTER 18

Judge Caesar Cargyle rolled into the living room of his palatial Rancho Santa Fe estate and saw all the female invitees engaging in harmless banter. When the women noticed him, silence draped the room and their attention turned to the Judge.

"Ladies," the Judge began," "welcome to our monthly meeting of the Female Optimization Group, better known as FOG. Before we begin, I would like to advise that we have a new member, Miss Linda Green."

Cargyle pointed to her and the women gave her a short round of applause. Cargyle continued.

"Ladies, let's go around the room and introduce ourselves. I only want you to state your first name and your profession."

The Judge motioned to the woman sitting immediately to his left. She was petite, with black, shoulder-length hair, and in her early 20s.

"Frida. I'm a paralegal."

"Claudia. I'm a lawyer," the next woman stated.

Claudia was in her late 30s, with a cherubic face and beaming smile.

"Daniela. I'm a lawyer."

Daniela had the body of a model and wore light make-up that caused her beauty to radiate.

"My name is Alexandra. I'm a law clerk," the next woman advised.

Alexandra had a cute, girl-next-door look. She appeared very down-to-earth. She weighed 105 pounds on a five foot, four inch frame.

"Cassie. I'm a paralegal."

Cassie was African-American and wore her long hair pulled back and held with a scrunchy. Like most of the others, her physique was close to petite and her beauty was undeniable. The way she sat communicated a refinement, like she was a princess to be noted.

All of the women exuded a desire to learn.

Finally, Leticia Harrison announced herself and the meeting was able to begin in earnest.

"Thank you, ladies," the Judge began. "We come here tonight to discuss the future. The FOG is a rather covert, invitation-only organization. You women all have one thing in common: You are survivors. Survivors of sexual assault, sexual coercion, and sexual harassment. All at the hands of men sworn to provide justice to those in need."

Cargyle surveyed the crowd while his comments sunk in. He continued.

"For too long, the San Diego legal community has been an 'old-boy's' network, where the lawyers protect each other, and women have been seen as nothing more than subservient machines that only exist to serve male lawyers. The consensus is that women don't belong in the courtroom.

"They don't allow you to become partners at the firm and if you take maternity leave, they hope it is forever. You cover for their mistakes and then they tell you how stupid you are. Then, if you do not comply with their requested shenanigans, they make your life miserable until you quit. And they replace you, like a copy machine, with another girl that is younger, cuter, and cheaper.

"If nothing is done to stop these predators, then they are allowed to continue unabated. This has gone on for too long. And I find these actions to be repugnant. The purpose of the FOG is to remove these men from the practice of law and send a signal to others that their actions against women will not be tolerated.

"Now, are you willing to do what it takes to accomplish this goal?"

All the women sheepishly replied, 'Yes.'

"Very good," the Judge advised. "From this point forward, we are no longer the Female Optimization Group. Exodus 33:20 of the bible states of God speaking to Moses, 'There shall be no man that sees my face and lives.'

"Now, if a lawyer sees us coming, the new FOG, the Face of God, their life will be over. It is time for comeuppance and atonement."

Linda Green was beginning to become uneasy with the Judge's rhetoric. She was not the victim of any sexual impropriety, but nothing would be more satisfying than seeing her old boss lose his law license.

CHAPTER 19

At the Starbucks Coffee Shop, located on Market Street in San Diego, Ruben Herrero sat at a table farthest from the ordering area to survey the activity inside the shop. It was nearly closing time, so activity was rather stagnant. For the past hour, Ruben had nursed a venti, Caramel Macchiato while scrolling through his phone.

Ruben was 48 years old, nearly 6 feet tall, with a full head of black hair. He was an imposing figure on a 240-pound frame and his visage boasted intimidation. He was proud of his 'take no shit' attitude. Ruben had a reputation for being reckless and disdaining authority. His police personnel file indicated as many heroic events as it did police department procedure violations.

Herrero wore a muted, blue Hawaiian shirt, size XX large, to conceal the fact that he carried two .45 caliber Smith & Wesson handguns behind his back. He kept another .380 caliber Berretta handgun on his ankle.

The quiet of the coffee shop was torn when a man entered and his body language evoked urgency. The man surveyed the coffee shop and saw Ruben. Ruben looked up and their eyes locked.

The man proceeded directly to Ruben and sat next to him. His name was John Donzen, a fellow police officer.

"What's up?" Ruben inquired.

"I just got the word: IA (Internal Affairs) put a tracker on your car."

"Are you sure?"

"It came from my inside guy."

The Internal Affairs Department of the San Diego Police had opened an investigation on Ruben two years earlier, when he was suspected in the murder of an Oriental rug trader in the Midway District of San Diego.

Ruben cogitated on his next move.

"Take my car down to the police garage. Tell Dutch to take it off and put it on your car. How far is it from here to your house?"

"Valley Center," John responded. "More than sixty miles."

"That's perfect. Your mother-in-law still live in Arizona?"

"Tempe."

"Go over and visit her for a couple of days. Dutch knows a mechanic in Scottsdale that we can trust. I'll have Dutch tell him to pull the tracker off your car and put it on a tractor trailer going cross-country."

"Sounds like a plan," Donzen concurred.

"That stupid, fucking IA Polack, Wokawski, thinks he's always one step ahead of me."

Ruben shook his head in disgust and handed the car fob to John.

"Hey," Ruben said seeking John's attention. "You know how you make a Polack go crazy?"

John shrugged his shoulders.

"Put him in a round room and tell him to piss in the corner."

Both men's faces conveyed a wide grin and slight chuckle.

Ruben now had some time free to fulfill several assignments that were requested of him. One of them, was Raul Verdugo.

CHAPTER 20

Annabella sat at a small desk in the bedroom where she was staying in Judge Cargyle's home. She was perusing photographs on her cell phone and trying to remember the events associated with them. Most of the pictures showed far-away places, exotic and beautiful. But the best ones showed Raul.

A knock at her door disrupted her focus.

"Yes," she called.

Farmington opened the door, just enough to see her.

"The Judge would like you to join the meeting now."

"Tell him, I'm on my way."

Annabella shut her phone off and looked into a mirror situated over a dresser. She touched her face lightly and realized that her make-up was flawless. She wore a black, long-sleeve, Nickie Lew dress. As requested by the Judge, it adequately covered all of her tattoos.

When Annabella entered the room, the Judge recalled all of her charms, and he smiled a bit too broadly. He quickly brought his smile down to 'low beam.'

"Annabella, please take a seat," the Judge requested. She sat opposite the Judge across the coffee table.

"Annabella is our guest speaker. I just want to touch on one more topic before we continue. The purpose and mission of the FOG is to correct those inequities that exist in the San Diego legal community. The very reason for a lawyer's existence is that the court battle will be fair to all participants. No one should be allowed to have an edge.

"But what happens if you dare to challenge one of these gods of the courtroom? They make your life miserable. They try to bankrupt you and they make sure that you never hold a legal job in San Diego County again. They make backroom deals that reward their legal friends and punish their perceived enemies.

"I know this because I was once part of the hypocrisy. Then one day, I said – No more! Together, Leticia and I came up with the idea of the FOG. An organization dedicated to the exposure and removal of abusive predators from the practice of law.

"If we have evidence to prove our allegations, that's fine. If not, we wish to associate certain lawyers with 'the taint.' The taint is merely he said/she said. We may lose in court, but the stain of the taint is indelible. Reputations are destroyed and clients are lost. As long as the story is compelling, we will win. Every good lawyer knows that the bigger the lie, the more people will believe it.

"Leticia and Cassie," he pointed to both of them, "have their first settlement conference tomorrow in one of the FOG cases. The evidence in that is iron-clad. I believe it will serve as a barometer for our success.

"Ladies," the Judge uttered with a degree of finality, "we are about to storm the castle."

All the women, including Annabella were mesmerized by his presentation. Now, it was Annabella's turn.

CHAPTER 21

As the Judge continued his efforts to proselytize the women and convince them of the morality of his crusade, the butler, Farmington, entered the room and walked over to the Judge. He bent forward to speak softly into his ear.

"We've received a message from Herrero. He's says that he needs to talk to you. It's important."

"Tell him I'm busy. Find out what he wants," the Judge told Farmington in a hushed, perturbed tone. He then turned his attention to the invitees.

"Ladies," the Judge declared, "Annabella has come to speak to us this evening about her journey. By virtue of her appearance here, she wishes to retain all of you to assist her with any future legal services. Therefore, as soon as you agree, an attorney-client bond will be formed that will prohibit you from disclosing any information that she shares with us this evening. Are you willing to accept this retention? I want individual responses. Those of you that are not attorneys shall be bound by virtue of your employment status with Leticia's law firm."

The Judge pointed to Frida.

"Yes," Frida replied.

Thereafter, in succession, each of the women agreed to have a legal relationship with Annabella. When the last woman, Leticia, gave her affirmative acknowledgement, the Judge nodded to Annabella to begin.

Annabella rose from her seat and surveyed the women.

"My name is Annabella and I am a *sicaria*. You may have heard the term, *sicario*, which has been made popular by the media, which means 'hitman' or 'assassin.' *Sicaria* is a female assassin. I kill people for money."

The silence in the room would require a jackhammer to penetrate. Every woman was aghast, with their mouths slightly open and faces frozen in shock.

"I did not start my life with the ambition to become a professional killer. Circumstances brought the profession to me.

"About ten years ago, I was a receptionist and secretary at an architectural engineering company. The owners of the company became involved with drugs and they tried to set-up my then boyfriend. I advised my boyfriend of the drug set-up and he told the drug suppliers about it. The drug suppliers said they would let him go if he would kill our bosses. My boyfriend agreed. He discovered that he had a knack for killing. My boyfriend was a man of precision. He studied the art of killing like it was a science. In addition to loving him, I admired him greatly. He had great patience and was an excellent teacher. So, I asked him to teach me how to efficiently take someone's life."

Annabella stopped for a moment and Claudia spoke up.

"How many people have you killed?"

"Fifty-six, as of last week."

"Do you use guns or some other way?" Daniela wondered.

"It depends on the situation. Everyone is different. Some are easy, some seem impossible."

"Ladies," the Judge interjected, "let's allow her to continue."

"I come here today to offer my assistance," Annabella apprised. "Look at me. I'm a waif. All I ever wanted to be was a good person. But almost every man in my life looked for the opportunity to take advantage of me and would only help me when they received something from me. I wanted to be liberated from that life. As the Judge points out, I wanted to level the playing field. So, I found a way to do it.

"My arms are tattooed with a history of those persons that have harmed me and those persons who I have harmed. I want those markings to serve as a reminder that no one will ever take advantage of me again.

"My suggestion to you is to remember the reason that you are here. Wear those indignities as a badge of honor. Learn from them. I will help you do what needs to be done. Let those events strengthen your resolve to stop these men from coercing another woman into submission."

"Wait," Linda spoke up, "are we talking murder?"

"No," the Judge adamantly replied. "Not murder. Not even retribution. What we are discussing here is . . . justice!"

Linda was becoming nervous that the Face of God organization was, in actuality, a murder squad.

CHAPTER 22

Every Friday morning at Legion & Associates, an attorney meeting went forward. Today was no exception. Fourteen attorneys entered the conference room and took seats at the conference table – a huge, oak table that could seat twenty-four people. The windows of the outside wall boasted a magnificent, panoramic view of the Pacific Ocean. The opposite wall divided the room from the reception area and was frosted, alabaster-trimmed glass with glass door entrances at each end.

The room had its share of infamy, being the venue of a hellacious gunfight, which took place nearly eight years earlier.

All the attorneys wore white shirts with Windsor-knotted, non-descript, silk ties. Anything less could invoke the wrath of Roger Legion.

The meeting was more than just an information-sharing event, it was a reminder to Legion's troops of their mission and purpose.

Legion entered the room and immediately canvassed the attendees.

"Is everybody here?"

"Clint's not here," one of the attorneys answered.

The attorney was referring to Clint Eversol, the lawyer who was with Roger and Linda Green when they obtained a defense verdict in a case earlier in the week.

"He's got something going on," Roger answered. "He told me he wasn't going to be here."

Roger then opened the door through which he entered and called out.

"Nina, we're going to start."

This was Nina's signal that once the meeting commenced, they were not to be disturbed.

"Gentlemen, I am meeting with a potential, new client today. It's an insurance company called Tecton Insurance. They're involved in a bad faith case that has the potential to destroy their company. They want our help. If we take the case, I am going to select two attorneys who will work only on this particular case. The rest of you guys have to pick up their slack. Understood?"

Everyone either nodded affirmatively or said, "Yes."

"Now, Clint's not here, but he did a good job with the trial. Our co-defendant took a severe hit."

One of the attorneys, Dan Clarkson, took an opportunity to make a comment in the form of a question.

"Did he do any dancing or sing any songs in the courtroom?" Dan asked trying to get anyone in the room to chuckle with his homophobic reference. They did not.

Dan was 31 years old, 6 feet 2 inches tall, and 190 pounds of muscle. He was a Marine for eight years prior to joining Legion & Associates. He had a penchant for bubble gum and chewed it continuously throughout the day, including this attorney meeting.

"How many defense verdicts have you obtained?" Legion asked.

"You have to be given the opportunity to try a case to get one." Dan's response was no nonsense and serious.

"Why do you think you have not been given the opportunity?" Legion again posed an inquiry.

"I've got my suspicions," Dan responded.

"I'll tell you why. You intimidate people. Their first impression of you is that you are ready to start a fight. And you don't know how to turn it off.

"While that stance may be beneficial when dealing with the plaintiff attorney, you are more than willing to intimidate the Judge, the jury, and even your client. A jury will punish you for that. The insurance company claim examiner, who is paying our bills, specifically asked for Clint to try the case. Do you think any of the insurance company people are asking for you?"

"That's bullshit. An excuse. It's obvious around here that you have guys you like."

"There are some guys who are better than others in the courtroom. You learn to tone it down and I'll put you in every time."

Dan gave Legion an angry stare, but backed down from the verbal sparring. Legion gazed out the windows for a moment before continuing.

"Gentlemen, it is necessary to remember when we deal with our adversaries that,"

His sentence was interrupted by Dan.

"No one stands alone at this firm," Dan sputtered, once again searching for an audience response, without success.

Everyone in the room knew what was going to happen next.

"Am I boring you?" Legion asked him in a bold, icy tone. "Because if I am, you can leave. Not only the room, but the law firm. Do you know why I have to repeat myself?"

Dan did not respond.

"Because of the short attention span of you and your fellow attorneys, I need to inculcate you," Roger spoke with a pejorative tone. "What does the word 'inculcate' mean?"

Initially, no one raised their hands, then a lone lawyer decided to put forth a response.

"Mr. Davenport, what does 'inculcate' mean?"

"To teach and implant information by repeating something or admonishing something," he responded.

At the center of the table, was a Polycom SoundStation, conference phone, used specifically for conference calls. Roger pointed at the phone.

"Dial zero-two and put it on speaker."

The attorney closest to the phone complied and it was answered on the second ring.

"This is Louise," the voice answered. Louise was Roger's secretary located on the twenty-third floor.

"Louise, this is Roger. Please tell the Accounting Department to prepare a bonus check for our attorney, Stewart Davenport, in the amount of twenty-five thousand dollars. Tell them to classify it as regular pay and deliver the check to my office this morning. Thank you, Louise."

With that, the call ended. The attorneys in the room were stunned. Legion's actions clearly agitated Dan, because his face turned on a low-burn scowl. Legion knew exactly what buttons to push.

"Be prepared, gentlemen. You never know when an opportunity may arise."

The flare of tempers seemed to be cooling and Legion decided to put the meeting back on track.

"You may all know by now that Nina, out here," he advised pointing to the doorway, "is pregnant. We are going to give her one of the offices to use in case she needs to lie down. If she needs a ride to the doctor or anything for her dog, I told her that we would give her a ride."

Dan Clarkson was looking down at the desk and decided to speak up without thought. If he had thought about it, he would have never said it.

"Are you the Baby Daddy, Roger? Did you inculcate her?"

The stillness of the air proclaimed cataclysmic action ahead. Everyone in the room knew that whatever happened, it would not end well.

Roger locked his piercing, blue eyes upon Dan.

"Get up," Legion told him.

Dan did not move.

"GET UP!" Roger screamed and his voice reverberated within the room.

Dan slowly rose, but appeared as if he was ready for a street fight.

"You see that window over there," Roger pointed to a pane of glass that was next to him at the end of the room. "I once threw a guy out of that window. Do you want me to show you how I did it?"

Everyone in the room was stunned by Roger's admission. On the day of the famous firefight, someone was thrown out of the window, but the police were never able to conclusively determine who the perpetrator was. There was always talk in the hallways of the law firm that Roger did it. Now, there was confirmation.

The attendees looked to Dan for a response to Roger's question. Don timidly shook his head in a negative fashion.

"Sit down and SHUT UP!" Roger commanded. "If I have to deal with you one more time, they're going to take you out of here on a gurney. And get rid of that gum! You look like you're trying to get the taste of a blow job out of your mouth."

Dan sat down, removed the gum, and wrapped it in a piece of paper. From that moment, until the day he died, Dan never chewed another piece of gum.

The other attorneys had all received a lesson in what Roger Legion does best: intimidate through fear with the use of shock and awe.

CHAPTER 23

In Room 612 of Scripps Memorial Hospital in La Jolla, California, a 78-year-old man lay dying from lung cancer. His grizzled hair was devoid of hue and his three days of beard growth made him look like a prospector from the California Gold Rush. A medical ventilator, attached to his nostrils, moved breathable air into an out of his lungs.

His name was Woodrow 'Woody' Tobag. He had no blood-related family and he spent most days thinking about the events of his past life, both good and bad. On this day, he would have a visitor.

Jack Prickett entered the room and Woody came to life. A smile beamed on his face and he was genuinely excited.

"Hey, what are you doing?" Jack asked, in a smart-alecky fashion.

They met with an arm-wrestling handshake and a quick hug.

"You know me," Woody was quick to respond, "trying to get laid. All these nurses in here think I'm rich, because they know I don't have any insurance, but somebody is paying cash for the place."

"You're just lucky, that's all," Jack told him. "Tell them you won the lottery."

"You should have left me in the gutter where you found me." Woody somberly imparted.

"You taught me everything I know, Woody. If it wasn't for you, I'd probably be pumping gas or working at a car wash right now."

"Don't underestimate yourself, Jack, my boy. The only thing that can limit you are your own words. How did that Gibson job go? I didn't read anything in the papers."

Jack had planned to assassinate a local Union official at a San Diego hotel during a speech.

"It didn't go. It got pushed back."

"I wish you could take care of it 'old school.' Blast him in a parking lot from a distance."

"Cargyle gave me the green light. If my plan doesn't work, then do what is necessary to get it done."

"Never trust Cargyle," Woody warned. "He likes to talk. You know my motto: I can't stand a bullshitter."

"My plan will work."

"Don't be married to it. Stay fluid. But, why take a chance?" Woody wondered. "I'll get out of here and come with you. We'll get it done."

"No, I can handle it. I have people in place. It's tough to get close to this guy. He uses different vehicles, all with bulletproof glass, and he changes up his route every day."

"Gibson," Woody shared, "uses the same security system as Hitler did. Three sets of security guys. All work independently of each other. You have the 'inner sanctum' guys, who are right on top of him. Then, you have guys on the interior perimeter of the room and the final set of guys are on the exterior of the building."

"For my exit plan, I'm going up to the top of the building." Jack advised.

"It's gonna be at least twenty guys, all strapped. I don't like one gun against twenty."

"I can do it," Jack relayed sternly.

"I know you can," Woody concurred. "Any chance you got a cigarette?"

"No," Jack replied in bewilderment. "Look at the stuff they got you connected up to. That's what got you in here."

"You know what I really could go for?" Woody asked rhetorically. "About two fingers of Jack."

Woody was referring to Jack Daniels whiskey.

Jack reached into one of the pockets on the leg of his cargo pants and pulled out a small hip flask. He showed it to Woody and shook it.

"That's my boy," Woody exclaimed in jubilation.

Jack grabbed a paper cup off a nearby counter and poured Woody a drink. Woody downed it all at once and motioned to Jack for another. Jack obliged.

"That's enough for today," Jack told him.

"You make my day," Woody told him sincerely. "You coming to see me, and me thinking about you, gives me a reason to live. You got a girlfriend?"

"I'm working on it," Jack replied.

"I got one for ya. A nurse. Nurse Patty. She's cute, got a nice personality, and she's a family person. She reminds me of my wife."

"Well, we'll see," Jack said.

"What you leave, is lost," Woody asserted.

Woody picked up the intercom device that he had tucked in between the mattress and his bed frame. He pushed a button on it and waited for a response.

"Yes, Mr. Tabog."

"I need to see Nurse Patty. Now. Please send her in here."

"Is this an emergency?"

"It will be if I don't see Nurse Patty."

Within twenty seconds, Nurse Patricia Chatsworth appeared in the doorway. She was 35 years old and strikingly beautiful. Woody described her perfectly. She spoke as she entered.

"Is there anything wrong, Mr. Tobag?" she asked with evident sincerity.

"I want you to meet this guy," Woody told Nurse Patty. "I consider him my son."

"I'm Jack. Nice to meet you."

"I'm Patty. It's nice to meet you."

They shared a handshake and gazed at each other for a moment.

Woody broke the tension.

"Get her phone number, stupid!"

CHAPTER 24

At 9:50 am, Roger Legion sat at his desk and studied an online pleading from the *Zantoff Transportation v. Tecton Insurance* case. Legion was about to have a meeting with representatives from Tecton Insurance to discuss Roger's possible retention for a bad faith case that had the potential to bankrupt the company.

A bad faith insurance case deals with an action against an insurance company due to their refusal to pay a policyholder's legitimate claim within a reasonable period of time. This generally occurs when an insurance company has an opportunity to settle a case against their insured, but they refuse for various reasons. The policyholder then proceeds against the insurance company and there is a potential for punitive damages. This could sometimes place a verdict in the range of millions of dollars.

Just as he was finished reading the last page of the pleading, his office phone rang.

"Yes," Roger answered.

"Your ten o'clock appointment is here. Several men from Tecton Insurance."

"Show them into the conference room."

Legion hung up the phone and lowered his reading glasses to the desk. He then dialed two numbers on his phone.

"Yeah, Roger," Clint Eversol, the attorney Roger was with earlier in the week when the defense verdict was reached, answered.

"Get Dan and come down to the conference room. Make sure you both have a pad and pen."

Roger again returned the phone receiver to its cradle and stood up to commence his trek to the conference room.

Inside the conference room, four gentlemen sat on the window-side of the table and did not utter a word. All were dressed in finely-tailored suits. Three of them had white shirts, with ties that matched a pocket square, in their suitcoats. The fourth man's shirt was red striped.

The men sat in the following order from right to left: Jesus Loredo (Chief Executive Officer), Estaban Flores (Chief Operating Officer), Alberto Adelardo (Chief Claims Officer), and Alejandro Lopez (General Counsel). All the men would speak with accents that indicated English was not their first language. Roger Legion and his lawyers entered the room at the same time. He directed Chris and Dan to sit across from the men. Roger would sit at the head of the table.

"I'm Roger Legion. Welcome to Legion and Associates."

The men exchanged names, handshakes, and pleasantries. Then, the meeting began with serious resolve. Roger began.

"Gentlemen, I've read the initial pleadings in this case and I have a few questions. During one period of time did your claims adjuster ignore the claim for more than ninety days?"

The General Counsel, Alex Lopez, spoke up.

"When we questioned the adjuster about it, he said it slipped through the cracks. May I explain?"

"Go ahead," Legion replied.

"We insured the tractor-trailer. The driver, who was an employee of our insured, said the claimant's car cut in front of him and slammed on their brakes. There was no way he could stop in time. He rear-ended the claimant's vehicle. The mother and father sustained soft tissue injury. The 4-year-old child, who is the subject of the bad faith litigation, was sitting in a belt-positioning mode car seat, but she was not strapped in. When the truck hit the back of the car, she flew out of the seat and slammed her head into the front windshield. She suffered severe TBI," he paused for a second, "traumatic brain injury and severe spinal cord damage."

"He let a policy limits case slipped through the cracks?" Roger wondered. "As you probably are aware, he was violating the California Department of Insurance regulations. He was supposed to send out a status letter to a claimant every thirty days, unless they're represented by an attorney. What was the policy limit?"

"One million dollars," Lopez responded.

"I would assume that the medical payments were well over a million dollars early on?"

"The highest amount we ever offered was three hundred thousand dollars. We felt that the parent's contributory negligence was significant."

"What percentage were you assigning to them?" Legion wondered.

"Ninety percent."

Roger shook his head in disgust.

"With a child injury, you will never be able to tag the parent with that high of a percentage. No jury would believe that a parent would ever put their child in that situation. You would need intentional gross negligence to get anything over fifty percent. Where is your claims examiner now?"

"We let him go," said Alberto Adelardo, the Chief Claims Officer.

"That was your first mistake. He'll align with the plaintiff and blame a failure of management oversight for these events."

"Mr. Legion," Jesus Loredo, the Chief Executive Officer spoke up, "We're having a problem with our re-insurers. Normally, we would be responsible for the first million dollars of any claim. Our next layer of reinsurance was placed into receivership by the Pennsylvania Department of Insurance. The layer above them is refusing to drop down. Without those two layers, Tecton Insurance would be responsible for forty million dollars of this claim. A judgment or settlement of that size would cause us to go into receivership. We don't know what to do. Will you help us?"

Legion gazed at the CEO. His face displayed stern, pensive thought.

"I'll help you, but I have some conditions. First, from this point forward, the only two words that anyone from Tecton Insurance will utter to any third party, regarding this claim, is 'No Comment.' If I read in the media that any information has leaked out, I will quit.

"Second, I want the cell number of anyone remotely involved with this claim, including you guys. If I call you in the middle of the night, on a weekend, I want you to answer the phone. I don't want to go through a filter.

"Third, I want the personnel file for the person who handled this claim.

"Fourth, if either of these two guys call you," he said pointing to Clint and Dan, "you treat it like its coming from me. If they have a question, get them the answer immediately. Are we understanding each other so far?"

They all uttered a chorus of 'Yes.'

"Now, who in the chain of command, of people involved with the claim, does not have an accent?"

"Our Claims Manager doesn't speak Spanish," Alex Lopez added.

"Is he a nice-looking *gringo*?"

"He is a very fine-looking gentleman." Jesus, the CEO, interjected.

"Tell him to clear his calendar. Anything we do in front of a jury, I want him sitting next to me. The courtroom is an arena and a theater. We have to play to the jury.

"I'm a lawyer who has a bloodlust to win. I teach my methods to all my lawyers. Whatever witnesses the plaintiff puts on to testify, my men and I will eviscerate them. Eviscerate is the proper word for this context."

Eviscerate means the removal of entrails or to disembowel.

"Mr. Legion," the CEO spoke again as he reached into the inside pocket of his suitcoat and retrieved a check, "This is a check for one million dollars to cover any expense and your fees."

Jesus placed it on the table and slid it toward Legion as far as he could.

"How much settlement authority do you want to give me?"

"What do you think?" the CEO asked Legion.

"Ten million dollars."

"We can do that," Jesus assured him. "Thank you."

"Don't thank me yet. Thank me when it's over."

Legion had just enlisted himself, in what was to become, the most dangerous case of his career.

CHAPTER 25

When Annabella returned, from a quick shopping trip for make-up, to Judge Caesar Cargyle's Rancho Santa Fe home, the Judge was waiting for her in the living room. His wheelchair was poised at the far end of the couch, as it had been during the FOG meeting.

"Annabella," he called out, "come and sit with me.

Annabella wore blue jeans, with a red t-shirt, and a jean jacket. She sat at the end of the couch, closest to him.

"My Annabella," he muttered sweetly. "You are the daughter I never had. Can I summon Farmington to get you a drink?"

"No, I'm fine."

"I was very proud of you at the FOG meeting. Your words were inspirational. Very heartfelt. It was just enough for the persuasion that was needed."

"I'm glad you're happy, your Honor. I believe in the cause."

"That is so good to hear. Your services will be needed quite soon for that organization. I'm still working on details. But I want to discuss some business with you."

"Sure, go ahead."

"I know that you were once very good friends with Raul Verdugo. And I know that you've also become quite fond of Jack, Jack Prickett."

Annabella just looked at Caesar with a slight, serious smile.

"I have received assignments for both of those gentlemen. They have to go."

"What? Why?" Annabella wondered.

"I don't know. I can only assume that the 'powers that be' have deemed their utility to be at an end."

"What about me? Do you think they would give out an assignment on me to somebody else?"

"I don't think so. That would come through me. I believe they realize that you bring some unique qualities to the table. Some deemed irreplaceable."

Annabella gazed forward without focus.

"So," pondered the Judge, "what do you think: are these assignments something you would consider, or should I give them to someone else?"

"They're not open, are they?" Annabella quizzed.

An open assassination contract means that anyone can fulfill it.

"Not if you want them."

At that moment, Farmington entered the room, carrying a Smartphone. Both the Judge and Annabella looked at him as he entered.

"You have a phone call, sir. The caller says it's urgent."

Farmington handed the phone to the Judge.

"Annabella, you will have to excuse me. But before you go, what about these matters that we discussed?"

"I want both of the contracts."

Annabella had just agreed to kill both Raul and Jack. She darted out of the room to contemplate her assignments.

The Judge could see from the Caller Id that the caller was Ruben Herrero, the rogue police officer who was running his own murder-for-hire business and unsuccessfully tried to kill Raul.

"Yes," he answered with a monosyllabic, no-effort tone.

"We need to talk," responded Herrero. "Now. Come and get me at the coffee shop and we'll go for a ride."

"I'll be there in forty-five minutes," he answered.

Herrero had always been a good source of information for the Judge regarding the interior workings of the police force. The Judge did not like his vulgar manner, but he tolerated it as part of the cost of doing business.

CHAPTER 26

At the conclusion of the meeting with the executives from Tecton Insurance, Roger Legion met with Clint Eversol and Dan Clarkson, the Legion attorneys that he selected to assist him in the defense of the _Zantoff Transportation_ case.

He sat at his desk and the other two lawyers sat across from him.

"Clint," Roger began, "you go through the depositions. Fine tooth comb. I don't think there are too many of them."

"Less than ten," Clint advised.

"Dan, you go through all the expert reports. Find the primary information upon which any report is based. Make sure we have the maintenance history on the truck. One of you guys call our private investigator, Glenn Edgarian, and retain him for anything that we may need in the future. Clear your calendars. Starting tomorrow, we meet every day at three o'clock in my office. Depending on the direction, we may have to establish a war room, so that all non-electronic documents are in one place."

"Dan, are you married?" Legion asked.

"Yeah," Dan responded.

"Starting tomorrow, I want you to wear your wedding ring. No lawyer from this firm appears in front of a jury without one."

Legion then opened the top, right-hand drawer of his desk and pulled out a gold wedding band.

"Here's yours, Clint."

Clint put it on.

"So, that's how you got the defense verdict," Dan uttered with a smile.

"Juries will hold it against a lawyer," Legion asserted, "if he is not wearing one. They must think he's defective to society."

"They probably figure he can't get a woman," Dan retorted.

"Should we tell him what else we did?" Clint posed his inquiry to Legion.

"Go ahead," Legion answered.

"We had a girl from the twenty-third floor, a real cutie, bring me a bag lunch one day. Just when there was a break between witnesses, she hands me the lunch, we share a kiss, and talk about our kids. All in front of the jury."

"His performance was magnificent," Legion added.

"Roger had us practice up here in his office," Clint advised.

"What did the girl get out of it?" Dan wondered.

"She got to take the rest of that day off," Clint conveyed, "and Roger and I have to take her out to lunch."

Dan chuckled and marveled at Legion's moxie. Legion would take no chances with a jury.

"Roger," Dan said, "I just want to thank you for this assignment. I thought that I would be the last guy that you would pick. Especially, after last Friday's staff meeting."

"This case needs a guy like you. I need your domineering presence and especially, your ability to intimidate others."

A moment of silence filled the air.

"All right gentlemen, let's make sure our powder is dry and our knives are sharpened. It has begun."

Clint and Dan nodded in agreement, stood up, and left Roger Legion's office.

Roger's defense team was now in place. He was confident that within a very short time, he would be ready for the courtroom.

Part 3

CHAPTER 27

The sun warmed the streets and sidewalks of downtown San Diego to a perfect seventy-two degrees. The sidewalks were filled with people, walking hurriedly to their destinations. Those that were not walking at a quick clip were, judging by their attire, homeless. They wandered aimlessly in search of sympathy and a handout.

Ruben Herrero was standing on the corner of Third Street and Market Street, not far from the Starbucks that he had visited the night before. This day, Ruben wore a red, Hawaiian shirt with a light, blue floral pattern. It was large enough to conceal his weaponry.

Judge Cargyle's black, Cadillac limousine pulled up and Ruben quickly entered the vehicle. He sat on the rear bench seat where the Judge sat.

"Caesar, how you doing?"

"In all honesty, my day has been disrupted," was his response. Herrero looked at him with a smirk.

"How you doing, Farm-boy?" Farmington looked at him in the rear-view mirror.

"I'm fine," he responded.

"Would you mind?" Ruben asked pointing his finger forward and swaying it from top to bottom.

A divider arose from behind the other seat that faced the men. It rose like a power window. When it was fully up, his head turned slightly toward the Judge.

"You," he began and swayed his index finger back and forth between them, "We, have a problem."

"What?" the Judge asked with little tolerance.

"*La Niña*. Your little girl."

"What's the problem?"

"Her mother lives down in Punta Banderas, just south of T.J. (Tijuana). She's dying, doesn't have much time left. *La Niña* has a brother, who was taking care of her. He was just picked up in the last forty-eight hours for trying to transport heroin across the border. They are trying to encourage him to contact her. Interpol is also looking for her. They have two warrants for her arrest for a murder and attempted murder in Berlin. The word is, that if she is willing to roll over on your murder-for-hire operation, then they'll let her and her brother walk on everything."

The Judge looked out the window in contemplation.

"Are you sure this information is solid?"

"As solid as it gets," Ruben assured him. "Are you going to take care of it, or do you want me to do it?"

"I'll take care of it," the Judge answered, sounding slightly perturbed.

"Were you tapping that?" Ruben matter-of-factly asked.

Ruben was inquiring if the Judge had a sexual relationship with Annabella. The Judge looked at him in disgust.

"Will you spare me the vulgarities?" the Judge demanded. "Where do you want to be dropped off?"

"The coffee shop, where you picked me up."

Caesar opened the divider in the car.

"Bring him back to where we picked him up."

They were back to the pickup point within five minutes. Ruben had one last comment before exiting the vehicle.

"Let me know if you need my help."

Annabella had become a liability and the Judge prided himself on removing liabilities far prior to their maturation. He would now ponder his next move.

CHAPTER 28

In the conference room at Legion & Associates, two African-American women awaited the arrival of Roger Legion and his client. Leticia Harrison, the lawyer whose firm employed all the female members of the FOG group, and Cassie Watsonak, who was also in attendance at the last FOG meeting, looked out at the magnificent view of the Pacific Ocean. The sun was low on the horizon, its rays glistened in blue highlights off the cresting waves.

The women were there in anticipation of a meeting with Roger Legion and his client, Andrew Stansworth. Stansworth was a founder and named partner at the law firm of Stansworth, Roberts & Martin. He had been a lawyer for nearly thirty-six years and was the former employer of Cassie. Cassie was a 'pool' paralegal at Stansworth's firm, not assigned to work for any particular attorney.

Leticia has alleged, on behalf of Cassie, that Stansworth coerced Cassie into performing sexual acts with him in order to retain her job. The purpose of the meeting was an attempt to settle the matter prior to the filing of any lawsuit. Leticia advised Roger that she would have evidence to share with him.

In Roger's office, Roger sat at his desk and Andrew Stansworth was seated across from him. Stansworth was sixty-one years old, with a full head of salt and pepper hair on a medium frame. He wore a gray, Brooks Brothers suit with a white shirt, and a blue, silk tie with a diamond pattern.

"I want to make sure," Roger stated, with a deliberate tone, "that you never touched this girl."

"Never. Perhaps an occasional handshake or congratulatory touch on the back, but nothing beyond that. This whole charade is a money grab. Please shut it down for me."

"All right, let's go."

Both men rose from their chairs and made the trek to the conference room. Stansworth entered first, followed by Roger.

"Hello ladies, I'm Roger Legion."

He moved toward them to shake their hands and Leticia began to speak.

"I'm Leticia Harrison. This is my client, Cassie Watsonak."

"This is my client, Andrew Stansworth."

"Nice to meet you," Leticia advised as she shook his hand. Cassie ignored him.

Each lawyer and their client sat opposite their opposing counterparts.

Roger began the discussion.

"Miss Harrison, please call me, Roger."

"Please call me, Leticia," she responded with a smile.

"Leticia, I've read your demand letter and you indicate that you have some evidence that you would like to share. What might that evidence be?"

"My client has a shoe. An Espadrille-type of shoe. We believe that it is stained with some of your client's seminal fluid."

"How do you believe it got on the shoe?"

"During an oral sex session, she gagged and some of your client's semen, fell out of her mouth and onto the shoe."

"Have you had it tested for DNA?"

"No, I wanted to see if we could resolve this prior to spending money on testing."

"Before we go any further, your letter did not mention any settlement demand amount. Did you have a number in mind?"

"Our non-negotiable demand is this: Fifty thousand dollars in cash and Mr. Stansworth shall resign from the State Bar of California, for cause, and shall not be employed as a law clerk, paralegal, or consultant for any legal firm or organization in the United States."

Stansworth was in shock. Legion remained stoic.

"That's a unique demand. Before we give it any consideration, we are going to need the testing on that shoe."

"We have one other piece of evidence," Leticia professed.

From her purse, Leticia retrieved a voice recorder. She placed it on the desk between herself and Legion.

"May I play you something?"

"Go ahead," Legion acknowledged.

Leticia pushed a button on the side of the recorder and it came to life. A conversation began:

STANSWORTH: For today, let's do the slave one. Don't forget – I'm the master. Understand?

CASSIE: Yes.

STANSWORTH: What did you say?

CASSIE: Yes, Masser.

STANSWORTH: Where were you?

CASSIE: Jenny in Accounting asked me to do a Starbucks run.

STANSWORTH: You got to tell Miss Jenny that you're a house nigger. Tasks like that should be given to a field nigger. We own a couple of those around here. Now, come here. Loosen that top so your master can put his hands on those fine globes of yours. (sounds of movement in the room). You're lucky your master has taken a shine to you. Otherwise, I'll make you a field nigger. Now, get on your knees. You got some man-milking to do.

"That's enough," Legion uttered in disgust as he pushed the stop button on the voice recorder.

"Perhaps, you would like to go out into the hallway," Leticia asked, "and ask your client if that's his voice on the tape?"

"We're going to step out for just a moment," Legion advised.

Legion and Stansworth stood and exited the room. Legion marched back to his office with Stansworth in tow. As soon as they entered, Legion began to speak.

"Shut the door." Stansworth complied. "Don't tell me it's not your voice."

"Roger, it was consensual. I even gave her cash after some of those sessions. That's prostitution."

"You have lost your mind," Roger told him bluntly and succinctly.

"Listen, go offer them three million dollars. I might be able to go as high as five million."

"Based on their demand, I don't think they're here for money. They're here for revenge."

"Stay here," Roger told him and left his office to return to the conference room.

Roger would not say it, but it was his personal belief that Andrew Stansworth deserved to lose his law license.

CHAPTER 29

Raul spent the day in search of Annabella. None of their mutual contacts had seen her and he was not on speaking terms with Judge Cargyle. They had a falling out a year earlier, when the Judge disagreed with Raul regarding the manner to handle a particular assignment. The Judge withheld payment to Raul, until Jimmy Flowers stepped in to negotiate a truce.

At 3:00 pm that afternoon, an idea struck him. He spoke into his cell phone.

"Call Detour Hair Salon in Encinitas, California."

Encinitas is the city located immediately west of Rancho Santa Fe. This was Annabella's favorite hair salon.

"Detour Salon. How can I help you?"

"I'm calling for my wife. She forgot the time of her appointment." Raul inquired.

"It's four o'clock today. Can she still make it?"

"She'll be there. Thank you."

With that, the call ended.

At approximately 5:00 pm, Raul stood at the corner of Highway 101 and E Street in downtown Encinitas. He casually looked around while watching the door to the Detour Hair Salon.

At 4:55 pm, Annabella emerged from the salon, radiating from her hair appointment. She wore a sleeveless, floral-print, Mikado dress. For shoes, she wore a burgundy, Doc Martens, Vintage boot. The boots accented her slender legs that were extremely defined by a muscular cut.

She had only taken a few steps, when Raul called out her name.

"Annabella."

She turned and did a double take. Annabella did not know what emotion to feel at that moment.

"Raul, what are you doing here?"

"I need to talk to you. It's important."

"What do you want to talk about?"

"Let's go in this restaurant over here and we can chat a little bit. Please?"

Annabella reluctantly agreed.

"All right. But not too long. I'm supposed to meet someone."

Angelo's Burgers was located on the adjacent corner. It had a 1960s décor and literally appeared to be from the sixties. Regardless of its age, or the condition of the restaurant, the food was good and the portions were large. Another unique feature was that the drive-thru went right through the center of the restaurant, creating two separate dining locations.

Annabella and Raul walked to the ordering counter.

"Do you want anything?"

"No," Annabella stammered. "Well, maybe an ice tea."

"Two ice teas," Raul told the employee.

"Can we get some French fries?" Annabella wondered.

"Sure," Raul told her. He turned to the employee. "An order of fries."

Annabella then spoke directly to the young employee.

"Do you have milkshakes?"

"Yes. Chocolate, vanilla, and strawberry."

"Can I get a chocolate one, instead of the tea?"

"What size? We have medium or large."

"Medium is fine."

Raul handed the female employee a twenty-dollar bill and told her to keep the change. They took a seat that was at a booth in the building separated by the drive-thru. There was no one at all in this portion of the restaurant.

"I know you like to dunk your French fries in your milkshake," Raul reminisced.

"Some things never change," Anabella responded with an air of despondency.

"How is your mother?" Raul asked.

"I haven't talked to her in seven years. You know she always liked you."

"I know. But I hear she isn't doing well. I wanted to know if you had any plans to go see her."

"No. But I hope she still prays for me. Why do you ask?"

"Interpol is looking for you. They claim there are two warrants out for your arrest as a result of a hit in Berlin. If you go near the border, with their facial recognition scans, they'll tag you."

"I guess it's just another reason not to go south of the border."

"One other thing: Your brother, Emile, was picked up for trying to transport heroin across the border. He was acting as a mule for one of the cartels. The deal they pitched to him was that if he could get you to flip on the murder-for-hire operation in Southern California, meaning the Judge, they would drop all the charges and the warrants would disappear."

"Did you come here today to kill me?" her tone was forlorn.

"No," he reassured Annabella. "I want to buy you time, so you can get out of here and go somewhere where you can't be found."

"You know, the Judge asked me today to kill you and another *sicario*, named Jack Prickett."

"With the sanction on you, I was also asked to take out Jack Prickett. I don't know him."

"I do. He's good. And he's a good person. Coincidence?"

"No. But I have to assume that Jack is going to be asked to kill you and I. We need to talk to Jack."

Just then their French fries, chocolate shake, and an ice tea arrived at the table. Annabella's eyes grew wide at the volume of French fries. She grabbed one immediately and dropped it.

"Oooh. They're hot!"

"That's why you needed the milkshake."

That's why Anabella needed Raul.

CHAPTER 30

Attorney, Leticia Harrison, proceeded to the Rancho Santa Fe home of Judge Cargyle immediately after her meeting with Roger Legion. As soon as she arrived, Farmington escorted her into the living room where she waited for the Judge.

He rolled into the room with a beaming smile.

"Good news," she began, "It looks like they are going to submit to our demand. I gave Legion until three o'clock to give us his decision. He offered three million dollars for a straight deal, but he hinted that he may be able to do a little better."

"What was the look on Stansworth's face?" the Judge anxiously inquired.

"Like he had just seen a ghost. He's probably still in shock."

"I'm glad. That stuck-up bastard deserves worse, but his removal from the profession is vindication for Cassie and every other female attorney in this County. Such actions will not be tolerated and the price to pay will be severe."

"Who is our next target?" Leticia wondered.

"Legion," the Judge answered.

"You know him quite well, don't you?"

"I gave him his first legal job in the City Attorney's office. I have regretted that decision every day since. When he left, I asked him to take me with him, but he refused."

"Why?"

"He was good. And he knew it. He thought I was past my prime. But he continued to use my services for unique insights into the machinations of the courthouse, the police department, and the political landscape of San Diego. Now, the time has come to punish him for his support of the old-boys club."

"Do you have someone lined up for 'the taint?'" Leticia quizzed.

"That would never work with him. Legion is a different type of animal. He fancies himself to be a military general and his lawyers are the troops. So, if you want to bring down a military general, you must bring down the troops. One by one."

Just then Farmington, the butler, entered the room.

"Jack Prickett has returned, sir. Would you like me to show him in?"

"Yes, please. Leticia, I think we're done for now. Excellent job, today. I'll call you tomorrow."

"Thank you, your Honor."

Leticia stood and left the room. She passed Jack Prickett in the hallway. The Judge began to speak as soon as he saw Jack.

"Jack, so good to see you. Come on in and sit down."

Jack sat the far end of the couch away from the Judge.

"I'm in a little bit of a time crunch, Caesar," Jack advised with urgency.

"This will only take a minute. Is everything shaping up well with the Gibson assignment?"

"I'm just going over details at this point, but there's a lot of them."

"I've got a few assignments that are of an exigent nature."

"If they can wait till Friday, I'll put them at the top of my list. Otherwise, I can't focus on them now."

"All right," the Judge acquiesced. "Just to let you know, the payout is doubled if they're done within seventy-two hours."

"I'm interested. Let's talk on Friday."

Jack left the room and the Judge shakily rose from his chair. He walked twenty feet to a window and grabbed the sill of the window for support. Caesar looked back at his wheelchair in disgust.

He then moved in a wobbly fashion back to the chair, concerned that he would fall at any moment. He dropped his butt into the seat of the chair.

His first thought was, 'I will walk again and other lawyers will bow down to me!'

His thoughts moved to the Gibson job that Jack was about to undertake. The Gibson job was very important to the people who hired Caesar to perform it. He would have to gauge Jack's reaction to killing Annabella and Raul on Friday.

CHAPTER 31

Roger Legion sat at his desk reviewing the claims manual from Tecton Insurance. This was the document that provided step-by-step direction for handling liability claims for the insurance company. This document would become a source of serious contention in the upcoming *Zantoff Transportation v. Tecton Insurance* case.

The landline telephone on Roger Legion's desk came to life and Roger answered it on the second ring.

"Yes."

"Pat Madore from Newford Casualty is on line 5," Nina announced.

Newford Casualty had been a client of Legion & Associates for the past eight years and the company was a significant source of revenue for the law firm. Pat Madore was their Claims Manager.

"Hello, Pat," Roger answered with a robust, welcoming voice. "How are you doing today?"

"I'm fine, Roger. How are you? Keeping busy?"

"Always. What can I do for you today?"

"I've got four new ones over here for you. Do you want me to drop them in the mail or do you want to send a runner?"

"I'll send a runner to your place," Roger advised.

"I'll have them ready for you first thing in the morning. I think the plaintiff attorney in one of them blew the statute of limitations. But he claimed there were some tolling issues."

"We'll look at it and let you know. Now, what about you? What have you been doing for fun? You and the wife need to go to the theater?"

Roger's hospitality to claims people was legendary. No expense was spared.

"No, that's okay," Pat told him. "But," he hesitated, "I do have something that maybe you could help me with."

"Anything," Roger retorted. "What?"

"I don't know if you remember my son, Jason?"

"I remember him."

"Well, he just turned twenty-one and he's been trying to get into law enforcement. Up in Carlsbad, they have this position with the police department called Community Service Officers. They help with traffic and crowd control and other things to assist police officers. My son went through all the interviews and they told him he was on a final list. Three people for two positions. He's one of them. The other two candidates are older ladies, who have worked for the police department over twenty years each." Pat paused for a moment. "I really don't know what to ask of you, Roger."

"Don't worry, Pat," Roger exclaimed in a calm, serene tone. "I know exactly what to do."

"Thanks, Roger," Pat's voice echoed relief.

"Okay, I'll be in touch."

Roger returned the phone receiver to its cradle and Clint Eversol appeared in his doorway. Roger waved him in. He stood behind one of the chairs across from Roger.

"We've got a problem."

Roger focused on Clint with concern. Clint continued.

"The plaintiff has been retaining private investigators all over Southern California for the _Zantoff_ case. He is having them do stupid, simple things. Dan and I have called twenty-one so far, including Glenn Edgarian, and they are all unavailable."

Roger's visage indicated that he was cogitating his next move.

"Our adversary is poisoning the well," Roger exclaimed. "We need to respond in kind."

"What are you thinking?" Clint wondered.

"Any discovery responses that we send out are to be sent on red paper. Most copiers can't copy red paper. No electronic copies."

"Doesn't the court require white copies?"

"They do. But let's wait until the plaintiff objects."

Roger viewed this development like a pebble in his shoe. It would have no real impact on his journey. But the plaintiff attorney needed to feel the repercussions from trying to slight the Legion law firm.

CHAPTER 32

At Angelo's Burgers in Encinitas, Annabella and Raul sat in a booth while they were finishing their French fries. Annabella took hold of both of Raul's hands.

"I don't want to do this anymore," she exclaimed with sincerity.

"What? Eat french fries?" Raul responded with a smile.

"What _we_ do," she said with maudlin serenity. "Years ago, I had something to prove. To all men, including you. It blinded me. But looking back, I wish I was a stay-at-home mom, who would wash the clothes, clean the house, make cookies, and take care of my babies."

"There's still time for that," Raul told her.

"I don't know, Raul. Do you ever see their faces?"

"Who?"

"The dead. The ones you've killed."

"Very rarely."

"I see them in my sleep all the time. I have this recurrent dream that I'm walking down the street and all I see are these people like a _día de los muertos_ (day of the dead). How do I get that to stop?"

"You need a change of scenery," Raul answered. "A life far away from this one." He paused for a moment. "Should we try again?"

"Too much time," she said, nearly in tears. "Too much damage."

"Think about it. You know me. I can make it happen."

Annabella made one final comment.

"If you decide you're going to kill me, just let me know. I won't fight it. I won't run. I'll surrender to it."

Raul looked at her with his trademark smile.

"Anyone who thinks they're going to kill you will have to kill me first."

Annabella smiled and a tear ran down her cheek.

"You call Jack and," he paused, "are you going to finish your milkshake?"

"You can have it."

Annabella pushed the shake toward him and he immediately began to consume it.

A sense of calmness flooded over her. It was something foreign to her, yet highly desirable.

CHAPTER 33

Roger Legion, Clint Eversol and Dan Clarkson entered the offices of Context Legal Services, located on West 'C' Street, just four blocks from the America's Finest City Building. The interior was bright white, with windowed walls that allowed illumination to pour in.

In addition to Court Reporting Services, Context Legal provided videography services, document depository services, trial technical services, and on-site facilities for attorney meetings and mediation services. It was the latter that brought Roger Legion there this day.

He was to meet the plaintiff attorney in the *Zantoff Transportation v. Tecton Insurance* case. This would be their last chance to mediate and settle the case prior to trial. Legion and his men approached the counter in the reception area.

"We're here for the *Zantoff* case," Legion advised the receptionist.

"Would you please sign in?" she asked. She then scoured a piece of paper on her desk. "You're the defense, so you're in Room five. Right down the hallway." She pointed them in the direction of the room.

Clint, Dan and Legion entered the room and there sat, around a table, the four executives from Tecton Insurance, who had met with Roger the day before.

"Gentlemen, how are you?" Legion proclaimed with a robust, strong tone. He moved around to each gentleman to share a firm handshake. Each of the Legion attorneys followed Legion's lead.

All answered 'Good.'

"Has the mediator been in to speak to us?" Legion quizzed.

"Just to say 'Hello' and introduce himself," Jesus Loredo, the CEO of Tecton Insurance, advised. "He said he was going to talk to the plaintiff first."

"Very well, gentlemen. Now we wait."

Legion and his men pulled out chairs from the table, but before any of them would sit, the door to the room opened and the mediator entered.

The mediator was Beauregard 'Beau' Lancaster. He would always introduce himself by his full first name and then include "of the Charleston, North Carolina Lancaster's." His Southern drawl was evident and he was extremely proud of it.

Lancaster was 72 years old, with a slight frame, wavy, gray hair (combed back) and a thick moustache. He looked like he could have been a veteran of the Confederate Army.

"Hello, Roger," he said immediately. "Hello, boys," he told Clint and Dan.

"We got a unique bird here today, Roger. He wants to talk to you and your group. Do you want to go in the other room or do you want him to come in here?" the mediator inquired.

"Have him come in here."

The mediator left and Roger immediately pointed to Clint, then Dan.

"Go to the far end of the table. Don't sit." He then spoke directly to Dan. "Don't forget why I selected you."

The two men walked to the back of the table and stood near their four clients. Roger reached the far end of the table, just as the door to the conference room opened.

The man who walked in, in no way exemplified his reputation. He was no more than 5 feet, 2 inches tall, quite slender and wore a crème-color, 3-piece suit. His colored, black hair was thinning.

His eyes locked with Roger's eyes and for a moment, his face was void of expression. Then, the smile of a Cheshire cat beamed.

"Mr. Legion, I've been waiting for you." His voice had a tone of finality. "Have you come to settle the case?"

"Maybe," Legion advised. "You wanted to talk to us, so, feel free to begin."

"Why don't you take a seat," the man suggested.

"I'll stand," Legion told him with a slight tone of defiance.

"Very well. My name is Ricky Ray Ransom. My law firm is the Triple R out of Houston. I specialize in bad faith cases against insurance companies. I've settled and obtained verdicts with a gross value in excess of half a billion dollars. I have never lost a case that I have taken to trial.

"You all know the facts of the *Zantoff* case, so I am not going to bore you by repeating them. The bottom line is that there was an underlying case in which a little girl was severely injured due to the negligence of your insured's truck driver. Your insured agreed to a stipulated judgment of twenty-one million dollars in exchange for a covenant not to execute it. Thereafter, your insured assigned their rights in your insurance policy to my client. Then, the current case was filed, and that brings us here. Any questions?"

The room was silent. Roger had a rather petulant look on his face.

"I am here to discuss damages," Ransom advised.

Ricky Ray turned to the door and opened it slightly. He snapped his fingers and was handed four, leather-bound, booklets, approximately the size of a legal pad and slid them down the table to the men. The cover of the booklet had the name of the case and a branding iron with the logo of his law firm.

"My time is too valuable to waste," Ransom admonished them. "If you people are serious about settling this case, then so am I."

Roger spoke up.

"You are not going to dictate how this mediation is going to be conducted nor how this case is going to be tried. The seas are not going to part for you here in San Diego, Ricky Ray."

"The way they do for you, Mr. Legion? I know all about you and your capabilities. I know about your unblemished record in court. But the facts of this case are going to bury you. Like Custer, you have met your Little Big Horn."

"Bring it on," Dan asserted with full intimidation mode.

"Very good," Ricky Ray told Legion. "You train your disciples well. He's ready for a street fight. I don't engage in street fights. I deliver death blows with laser precision without even breaking a sweat."

The room went silent and the men looked at each other for a second.

"I'll tell you what. I'd like to talk to Mr. Legion alone. We can go to another room or, if you people don't mind, you could step out for a moment."

The group decided to step out. Ricky Ray began to speak as soon as the door closed behind the last person.

"May I call you, Roger?"

"Of course," Legion answered.

"I don't want to get off on the wrong foot, because I know we have to work together regardless of the direction this lawsuit takes. If you look at the last page of the booklet that I handed out, my demand is fifty million dollars?"

Legion remained stoic.

"I'll tell you what," Ricky Ray stated. "You seem like a nice guy. I'm going to give you one chance to get out from under this. I'm going to let you tell your client that you beat me up terribly, because you're the greatest lawyer in the world, and I cut my demand to forty-five million dollars. But not a penny less. Do we have a deal? Because if we don't, and this case sees the inside of a courtroom, there's gonna be blood on the floor."

Legion just stared at him.

"Your braggadocio only serves to embolden me. My client will never pay anything near forty-five million dollars."

"What are you willing to offer?" Ransom wanted to know.

"The policy limit. One million dollars."

"That's a non-starter. We're done here."

Ricky Ray turned to the door and started to open it in disgust. Legion caught his attention.

"Ricky Ray - there's one significant thing you're wrong about: I am not a nice guy."

Roger was now fired up to quash Ricky Ray Ransom like an ant.

CHAPTER 34

Annabella had no luck contacting Jack. He did not call her back until eleven o'clock the next morning. This evening was the date that the Union official, Terry Gibson, was targeted for assassination. Jack was working on details that needed to be placed in motion prior to the hit, which was set for the early evening.

Raul and Annabella set a rendezvous point to meet Jack in the parking lot of the Home Depot Hardware store in Encinitas, located approximately five miles from the Rancho Santa Fe home of Judge Cargyle.

Shortly after they pulled into the lot, Annabella spotted Jack's late-model, gray, Dodge Challenger. She and Raul parked in a space where they could observe the car. When Jack emerged from the store, Annabella and Raul were standing by the back bumper of Jack's car.

"Jack," she said and met him with a smile, a kiss on the cheek, and a quick hug. She was sincerely glad to see him.

"Hey. What's going on?" Jack wondered.

"Jack, this is Raul Verdugo." They shared a handshake and a smile.

"The executioner," Jack declared. "I've heard a lot about you."

"All good, I hope, Clipper," Raul retorted with a smart-alecky grin.

"I don't think anyone has lived to say anything bad," Jack shared.

"Jack," Annabella began, "has Judge Cargyle,"

Jack's phone began to ring and it cut off Annabella's sentence.

"Let me take this," Jack conveyed, then swiped the phone to answer the call.

"Yeah, Woody."

Woody Tabog was the old man in the hospital, who was dying from lung cancer. He was Jack's mentor in the art of death.

"You ready for tonight?" Woody asked with a concerned tone.

"Just about there."

"Did you remember about the fingerprints? Get spray silicone and spray it until you get it to liquid. Then put your fingers in there and no prints for at least two weeks."

"I already did it."

"Did you check the loads on the guns to make sure there was no moisture? Moisture could cause the gun to jam."

"Done."

"Did you check the springs in the gun magazines? If they're compressed for too long, they lose their strength. That could cause a jam."

"It's done."

"Don't forget to make sure that the Velcro is loose."

"I won't forget."

"Sounds good," Woody added. "Remember what I told you. Stay fluid. Things can go to shit in a heartbeat. Just keep your eyes open."

"Will do."

"Listen, Jack. Come and get me. I can help you. You know I'm good with a gun. I can at least be a lookout."

"No, Woody, I've got this under control. I'll call you as soon as it's done."

"You better. I'll be waiting. I would wish you 'good luck,' but you don't need it. You're the second best hit man that ever lived."

"And I'm talking to the first."

"Damn straight, boy. I love ya. Take it easy or any other way you can get it."

With that, the call ended. Jack turned to Annabella and Raul.

"We have a little situation," Raul told him.

"The Judge has asked me to kill you and Raul," Annabella revealed.

"And I was asked to kill you and Annabella," Raul advised. "Has anybody talked to you about us?"

These revelations placed Jack into deep contemplation.

"No," Jack replied. "But Caesar wants to talk to me on Friday about some high profile work that pays double if it is completed within seventy-two hours."

"Well Annabella, did you know we were 'high profile,' Raul sarcastically uttered.

"What's our next move?" Annabella asked.

"Why don't I take out Caesar?" Jack answered.

"I'm afraid that would not get rid of the problem," Raul surmised. "We need to find out who gives the orders to Caesar."

"I can't focus on this right now. I've got a lot of things to do," Jack declared with a tinge of desperation in his voice.

Raul looked at Annabella, then back to Jack.

"You need some help?" Raul asked with a cool, calm and collected voice.

Jack began to smile.

CHAPTER 35

At 2:59 pm, Clint showed up at Legion's office for their daily meeting regarding the *Zantoff* case. This was the fourth day, and fourth meeting, since the mediation with Ricky Ray Ransom. The men were becoming more enlightened with the case every day.

Legion waved him in, and before he sat down, Dan was in the doorway.

"Come on in," Legion told him and Dan sat in the other chair, next to Clint. "What's new, gentlemen?"

"I just got a call from one of Ricky Ray's associates. They are withdrawing any claims to medical costs as a part of their damages."

"Why would they do that?" Dan asked in wonderment. "They have to be in excess of four million dollars."

Legion was quick to respond.

"Because, with those medical damages, it will never get him to fifty million dollars. He's going to pitch an argument that society has to punish the insurance company for its conduct. He is going to look at the insurance company and its overall value and income, then ask the jury for a percentage of it. It's dangerous. But I've seen it work before. What else?"

"I have now read all the deposition transcripts," Clint advised. "There are summaries in the files, but I haven't read those. The parents testified that they did connect the seat belt on the little girl. It was the little girl who disconnected it."

Legion was in deep thought with every word.

"Whenever we refer to the girl in front of the jury, it's important to say her name, Rebecca. They are going to call her 'baby', 'little girl' and 'Becky.' Ricky Ray will search for sympathy. We need to diffuse that with cold, hard facts whenever we can.

"What about the driver?" Legion quizzed.

"Clean driving record," Dan answered. "But he testified that he was texting right before the impact and didn't have time to stop."

"Were there any skid marks?" Legion queried.

"No," Dan answered. "Our expert found that to be odd. He has not yet prepared a written report, because it would not be very beneficial to us."

"Wouldn't you think he would have slammed on the brakes upon impact, instead of allowing the truck to plow into these people unabated?"

Clint and Dan nodded their heads in agreement.

"Are all the depos videotaped?" Legion asked.

"Yeah," Clint answered.

"Line them all up for viewing tomorrow in the conference room. I want to see a few minutes of each one."

"Will do," Clint responded.

"As of right now, the driver is M.I.A. (missing in action)" Dan disclosed. "The owner of the company thinks he may have gone home to Vietnam. His mother was usually able to contact him, but she died about six weeks ago."

"Find out if the police may have his phone. If they do, subpoena it."

Dan nodded his head in concurrence.

"Clint," Dan questioned, "was there anything in the depos about the father having a girlfriend?"

"Nothing. Did he?"

"Before this claim was in litigation, the claims adjuster took recorded statements from a variety of individuals, including the mother, father, the insured truck driver, and the insured owner of the trucking company. But I saw that he also took a recorded statement of a bartender, named Michael Lim. He was a bartender at a place called the Liftoff on Adams Avenue. Apparently, they thought the father may have been drunk at the time of the accident. There was never any proof of that. He took a breathalyzer test at the scene and blew a .04."

Dan was referring to the father's blood alcohol content. In California, a person's blood alcohol content would have to exceed .08 to be considered intoxicated.

Dan continued.

"The bartender said the father was at the bar for a couple of hours prior to the accident with a woman whose first name was Sharifa, but she goes by 'Shy.' He thought she was a crack whore. The bartender heard she was from Chicago and she owed some drug people there a lot of money."

The wheels in Legion's mind were smoking. Suddenly, you could see on his face that he had just experienced an epiphany, a moment of clarity.

"Gentlemen," Legion asserted as if he was about to disclose the name of a murderer, "I think I know what happened here. Now, I need to prove it. Keep doing what you're doing."

Roger Legion's hunch would either lead down a dark alley to the truth or be a colossal waste of time.

CHAPTER 36

The Union of Technical, Informational and Commercial Workers of America (UTICA) were holding an informational membership meeting at the Doubletree Hotel, located in the Carmel Del Mar area of San Diego. The 4-story hotel was not overly plush, but it would send the perfect message to potential members: that the Union will take members from a comfortable place to an extraordinary place.

The President's Room at the hotel held two hundred twenty people. The Union invited one hundred fifty people who either expressed an interest in joining the Union or held positions of influence inside their company.

Over the last several years, various technology companies had opened in the Rancho Bernardo and Scripps Ranch areas of San Diego. The number of employees had now reached into the thousands and the UTICA Union thought it was time to plant their flag.

Terry Gibson was a firebrand Union organizer, whose speeches were reminiscent of a Baptist preacher. He was 47 years old, average height and weight, with wavy blonde hair. He had been arrested three times for trespassing on the property of various technology companies. The management of the companies viewed him as a guerrilla malcontent. A rabble-rouser, who was looking to make trouble.

Gibson's message was simple: workers should throw down their shackles and be paid a decent wage, commensurate with their value. They should also share in the abundant profits that are gorged upon by a selected few.

As expected, management wanted to extinguish this revolution before it caught fire. Jack Pickett was the man summoned to accomplish this task.

One hundred fifty people were invited to this dinner. Fifteen circular tables were set-up that allowed ten people to sit at each table. Gibson was to sit at a dais at the far end of the room. There was a cocktail hour from 6:30 pm to 7:30 pm, followed by dinner.

There were eight men from Gibson's security detail already in the room. It was two men for each wall. All stood close to the walls with their backs to the surface of the wall. There was a man placed by each exit door and the other man would be placed equidistant between the exit door man and the adjoining wall.

The men were all former members of the Mossad, the Israeli secret police. Their ability to protect and guard was somewhat legendary.

At the end of the room, opposite the dais, near the kitchen area stood Jack Pricket dressed as a beverage waiter. He wore a black wig and moustache, along with some facial bronzer to darken his skin tone. This was all courtesy of Annabella. He wore a white, long-sleeve shirt, with black trousers, a black vest, and black bowtie.

Jack held a circular serving tray under his arm and compulsively scanned the room to know the exact location of the exits and Gibson's security detail.

The attendees began to arrive in waves. One of the first attendees was a small, blind woman, with gray hair, Wayfarer sunglasses, and a white, foldable cane. She also carried a large, circular handbag, which she carried by strap across her chest.

The woman slowly meandered to the closest table, folded her cane, and claimed a chair.

In the next wave of people, an elderly, debonair gentleman entered. He wore a blue suit, with a light pinstripe, white shirt, and a red tie with a blue diamond pattern. He had not a gray hair out of place and his pencil moustache highlighted his movie-star looks.

The woman was Annabella and the man was Raul. Each one locked eyes with the other, including Jack. They were all awaiting the target.

Into the room entered a Loomis armored truck security guard carrying a chest that looked like a small, foot locker. It was eighteen inches long, twelve inches wide, and ten inches deep. The truck security guard was flagged down by a woman, who showed the guard her identification, and signed for the chest. The woman carried it to the dais and placed it within the podium where union-organizer Gibson was set to give a speech.

The activity, involving the Loomis guard, did not go unnoticed by Jack, Annabella, and Raul.

CHAPTER 37

That evening, Judge Caesar Cargyle sat at his desk in his Rancho Santa Fe home and reviewed charges from his online American Express Centurion Card also known as the Amex Black Card. The total charges for the month exceeded twenty-four thousand dollars and the Judge wanted to make sure there were no inaccuracies.

As he perused the bill, his KryptAll phone, which lay on the desk, sounded. The KryptAll phone was a high technology device that prevented eavesdropping on a telephone line and prevented a call from being traced. Caesar answered it.

"Hello," the Judge greeted with a deadpanned, perturbed voice.

"Caesar, it's Seesay."

Oziel 'Ozy' Seesay was a mysterious, shadowy figure, who supplied assignments to the Judge from an organization referred to as 'the Company.' Not much was known about either the Company or Seesay, other than a chance encounter between the Judge and Seesay, nearly thirty-five years earlier at a meeting of Southern California Defense Counsel at an upscale hotel in Century City, California.

"Hello, Mr. Seesay. How are you?"

"I've been better. You did receive the list, didn't you?" Seesay wondered.

"I did," the Judge advised.

"Then, what's the problem? I'm not seeing any progress."

"I've got one of my best guys handling the Gibson assignment tonight. Tomorrow, he can handle two at a time."

"Who might that be?" Seesay queried.

"Jack Prickett."

"The same Jack Prickett who's on the list?"

"Yeah. But, let me get some mileage out of him. Then, if you still want him to go, I'll take care of him, too."

"What about Raul Verdugo?"

"It's in the works."

"Caesar, that guy is perceptive. He sees it coming from a mile away. The last three people that I've asked to kill him have wound up dead."

"You should have come to me first. Don't worry about Verdugo. His hours are numbered."

"Herrero told you about your little girl, right? That's a major concern and a big problem. What are you doing about it?"

"I'm going to let her take care of a few of the assignments, then I'll get it taken care of."

"Time is not a luxury that we have. The powers that be want to wind down affairs. A lot of people, including you, have made a lot of money from this operation. People in high places are asking questions and it's becoming," Seesay paused for a moment, "uncomfortable."

"Let me do what I do best," the Judge told him.

"All right, Caesar. But let me tell you that if I do not see significant progress on your efforts in the next three days, then I am going to call in men from out-of-town. They will be ruthless, relentless, and merciless. And you will be on the next list."

With that the call ended. Caesar slowly returned the phone to the desktop and gazed forward without focus. He could feel the vice begin to tighten.

CHAPTER 38

As 7:00 pm approached, nearly all of the invitees had arrived at the President's Room of the Doubletree Hotel. Alcohol was flowing and the sound level in the room continued to elevate. Most of the people were sitting and chatting, while waiters offered various hors d'oeurves. Just as the top of the hour arrived, so did the Master of Ceremonies.

Terry Gibson, the union organizer, entered, flanked by two security guards. He glad-handed the crowd, like a politician nearing election, all smiles and perceiving victory.

Both Raul and Annabella took a quick look at Jack.

Jack went to the location where a bar was set up to serve alcoholic drinks. Amidst the flurry of activity, no one questioned why he was there. He grabbed a cocktail shaker and poured approximately 1.25 ounces of vodka and .25 ounces of vermouth into it. Jack then stealthily added a powder to it. He took a martini glass and poured the contents of the shaker into it. Jack placed two large, green olives on a large toothpick into it and the vodka martini was complete.

The powder that he placed into the drink was cyanide, an extremely fatal poison, which can cause death within one to fifteen minutes.

Jack picked up the drink and walked briskly to the back of the kitchen. There was no activity near a series of cabinets and he opened the farthest cabinet door. He grabbed a small bag that looked like a shaving kit, off the shelf. Jack immediately proceeded to the employee bathroom, with the bag and the drink, located ten feet away.

Once inside the bathroom, Jack locked the door and went to his knees. From the bag he pulled out a 9 mm, P320 Sig Sauer pistol. Jack rapidly checked the pistol to make sure the magazine was loaded with ten bullets, there was a bullet in the chamber, ready to fire, and the safety was off.

Along the handle and barrel of one side of the gun were pieces of Velcro that matched two pieces of Velcro that was adhered to the bottom of Jack's serving tray. This is the Velcro that Woody, Jack's mentor, made reference to. Woody wanted Jack to make sure the Velcro would not be too tight when you pull the gun off. Jack placed the gun against the Velcro of the tray and pulled it off several times until he was confident that there would be no problem in pulling the gun from the tray.

Jack then retrieved a black piece of cloth from the small bag and covered the tray. He stood up and placed the Vodka Martini on the tray. With the cloth hanging down, no one would be able to see the gun under the tray.

Jack proceeded at a brisk clip out of the kitchen and directly in search of his target.

Terry Gibson had made his way to the dais and stood at the podium speaking to several people on the floor level. His two security guards stood on each side, scouring the room for any unusual activity.

While Jack walked toward the stage where Gibson stood, he took his right hand and started to grab the gun. He did not want to pull it off the Velcro, but he did want to loosen it. Both Annabella and Raul tracked Jack as he made the journey to his destination.

Jack stepped up onto the dais from one end and walked toward Gibson. One of the security guards turned and stood between Jack and Gibson.

"Someone ordered a drink for Mr. Gibson," Jack advised.

The security guard looked back at Gibson and Gibson looked to see what was on the tray.

"Set it down," Gibson told Jack.

Jack took has left hand and complied, placing the drink close to the end of the table that abutted the podium.

In that second, Jack realized that he could take a clear shot at Gibson and the two security guards. If Gibson would drink the martini, then Annabella, Raul and himself would have an easy exit.

Gibson reached for the drink, but as he did, he caught the eye of someone to share a handshake. As he reached down, he knocked over the drink. Gibson had just made the decision for Jack.

Jack easily pulled the gun off the Velcro, and fired three headshots into Gibson and two bodyguards within two seconds. Gibson fell forward, onto the now blood-stained podium, and both he and the podium fell off the dais. Jack then shot Gibson a second time, or double tap, to ensure his assignment was complete.

The first gunshot was the call to action for Annabella and Raul. Annabella reached into her bag and retrieved two flashbang grenades. She immediately pulled the pins on them and hurled one to the front of the room near the dais and the other to the opposite end near the kitchen.

The grenades went off, causing an intense, deafening explosion, coupled with a blinding light. Most attendees covered their ears as all they could hear was a masked ringing and held their eyes closed tightly.

Annabella, Raul and Jack all wore earplugs that set deeply within their ear to avoid detection.

As soon as the flashbang grenades went off, Annabella pulled four smoker grenades from her bag. She would pull the pin on each and launch it into each corner of the room to lay down a heavy, blinding fog. Raul put on sunglasses.

When the first bullet was sounded, Raul pulled a nearby fire alarm, to add an additional layer of confusion to the mix. He pulled a 9 mm Ruger LC9 from his waistband behind his back. He saw the first security guard start to move to the dais. Raul took one shot and hit the guard in the side of his left knee, blasting apart his kneecap. The guard went to the floor, writhing in pain.

Raul re-positioned as the second guard was about to disappear into the fog. Raul again stopped for a moment, took aim and shot the second guard in the back of his right knee. The hallow-point bullet exploded upon impact. The guard's tibia (shinbone) and patella (kneecap) shattered. He also dropped to the floor.

After all the grenades had been launched, Annabella moved toward one of the guards, who had drawn his pistol and held it with both hands, aiming down, when she was within three feet of him, she screamed.

"HEY!"

He turned his head instantly to look at her. As he did, Annabella pirouetted on her right foot around at lightning speed for a reverse roundhouse kick. Her booted foot slapped the guard in the face with such power that he was immediately knocked unconscious.

Annabella spotted the other guard that she was assigned to watch. She ran up behind him and as she ran, she pulled a small, circular ring off the face of the watch she was wearing. That ring was connected to a wire, like a piano wire, that connected to the watch. The wire had a slight, coarse texture that was hardly visible.

When Annabella was within one foot of the guard, she vaulted, her hands outstretched, with the wire between them. She swooped the wire over the guard's head and caught his neck. Annabella was now hanging from the wire, pulling it back as hard as she could in a saw motion. The coarseness of the wire was cutting more and more into his skin with each of Annabella's movements.

Annabella and the guard fell to the floor. He attempted to maneuver his gun to shoot Annabella without success. She pinned the gun down with her Doc Marten boot.

When she realized the guard was no longer a threat, she kicked his gun away and allowed the wire to retract back into the watch. He continued to bleed, but it did not appear to be fatal.

The room was fully enveloped in fog from the smoker grenades. Four guards were down and four remained. One of the guards was slowly making his way to the podium area, where Gibson was killed, when a chair flung around with baseball bat fury. The blow took him off his feet and sent him to the ground. Jack threw down the chair as he evidenced the reason for his nickname, the Clipper.

Raul met a sixth guard that he swiftly incapacitated by punching him in the throat while holding his gun. The barrel of Raul's gun cracked the guard's windpipe, placing him in a life or death struggle to breathe. The guard went down to his knees, hoping that help was on its way.

The other two guards made their way to the exits, realizing that any defensive posture was compromised. Jack grabbed the chest that was brought in by the Loomis armored car guard. He would now meet with Annabella and Raul at a pre-determined rendezvous point within the room,

The exterior security guards had now entered the building and were in the process of sealing it off. Time was of the essence.

CHAPTER 39

Judge Caesar Cargyle sat at his desk and contemplated what he needed to accomplish. He made a call to Leticia Harrison, the attorney who was the executive member of the FOG, which was known to the public as the Female Optimization Group and the Face of God to its members. She answered her phone on the second ring.

"Yes, your Honor," her voice indicating urgency to respond.

"I want to call a special meeting of the FOG this week" he told her. "Let me know if there are any days that don't work for you."

"All right. I should be pretty open. Anything in particular that you wanted to discuss."

"Our plan is about to move to the next level. I want all the ladies to be onboard. I don't want them to be dissuaded by anything they may hear in the media. It will basically be a pep talk, but I hope to outline our trek for the next twelve months."

"All right. I'll contact all of them. You just let me know the date."

"Thank you, Leticia. I'll be in touch."

With that the call ended. The Judge's next call had a more sinister intention.

"Hey, Caesar," Ruben Herrero answered.

Ruben Herrero was the rogue San Diego Police captain of the SWAT unit, who assisted the Judge with his murder-for-hire operations.

"I may have to press you into service," the Judge advised.

"Ready, willing and able," Herrero replied.

"I've got a list I need to share with you."

"How many on it?"

"Six."

"Does it include the Executioner and the Little Girl?"

Ruben was referring to Raul and Annabella.

"It does, but I'm not worried about them right now. It's the ancillary people on the list. How soon can you start?" Caesar inquired.

"Get me the list tonight and I'll start tonight."

"Where are you? I'll have Farmington bring it to you. The coffee shop?"

"I think Internal Affairs either has that place staked out or they have it wired for sound."

"Is this work going to be a problem?" the Judge voiced concern.

"No. The IA guys are dogs chasing their tails. I've been two steps ahead of them at every turn. Tell your guy to meet me at the Mission Valley Shopping Mall. I'll be sitting on a bench, just outside the Target."

"Okay. Thanks, Ruben."

Judge Cargyle felt some relief that the assassination list would clear quickly with Ruben's intervention. He wondered if it would be quick enough to satisfy Mr. Seesay.

CHAPTER 40

Annabella, Jack and Raul made their way to the rendezvous point, which was at the base of a staircase, outside of the room, with stairs all the way to the roof. The trio ascended the stairs with competition-like speed. As they reached the staircase between the fourth floor and the roof, sounds of someone entering the staircase on the first floor could be heard.

The marine layer that evening was extremely thick. Visibility had been deemed to be zero miles, so unless you had some form of lighting, you could not see beyond your hand in front of your face.

Once they reached the roof, Jack led them to the west side of the building. The adjacent building was a four-story office building that had a parking garage at the south end. It was only separated from the Doubletree Hotel by a driveway. Earlier in the day, Jack had run a cable from a steel girder on the top of the hotel to a concrete post on the third floor of the parking garage in the adjacent building. The third floor was selected because Jack needed a downhill grade to accomplish his desired task.

From one of the nearby air ducts, Jack retrieved a zip line trolley. This was a device with two small wheels that would allow a person to slide down the cable. The device also had a built-in 'T' bar that would provide the rider stability. Jack connected the device to the cable and tied an end of a parachute cord rope line to it. This would allow Raul to pull the zip line trolley back for the next rider.

Jack was going first, but not before Raul took off his belt and put it around the belt that Jack was wearing. Raul then connected the belt to one of the side handles of the small footlocker chest that was brought in by the Loomis guard.

Jack made it across.

Raul pulled the zip trolley back as fast as he could. Annabella grabbed it and looked at him for a second. He took his index finger and middle finger and blew a kiss to her. She smiled and he pushed her. Annabella zipped across the cable and into Jack's waiting arms.

Raul could see that the tension was off the cable from Annabella's ride. He immediately uncoupled the cable from the steel girder and it fell to the street. Amidst the thick fog, Raul heard the sounds of the San Diego Police Special Weapons and Tactical Unit arriving on the rooftop.

Annabella was incensed as she heard the sound of the cable slap against the building.

"Oh my God, Raul!" she exclaimed, looking at the hotel. She then turned to Jack. "We've got to go get him!"

"No," Jack sternly advised. "One more diversion and then we're all in the clear."

"Jack, let me go help him."

"No, it's too dangerous. He wants you and me to get out of here, now."

"Jack, there's a saying in Mexico, *Cree que es la única Coca en el desierto.*"

"What's it mean?"

"He thinks he's the only Coke in the desert." She paused. "He's not."

"Here's a Mexican saying I learned long ago, *Lo que un capitán ordena, un marinero tiene que aceptar.*"

Annabella looked at Jack with calm surrender. Jack told her, "What a captain orders, a seaman has to accept."

Annabella proceeded to Jack's car and got in.

Meanwhile, Raul sought the best offensive/defensive position to deal with the SWAT team. He could hear their movements from the metal jangling of objects they carried.

The first SWAT member he located was taking a position behind an air duct only four feet away from Raul. He crept up on the SWAT officer, and when he was close enough, Raul pounced and placed him in a headlock. As the officer struggled, Raul pulled the officer's Taser out of its holster right in his side that was not covered by a bullet-proof vest. The burst of electricity froze him and he lost all power. He fell to the ground like a dishrag.

Raul removed the officer's handgun and tossed it off the roof. He grabbed the officer's AR-15 rifle and continued his hunt. The next two officers that Raul encountered were both incapacitated by a quick, sharp smash to the face by the butt of the rifle. In each instance, Raul would remove their handgun, rifle, or both, and toss them off the rooftop.

He stopped to listen to the chatter on one of the walkie-talkies. Their commander was calling out to them without receiving a response.

Raul approached a fourth SWAT officer with his handgun leveled at him. With the thick marine layer, he did not notice Raul, until Raul was right on top of him. His locked eyes evidenced concern.

"Drop the rifle."

The officer complied. Raul picked it up and whipped it off the roof.

"Left hand. Remove the handgun."

"I've got a safety on the holster. Can I use my right hand to take it off?"

"Go ahead."

The officer complied and pulled his gun out of the holster with his left hand. He gave the gun to Raul, who promptly threw it off the roof.

"Give me your handcuffs."

Again the officer complied. Raul had him turn around and he placed the handcuffs on him. He then placed the barrel of his handgun against the side of the officer's head, next to his ear, right below his helmet.

"Call your Commander," Raul told him in a low, chilling voice.

"Push the talk button on the walkie."

Raul complied.

"This is Nelson to Command. Over."

"Nelson, do you see him?" A voice asked with urgency.

"He's standing right next to me. He's got a gun to my head."

There was silence from the Commander.

"Tell him to stand down," Raul ordered. "And tell him to get everybody off the roof. Three of your men are down. I don't plan to kill anyone unless I have to."

Officer Nelson conveyed the information and the Commander cleared the roof within fifteen seconds.

"We're going to take a ride."

Raul walked the officer to the rooftop freight elevator. There was a keypad on it and Raul punched the necessary number to open its doors.

Meanwhile, at the reception desk, police officers were monitoring movement within the hotel, which included the elevators. The manager of the hotel, who was also watching an electronic video screen, with a schematic of the hotel, suddenly spoke up.

"The freight elevator is moving from the roof," he uttered with surprise.

"Where's it going?" one of the police officer's asked.

"Whoever is in it," the manager advised, "pushed the buttons for all four floors." There was a pause. "Wait a minute. It's stopped on the fourth floor.

"Pull up the fourth floor hallway cameras," an officer exclaimed with urgency.

There they saw the back of a man scurrying down the hallway. From the back, he fit the description of the debonair assassin. The man entered room 426.

"Bravo team in position."

Four SWAT officers ran down the hallway and encircled the door to Room 426. Each SWAT team had been provided with a master key card for ease of entrance into any room.

The lead officer caught the eyes of the other three men.

"Guns up," he told them and the men leveled their rifles.

The lead officer slipped the master key card into the slot for the door and a blinking red light turned green.

The SWAT team made a single-file entry.

"FREEZE!" the first officer yelled and all four officers held a deadly aim on the occupant.

Ninety minutes later, Annabella and Jack were sitting in the parking lot of a 7-11 convenience store on 'D' Street in Encinitas, each with a fresh, cold bottle of water. Annabella's phone started to buzz and the Caller ID indicated it was Raul.

"Raul, where are you?" Annabella asked with urgency and concern.

"I'm at the McDonald's on Via de la Valle in Del Mar. Can you come and get me?"

"Sure, but what happened?"

"I'll tell you when I see you. You guys want anything from McDonalds?"

"I'll take a Big Mac and a Coke," Jack answered. "We'll be there in twenty minutes or less."

"I'd like a large French fry," Annabella said.

"Okay. I'll see you guys soon." With that, the call was ended.

Jack's assignment was complete. And the legend of the Executioner was catapulted to a new level. Perhaps, Raul was as good as he thought.

Part 4

CHAPTER 41

On the night of the Gibson hit, Jimmy Flowers sat in his office at the Bagheria Bedda restaurant, reviewing receivables from the previous day. He wore a dark, green Polo shirt that was buttoned to the neck and black, Haggar slacks. A knock at his door broke his focus.

Domenic, his usual sentry, poked his head in. Jimmy looked at him in anticipation of a message.

"Roger Legion is here to see you," Domenic advised.

Jimmy was somewhat surprised, but pleased at the same time. Roger Legion had provided legal representation to Jimmy in the past, both personally and for Jimmy's various business entities. The men each had a great respect for the other.

"Show him in," Jimmy commanded. "Don't frisk him."

Within ten seconds, Roger entered. He wore a tailored gray suit, tailored white shirt, Italian leather shoes, and a yellow tie. The two men met each other with a smile and a strong handshake.

"Hello, Jimmy, how are you?" Roger inquired with a sustained ebullient voice.

"I'm good, Roger. How about you?"

"Good," he answered with a nod.

"How's the family?" Jimmy wondered.

"They're all fine. And yours?"

"They're fine, too. Have a seat," Jimmy told him as he pointed to the other side of the desk. "Can I get you a drink? You hungry?"

"No, I'm fine right now, but thanks."

"You know what I'm going to do? I'm going to send you home with two orders of the Special of the Day. *Gnocchi al la Zillia Theresé*. That's Sicilian for "Gnocchi of Saint Theresa." It's like baked ziti, but with gnocchi."

"I'm gaining weight thinking about it."

Both men shared a quick chuckle and Jimmy changed the subject.

"I see that guy you're going against in court on television every day. The guy looks like a midget, carnival barker."

"That's a pretty good description. He's the reason that I've come to see you this evening."

Jimmy focused on Roger, listening intently.

"This guy, Ransom, has contacted all the good private investigators in Southern California and hired each one for some stupid, useless purpose. By doing that, the investigators are precluded from working for me. I've got a woman I'd like to find."

The men looked at each other for a moment.

"We've been friends for a long time, Roger. So, let me ask you this: Do you want to settle the case out of court?"

Roger knew exactly that Jimmy was inferring that he would kill Ransom, if Roger wanted him dead.

"I'm not going to say 'No' to that right now, but I think with this woman I can take this guy down in court."

Jimmy reached for a Post-it note pad and picked up a pen.

"What information do you have?"

"Her name is Sharifa, but she goes by 'Shy. She's in her thirties. My information is that she is heavily into drugs. She was doing cocaine and recently moved to meth. She owes some people in Chicago a lot of drug money. That's all I've got."

"I've got a guy working for me, named Raul Verdugo. He's real sharp. I'll see if he can hunt her down."

"I greatly appreciate it," Roger told him.

Organized crime had just stepped in to assist Roger in the defense of Tecton Insurance for the *Zantoff* case. But the question remained: Would it be enough?

CHAPTER 42

As the dense, marine-layer fog continued to blanket the coastline, Jack's late-model, gray Challenger pulled into the parking lot of the McDonald's on Via de la Valle in Del Mar, California and found a parking spot right by the door. Jack and Annabella got out of the car and spotted Raul sitting at a table in the playground area with a young woman and a small child.

Raul was enjoying an ice cream cone and speaking to the woman in Spanish. He was wearing black shorts, a light, blue t-shirt and sneakers.

"*Mis amigos están aquí* (My friends are here)," he told her.

The young woman looked over at them, then looked at Raul and nodded. He slid a small piece of paper across the table to her. Raul's cell phone number was written on it.

"*Si necesitas algo, llámame* (If you need anything, you call me), Raul said.

Raul stood from the table and gave the woman a kiss on the forehead. He glanced over to the small girl and waved.

"*Adiós, Julieta* (Goodbye, Juliet)"

Raul walked out of the playground area to meet his friends. He was holding his suit bag, a soda for Jack, and a bag that contained a Big Mac and a large french fry. Annabella greeted him with a tight hug. Jack offered him a fist bump.

"How did you do it? I've never seen so many cops at one place," Annabella asked in amazement.

"You see the girl and the little kid I was sitting with?" Raul quizzed. "That's how I did it. Let's go. I'll tell you about it on the ride."

"That baby's name was Julieta? That was your mother's name," Annabella recalled.

"Thanks for remembering that," Raul advised with sincerity and a smile.

Annabella reciprocated with a melancholy smile, as she thought about her own mother for a moment.

They were heading to Raul's condominium in the Little Italy section of San Diego. Annabella sat in the back seat of the car, hanging on Raul's every word. The condo was seven blocks from the Bagheria Bedda restaurant that was owned by Jimmy Flowers.

"After you guys were safe, I was pulling a classic 'divide and conquer' move. I would locate a SWAT guy, incapacitate him, and move on to the next guy. When I got to the fourth guy, I had him talk to his commander and tell the commander to clear the roof. Then, I put that last SWAT guy in the freight elevator and pressed every floor. But I never got in the elevator.

"While the cops were chasing the elevator, I was able to go down an exterior ladder to the second floor. I went to the maintenance closet, where I hid my clothes, and changed into what I am wearing right now. When I came out of the maintenance closet, I spotted the young girl you saw at McDonalds, pushing a stroller.

"Her husband was in the Navy and he had just deployed to the Persian Gulf. She spoke Spanish and was not very fluent in

English. I asked for her help and she agreed. She said she heard the fire alarm, but did not smell any smoke."

Raul let out a slight chuckle.

"She asked me if all the police were there for immigration. *La migra.* I told her that I didn't know. I carried the baby and she and I walked out the front door amidst dozens of cops. There must have been a hundred people trying to get their car keys from the valet to get out. I tipped him a hundred dollars and we went to the front of the line.

"She let me drive and we drove off. It was her plan to go to McDonalds for dinner tonight."

"Hope you paid?" Jack chimed in.

"I did," Raul answered.

"Wait a minute. I know my Raul" Annabella interjected. "What kind of gratuity did you leave with her?"

"I had four, one hundred dollar bills in my wallet. I gave them all to her."

"Raul," Jack conveyed. "I like the ending of that story the best."

Jack then recalled something that he had to do. As he drove, he picked up his phone and for a quick second, perused the keyboard and dialed a number on speed-dial.

"Jack, I've been waiting for you, boy," answered Jack's mentor, Woody, in a robust, ebullient tone. "How did it go?"

"It's done," Jack proudly answered.

"Clean?" Woody inquired, wondering if there were any problems.

"Yeah."

"That's my boy. I knew you could do it," Woody gushed with enthusiasm.

"I couldn't have done it without you. The Velcro made the difference."

"You made the difference, Jack. What's my second favorite saying after 'I can't stand a bullshitter'?"

"Action – not words."

"Damn straight. Until a plan is put into action, it's just something in the air. In the ether. It takes brains, determination, and a lack of fear to bring it to life. It's all you, Jack."

"Listen, I'll come to visit either tomorrow or the day after."

"I want details," Woody told him. "And bring that hip flask and maybe a cigarette."

"No cigarettes."

"All right. Take care, boy. I love ya," uttered Woody proudly.

All three had experienced a pleasant thought of family. It was something they had not done for a very long time.

No one thought about the small chest that was in the trunk of the car. The one that was brought into the Presidents Room, by the Loomis armored truck guard, where the Gibson hit took place. Would it contain more secrets or more answers?

CHAPTER 43

At ten o'clock the next morning, Roger Legion had an appointment with Chief Benjamin Aceti of the Carlsbad Police Department. Roger had been asked by Pat Madore, the Claims Manager of Newford Casualty, for assistance to help his son secure a job with the Carlsbad Police as a Community Service Officer.

Legion entered the police headquarters located on Orion Way in Carlsbad. He proceeded to a counter in the lobby where several windows had either civilian employees or officers to greet visitors.

"Hello," Roger greeted the receptionist. "My name is Roger Legion. I have an appointment with Chief Aceti."

The receptionist pressed three keys on a telephone keypad.

"Roger Legion is here to see the Chief." She waited for a response, then turned to him. "The Chief's secretary is going to come and get you."

"Thank you," he told her.

Within sixty seconds, a portly woman, in her early sixties, arrived in the lobby.

"Mr. Legion," she greeted him, "please come with me."

Roger and the woman took an elevator ride to the second floor and he followed her to the Chief's office.

"You can go in."

Roger entered the room. It was large, clean, and sterile. The walls held awards and the desk and credenza were filled with photos of family and police outings.

Chief Benjamin Aceti was in his late fifties, thin-build, physically fit, and had a full head of black, curly hair with a tinge of gray on each side. His police uniform appeared to be tailored to his body and he had four golden stars on each side of his collar. He rose from his desk chair to greet Roger.

"Mr. Legion," as he spoke, they shook hands. "It's a pleasure to meet you."

"Same with me. But please, call me Roger."

"Bill Piersol told me to make time for you. He told me that you've been good to the San Diego police force."

William Piersol was the Chief of the San Diego Police Department.

"I've known Bill for a long time and I consider him a friend," Legion told the Chief.

"Well, listen," the Chief told Roger, pointing to a chair on the opposite side of a chair from where the Chief sat, "have a seat. What can I do for you?"

"I'm here to talk to you about the son of a client of mine. He applied for a job in your department as a Community Service Officer. He made it to the last stage, but was told informally that he wasn't going to get the job. That's what I wanted to discuss with you."

"What's his name?" the Chief asked.

"Jason Madore," Roger responded.

The Chief made several keystrokes on his desktop computer and was immediately reading the file of Jason Madore.

"I remember this young man. He seems qualified, but he lacks life experience. Give him some time," Aceti paused, "and then he can re-apply."

"Isn't one of the main duties of a Community Service Officer to control traffic and control crowds?" Legion inquired.

"Yes."

"This young man has been working as a security guard at a shopping center for the past two years doing exactly that. How much more life experience do you want him to have?"

"I'm sorry, Mr. Legion. The decision has already been made. We are currently conducting background checks on the candidates before we extend an offer. There's nothing I can do."

Roger gazed at him with slight disdain.

"I notice that all your Community Service Officers are elderly, heavyset women, who have been working for the department in some capacity. I did not notice a requirement for that in the job description."

"Not all the women are elderly," the Chief advised, "and not all the women are overweight."

"Well, perhaps, I should advise my client, Mr. Madore, to commence an action against the City of Carlsbad for gender discrimination. Then, through discovery, I'll find out how many other men have been denied a position in place of a woman. I can amend the lawsuit to be a class action. And this city will be liable for millions of dollars. What do you think about that?"

"Mr. Legion, do you think that you're going to come into my office, bark an order, and I'm going to jump? I don't care whose friend you are, I would like you to leave right now."

The Chief stood from his chair behind the desk as did Roger from his chair.

"I apologize if you're offended," Roger said, "but I also came to offer you some help."

"What sort of help?"

"Do you want to know where your officers are purchasing their recreational drugs? I know. The *San Diego Union Tribune* thinks that they know, and they're trying to find someone to corroborate it. I think you know. Now, I can have that story killed. You've put in more than twenty years here. Do you want to throw it all away?"

The Chief stared at Roger and Roger saw surrender in his eyes.

Two weeks later, Jason Madore received an offer of employment to be a Community Service Officer with the Carlsbad Police Department.

CHAPTER 44

Raul carried the small chest into his apartment, followed by Annabella and Raul. He set it down on the coffee table in his living room and examined the lock. He then proceeded to his bedroom and returned with several keys for foot lockers. The third key that he tested, worked. He undid the latches and opened it.

Contained within it was a list of the one hundred fifty attendees at the event plus one hundred fifty envelopes. In each envelope were five, one hundred dollar bills. These envelopes were to be gifts given out to the attendees in gratitude for the potential support of the Union. Therefore, the small chest contained seventy-five thousand dollars in cash.

They looked at each other and Jack was the first to speak.

"You guys divvy it up."

"No," Raul said. "It was your gig. Your booty. Your spoils."

"I agree with Raul," Annabella chimed in.

The next day, Annabella went to see Judge Caesar Cargyle and Raul went to see Jimmy Flowers. The Judge advised Annabella that the 'powers that be' were so happy with the results of the Gibson hit, that they cancelled the contracts for assassination of Raul and

Jack. Jimmy Flowers told Raul the exact same information about Jack and Annabella.

A copy of the list of attendees was also provided to the Judge. The Judge said that his client would be extremely pleased because now they would be able to identify those individuals who should be monitored for any further treacherous behavior against their companies.

Before Raul left Jimmy Flowers, Jimmy had some information that he needed to share with Roger Legion. He asked Raul to visit Roger Legion for the answer to a quick question.

CHAPTER 45

Annabella returned to the Rancho Santa Fe home of Judge Caesar Cargyle later in the night. The Judge had retired for the evening. She proceeded to her bedroom, undressed, and laid down for the night.

Discordant thoughts filled her head about her life, Raul, Jack, and the various people that she had killed. These thoughts ran through her mind like the wheels on a slot machine. They were moving quickly and she had no idea where they would stop. Amidst the confusion, she realized that there was one voice that she wanted to hear.

According to her telephone, it was 1:59 am. Annabella knew that the person, whose voice she wanted to hear, would be awake. That person was a night owl, who would stay up late at night and sleep late into the morning. That person was her mother.

Rosaria Romero lived in Hermosilla, which was centrally located in the northwestern Mexican state of Sonora. She had spent her life as a homemaker and was fiercely devoted to her two children, Annabella and Emile, and to her Catholic faith.

Rosario's husband, Federico, died ten years earlier after a career as a Professor of Economics at the *Universidad Estatal de Sonora* in Hermosilla.

Annabella found her mother's phone number in her contacts and touched it to commence a call. It was answered after the third ring.

"*Hola* (Hello)," it was answered by the voice that she longed to hear.

"*Mamá, es Annabella* (Momma, it's Annabella)".

"*Annabella*," she uttered with a weakened voice filled with as much joy as possible, "*Mi bebé. ¿Dónde estás? ¿Estás aquí?* (My baby. Where are you? Are you here?)"

"*No mama. Estoy en San Diego. Lamento no haberte llamado durante tanto tiempo. Quiero saber como estas* (No, mama. I'm in San Diego. I'm sorry that I have not called you for so long. I want to know how you are.)"

"*No te preocupes por mi. Tu tía, Ada, me está cuidando. Dejaron de darme la medicina porque no me ayudó. El cáncer se diseminó desde mis pulmones a muchos otros lugares. Rezo todas las noches para que Jesús me lleve, pero sé que él quería que yo te hablara primero.* (Do not worry about me. Your aunt, Ada, is taking care of me. They stopped giving me the medicine because it did not help me. The cancer spread from my lungs to a lot of other places. I pray every night for Jesus to take me, but I know he wanted me to talk to you first.)"

"*Mamá, ¿Necesitas algo? ¿Cualquier dinero?* (Mama, do you need anything? Any money?)"

"*No. Antes me preocupaba la medicina, pero ahora no tomo ninguna medicina. Perdí mucho peso. Ahora soy como tu.* (No. I used to worry about the medicine, but now I do not take any medicine. I lost a lot of weight. Now, I am like you.)"

"*Desearia ser como tu* (I wish I was like you)," Annabella's voice echoed surrender.

"*¿Estás casado? ¿Tienes algún nieto para mí?* (Are you married? Do you have any grandbabies for me?)" her Mother asked with excited anticipation.

"No, Momma."

"*Hay tiempo, mi bella Anna. ¿Qué le pasó a Raul?* (There is time, my beautiful Anna. What happened to Raul?)"

"*No funcionó.* (It did not work out.)"

"*El fue un buen hombre.* (He was a good man.)"

"*Lo sé. Debería haberlo escuchado.* (I know. I should have listened to him.)"

"*Cuando eras niña, jugabas a fingir y siempre quisiste ser madre. Sostendrías una de tus muñecas en tus manos y era tu bebé. Mecerías al bebé, harías galletas para el bebé y dirías que estás esperando a que tu esposo regrese a casa del trabajo. Siempre pensé que eso era lo que querías.* (When you were a little girl, you would play pretend and you always wanted to be a mother. You would hold one of your dolls in your hands and it was your baby. You would rock the baby, make cookies for the baby, and you would say that you are waiting for your husband to come home from work. I always thought that is what you wanted.)"

"*Yo tambien.* (So did I.)" Annabella's voice cracked as she uttered those three words.

"*¿Cuándo puedes venir a verme?* (When can you come to see me?)" her Mother wondered.

"*Es difícil con la frontera en este momento, mamá. Encontraré una manera.* (It's hard with the border right now, Momma. I'll find a way.)"

169

"*Voy a orar por ti, mi bebé, para que obtengas todo lo que quieres.* (I am going to pray for you, my baby, that you get everything you want.)"

"*Te amo mamá.* (I love you, Momma.)"

"*Te amo mi bebé.* (I love you, my baby.)"

"*Vas a descansar,* (You go rest,)" Annabella told her.

"*Ve con Dios.* (Go with God.)"

With that, the call ended. Annabella began to cry uncontrollably. She sat up in the bed and threw her legs off the side of it. She slowly regained her composure and wiped her face with tissues from a box on an adjacent nightstand. Her sadness began to percolate anger and she wanted to focus on anyone responsible for the life she had.

In the morning, she would tell the Judge that she was ready for another assignment. There were men who needed to be killed.

CHAPTER 46

In the lobby of the America's Finest City Building, Raul waited for a non-stop elevator ride to the twenty-fourth floor. A unique feature of the building was that during non-rush hour time periods, an elevator rider was able to request a direct ride to their floor.

On this day, Raul was wearing black slacks, with a white shirt, red tie, and a black sport coat. His shoes were saddle tan, wingtip Oxfords.

When the elevator car was ready, a mechanical voice announced that the non-stop trip to the twenty-fourth floor was ready.

Raul entered the car and saw the button was already pushed. As the doors began to close, a voice called.

"Excuse me! Please!"

Raul stuck his arm out to stop the doors and they retracted open. The young lady who called out was Linda Green. She was in court with Roger Legion two weeks earlier, lost her job, and was recruited to be a member of the Female Optimization Group or FOG. This was the legal organization, mentored by Judge Caesar Cargyle, who was developing nefarious plans to deal with perceived slights by their legal counterparts.

Linda wore a teal, short-sleeve A-line dress with dark, denim Espadrille wedge shoes.

"Thank you so much," she told Raul.

"It's always nice to have company."

"Are you going to see Roger Legion?" she wondered.

"Yes, I am."

"Do you have an appointment? Because I was going to see him and I don't have an appointment."

"No, I don't have an appointment," Raul told her. "I just need to talk to him for about a minute."

"Are you a lawyer?" she asked.

"No. Are you?"

"Yeah. But I'm between jobs right now. What kind of work do you do?"

"I'm an engineer by trade. I do logistics. Problem solving."

"I find that very interesting. I'd love to talk to you more about it."

Raul was smitten with her cuteness and her curves.

"After we're done talking with Mr. Legion, would you be available for a cup of coffee or maybe even lunch?" Raul suggested.

"Yeah. That sounds good."

"My name is Raul. Raul Verdugo." He extended his hand for a quick shake.

"My name is Linda. Linda Green."

"It's nice to meet you Linda."

"Same here."

As Linda finished her sentence, the doors to the twenty-fourth floor opened and they both exited the car into the lobby of Legion & Associates. They both stood in awe of its opulence. The teal and white marble floor boasted success and a large, cursive 'L' was embedded into the floor. The walls to each side were glass from ceiling to floor with alabaster carvings within the glass.

Directly in front of them was a raised granite counter that matched the marble floor. There was a place card on the counter that read, "Be Right Back."

"Should we wait?" Linda asked Raul.

A hallway ran down each side of the floor. Raul looked down the western hallway. He looked at her with a wide smile.

"Let's take a little walk," he said.

He took her left hand and began a casual stroll. They saw the name placards outside the doors of the various offices, but only one office door was open. The last office on the western side of the hallway belonged to Roger Legion.

Roger was sitting at his desk reviewing a report from the Accident Reconstructionist that was retained by Ricky Ray Ransom in the *Zantoff* case. A knock at his door suspended his focus.

"Come on in," Roger told them as he lowered his reading glasses to the desk and stood.

"Hello, Roger," Linda exclaimed with a strong, confident tone. "How are you?"

"I'm fine," he told her as they met with a handshake.

Roger immediately turned his attention to Raul.

"Hello, Mr. Legion. I'm Raul Verdugo."

The handshake they shared was more powerful than the one Roger just shared with Linda.

"Hello, Raul," Roger told him with a smile. "I've heard a lot of good things about you."

"Sorry to come in without an appointment," Linda advised. "But I was just in the neighborhood. And your receptionist wasn't at her desk."

"It's no problem. Have a seat." He pointed to the two chairs on the opposite side of his desk. "How are you doing?"

They sat and Roger reclaimed his seat.

"Okay," she replied in a nonchalant tone. "You probably heard I got let go at Rayne, Lindstrom, & Avici."

"I heard you quit."

"Technically. Monty Lindstrom verbally berated me and called me all kinds of names and said this carrier, Oneonta Mutual, wanted all my files pulled."

"He lied about that," Roger shared. "I was speaking to the people at Oneonta Mutual shortly after the verdict came in. They blamed Monty, not you."

"That asshole," Linda declared. "I was the one he needed to blame. But anyway, I was offered a job the same day."

"Congratulations," Roger conveyed. "Where you going?"

"Do you know a lawyer named Leticia Harrison?"

"As a matter of fact, I do."

"Well, she said she saw me in the courtroom in the *Nastasi* case and she liked what she saw."

"I met with her recently. She was sharp."

"Yeah, she's the executive member of this female empowerment group."

"What's that?" Raul chirped in.

"Well," she began, turning to Roger, "do you know a judge, a retired judge, named Caesar Cargyle?"

"Quite well," Roger answered. "He gave me my first legal job."

"He mentors this group of young women that are either lawyers, paralegals, or law clerks that have had some terrible interactions with their male counterparts. I've only been to one meeting, but the Judge has some ideas about justice."

"What's the name of the group?" Raul queried.

"FOG," Linda told him. "I guess it originally meant Female Optimization Group, but now I think it means Face of God."

"Face of God?" Roger wondered.

"Apparently," Linda told them, "according to the Bible, once someone saw the Face of God, they were done."

Roger pondered on her comment for a moment.

"What can I do for you, Raul?"

"Linda, would you mind waiting for me down in the lobby? I should only be a few minutes. I'll be right there."

Linda left the room and Raul waited an additional few moments before he started to speak.

"*La bella chica* (Beautiful girl)" Raul told Legion with a smile and a head nod toward the door.

"*Si* (Yes)." Roger answered.

Raul then turned cancer-serious.

"Jimmy Flowers wanted me to share with you a development and get your input on it. That lawyer that you are going against, the short one that's always on TV, he's bringing in some high-end technology guys from Philadelphia. Jimmy thinks they want to get eyes and ears on you."

Roger's face evidenced a slow boil anger.

"Jimmy would like to send these technology guys a message. Would you have a problem with that?"

"Not at all," Roger conveyed without thought.

"We're going to send our telephone guy over here. Do you know Fred?"

"I know Fred," Roger asserted.

"Let him sweep your office and it might be a good idea to put some small cameras in your hallways to detect motion when you're not here. All right?"

Raul extended his hand to Roger as he stood and they shared a handshake.

"Thanks, a lot, Raul. And thank Jimmy."

"I'm still looking for that girl."

"If you find her, let me know," Roger responded.

"You'll know immediately. I'll be in touch, Mr. Legion."

Raul left Legion's office and proceeded at an accelerated gait down the hallway for his rendezvous with his new female acquaintance.

Raul and Linda had visited with Roger for just a few minutes, but they left him with much to ponder.

CHAPTER 47

One half of the entire tenth floor of the Westin Gaslamp Quarter Hotel, located on Broadway, across from the Courthouse, in downtown San Diego, was occupied by the Triple 'R' Law Firm. Ricky Ray Ransom set up residency and had a small army at his disposal that could handle any contingency.

One of the suites was their War Room that contained two television monitors, three whiteboards, and special telephone equipment that allowed Ricky Ray or any of his underlings to have direct access to their Houston office.

One side of a long, dining room table contained seven computer monitors, which allowed direct access to the internet and websites, such as Lexus/Nexus for ease of legal research.

Another room on the floor was for clerical people to respond to pleadings and produce any correspondence as necessary. There was a room for storage of paper goods and technology equipment. Part of the team was a person devoted to the technology equipment to make sure it ran smoothly.

Security guards were posted twenty-four hours a day in the hallway to keep an eye out for suspicious activity.

None of the rooms were to be cleaned without Ricky Ray's permission.

The room with the most activity was the one that was designated as Ricky Ray's office. He reviewed documents incessantly and if he had any questions, he would summon one of his associate attorneys and demand an answer. Ricky Ray would never accept an excuse. Excuses resulted in termination.

On this day, Ricky Ray sat in his office at the hotel's desk. He reviewed a schedule of upcoming promotional interviews to discuss the _Zantoff_ case. His concentration was broken when one of his associate attorneys, Joyce Adler, stormed into the room. She held in her hand a red piece of paper. She placed it on the desk in front of Ricky Ray.

"What's this?" Ricky Ray inquired.

"It's a supplement to their Witness List," Joyce advised.

"Why is it on red paper?"

"That's the way it came in."

Ricky Ray picked up the piece of paper and inspected it.

"Who is Michael Lim?" Ricky Ray asked.

"He's a bartender at a place called The Liftoff. Our client, Bernie Kaylic, was drinking there right before the accident."

"I thought the drinking issue was dead?"

"Everyone did. But I think the bartender has something to do with the second name on this list."

Ricky Ray again browsed the paper.

"Who is Sharifa?

"I have no idea," Joyce answered.

"Neither does Legion. Otherwise, he would have included her last name." Ricky Ray was pensive. "Call our client, Bernie. Get him over here, now. Tell him it's urgent. Then, find out if we can bring a motion against Legion for sanctions for using the red paper. If we're allowed to do it, proceed."

Joyce ran out of the room as quickly as she ran in. Ricky Ray would have an answer to all his questions within the hour.

CHAPTER 48

Judge Caesar Cargyle rolled into his living room and parked his wheelchair at the end of the coffee table in the area reserved for him. He set the brake on the chair and shakily stood up. The Judge quickly gained his composure and Annabella entered the room.

"Take the chair away from me, my dear."

She took off the parking brake and pulled the chair away from the Judge. He turned slightly toward her.

"Someday, Annabella, the utility of that chair will be history. Soon to be forgotten history." The Judge paused for a moment. "Bring it back to me."

Annabella returned the chair to its original position and the Judge lowered himself into the chair.

"I need it, but I hate it," he advised, referring to the chair.

"Keep working at it, your Honor. You can do it."

"Your words of encouragement are most appreciated. But there is work to be discussed. The next target for the Face of God is Roger Legion. Do you know him?"

"I know of him. Do you have some solid evidence against him or are you going to go with the taint?"

The 'taint' is a process whereby a female acquaintance would make a fictitious allegation against a male in the hopes that the bad publicity would promulgate a settlement.

"The taint would never work with Legion. He's a different kind of animal. He never deals with a woman on a one-on-one basis. Always has somebody with him. He teaches this to his other lawyers."

"So, do you just want him taken out?" Annabella inquired.

"No. Over the past several years, Legion lawyers have been killed in their attempts to emulate him in a criminal enterprise. Now, he would never blame himself. He considers himself to be the general of an army that has never lost a battle. So, how do we take out the general?" he postulated.

"I'm guessing it has something to do with his troops."

"Exactly," the Judge proclaimed. "In a public arena, with the world watching. Legion must realize that there is only one way to stop it. He must step away from the practice of law."

"Are you sure about this?"

"I know Legion. I know his vanity. And I know his weaknesses. He will fall on a sword to save his troops."

"Who's first?" Annabella asked nonchalantly.

"I will have all that information this afternoon. I have someone in the law firm who is going to help us achieve our ends."

Judge Cargyle's plan for the destruction of the Legion law firm was now set into motion. Roger Legion did not know it, but he was about to be hit by a runaway freight train.

CHAPTER 49

Less than an hour after Ricky Ray Ransom ordered his associate lawyer, Joyce Adler, to bring their client into their makeshift office at the Westin Hotel, there was a knock at his door.

"Com'on in, y'all," Ricky Ray called out.

Joyce entered followed by their client, Bernie Zantoff. Bernie was an African-American, five feet, ten inches tall, medium build, with a fully, bald head, moustache and a growth of chin hair. He wore dark trousers with a white t-shirt and a red, plaid sport coat.

"What's up, my man?" Bernie inquired as Ricky Ray stood to greet him.

"I'm fine, Bernie. How you doin'?"

"Just sha-boomin, gangsta'. Making sure the hood don't burn down."

"That sounds like a noble effort. Have a seat," Ricky Ray told him.

Bernie sat at the end of the couch in the room. Joyce Adler stood, while watching the proceedings.

"Who's Sharifa?" Ricky Ray demanded an answer.

"Shy?" Bernie responded with a curious interrogatory. "She's just a friend."

"What's your definition of 'friend'?"

"Somebody you know, hang around with, grab a drink every once in a while. It's no big deal."

"It might be." Ricky Ray's tone became ominous. "Did you ever have sex with her?"

"No," Bernie uttered sheepishly.

"Don't lie to me," Ricky Ray's voice commanded.

"Can Miss Joyce step out for a minute?"

"No, she can't. She needs to hear it."

"Once, maybe twice, we had a little 'some-un, some-un.'

Ricky Ray was incensed.

"Didn't I ask you, point blank, if you had a girlfriend?"

"She wasn't my girlfriend. She was, was just a booty call."

Ricky Ray walked around the desk and stood in front of it.

"You're not going to talk this way when we're in trial, are you?"

"What way?"

"Like an ignorant, nigger pimp. I apologize for the use of the word, nigger, but I find it appropriate in some instances. Now, when we're in court, you're going to be an eloquent, non-threatening black man, who is grieving over the condition of his baby girl. You address everyone as either 'Mister' or 'Miss.' You understand me?"

"Yes," Bernie answered with a mix of defiance and solemnity.

Ricky Ray turned to Joyce.

"Make sure he has conservative suits to wear. White shirts and normal ties."

Ricky Ray turned back to Bernie.

"Now, back to the bigger problem at hand. What's her last name?"

"Who?"

"Sharifa," he replied in disgust.

"I never knew her last name."

"What's her address?"

"I didn't know that, neither. I'd call her and we'd meet up at a bar."

"The Liftoff?"

"Yeah."

"What's her phone number?"

"I'll give you the number that I have, but it's been disconnected."

Ricky Ray turned to Joyce.

"Subpoena the phone company. See if we can get some anchor information on her. Contact our best investigators, tell them we want her found, and put a bounty on it of one hundred thousand dollars."

Ricky Ray was willing to pay a bonus of one hundred thousand dollars to anyone who could locate Sharifa.

"If Legion finds her first, that could be a big problem. Will she keep her mouth shut?"

"I hope so."

"You don't win a lawsuit based on hope. All hope does is heightened the blow once you lose. Is there anything else you haven't told me?"

"No."

"Are you sure?"

"I'm sure."

"You better be."

Ricky Ray's platinum case was starting to show evidence of cracks. This was only the beginning of the surprises yet to come.

CHAPTER 50

The last meeting of the Legion defense team for the *Zantoff* case took place on a Friday. For the past five weeks, Roger Legion and his attorneys, Clint Eversol and Dan Clarkson, met at precisely three o'clock to discuss status, strategy, and future handling. Legion was pleased with their work and their work products. It was now time for a final pep talk.

"Gentlemen," Legion began, "we pick a jury on Monday. Jury selection is where you win or lose a trial. I want you both to display a calm, inviting, pleasant demeanor. I'm talking to you, Dan."

Dan acknowledged him with an affirmative nod. Roger continued.

"We have six peremptory challenges. That means we can throw off any potential juror without a reason. I want one of you guys to focus on responses and the other to focus on physical appearance. Look for tattoos or piercings. People who brand themselves or engage in self-mutilation are easily persuaded and have no problem in awarding outrageous jury sums. The other extreme are people in the military. They often have a laser focus and are tough to persuade once they have made up their minds. I don't want any of these types of people on my jury."

"Roger, how did this case get to trial so quick?" Dan asked.

"Because it involves a minor. The California Code of Civil Procedure section thirty-six mandates that trial for minors under the age of fourteen, go forward within 120 days. All Ricky Ray had to do was file a motion for preference. I'm sure he feels that the expedited trial puts us in a pressure cooker."

"Chaos is what they want," Clint spoke succinctly.

"Did they get it?" Legion inquired.

"Absolutely not," Dan replied without thought.

"Gentlemen, we are ready. We leave kindness and civility at the door of the courtroom. We enter that arena with one thought: the absolute and total destruction of the plaintiff attorney and his case."

Both of the attorneys focused on Legion and concurred with his every word.

"I want to ask each one of you: what do you think of our case?"

They looked at each other and Clint spoke first.

"It's difficult. The facts don't favor us and the law doesn't favor us. But we are in the exact place that I want to be in."

"Rise up. Strike down," Dan interjected.

"Gentlemen, it's time to slay a dragon."

The Legion lawyers put forth the exact mentality that Roger wanted to instill in them. But in his mind, he knew how dangerous it was to take this case to trial, because it was a loser.

CHAPTER 51

At approximately seven o'clock that evening, Gerald 'Bell' Bellamo drove into the parking garage of the America's Finest City Building from the India Street side. He drove a late-model, Ford F-150 pick-up truck. Bell proceeded down to the second lower level of the garage. He parked and stepped out of the vehicle. Bell retrieved a tool bag and walked to the elevator area.

Bell lived in Willistown, Pennsylvania, just outside of Philadelphia. He was forty-six years old, medium-build, clean shaven with a flattop military haircut. Bell wore jeans, a black t-shirt and a vest with a logo for the local telephone company on the back and, in the front, over one of the breast pockets, was a patch that said 'Steve.'

Bell was a 'consultant' retained by Ricky Ray Ransom at a cost of one hundred twenty-five thousand dollars a month. He graduated at the top of his class at Massachusetts Institute of Technology and held twenty-four patents dealing with Voice over Internet Protocol (VoIP). Ricky Ray would utilize Bell as an expert if there was a technology issue in one of his cases.

Ricky Ray would also press Bell into service to obtain an edge over the competition in any high stakes lawsuit. The _Zantoff_ case met this criteria.

Bell's task was to set up a tap on the Legion phone lines and any video feeds that he would be able to monitor remotely from any computer.

His destination was the Communications Center of the building. It was located on this floor and consisted of a small room that had a computer monitor on a shelf against one wall and two other walls that were lined with thousands of feet of communication wiring, neatly organized, and behind locked cabinet doors.

If anyone asked why he was there, or what he was doing, he had a work order that indicated that he was there to repair a dead line in Legion's system.

Bell entered the Communication Center without any problem. He had an entry card from the phone company that he swiped to allow entrance. Once inside, he planned to take down a firewall on Legion's telephone system and install a ghost-sharing program. This would allow him to tap all telephone calls covertly. He would then return the firewall to its original condition and Ricky Ray would be able to listen to all telephone calls.

Bell started typing at a furious pace when he heard the door to the room start to open. He turned to look as a tall man, with glasses and green coveralls, entered. The man looked at Bell with a smile.

"How long do you think you're going to be?" The man asked.

"Fifteen, twenty minutes," Bell answered.

"Do you mind if I leave my tools here, I want to go upstairs for a sec?"

"Nah, go ahead."

The man set the bag down and moved around a few tools looking for something.

Bell returned to typing when he suddenly stopped and looked up. He saw a reflection of something in the monitor. Everything went silent as blood splatter and brain matter soiled the computer monitor. A second bullet completed the task.

The man in the coveralls was Raul. He was sending a message from Jimmy Flowers that Roger Legion had condoned.

Two hours later, Ricky Ray Ransom received the news that Bell had been murdered in the Communications Center of the America's Finest City Building.

He sat at his hotel-room desk in silence contemplating the reach of Roger Legion.

CHAPTER 52

On the following Sunday evening, the marine layer was once again thick enough to bring visibility down to less and one-eighth of a mile. At 9:30 pm, the Baheria Bedda Restaurant was preparing for its ten o'clock closure time when it was visited by two new guests.

The first was Roger Legion. He wanted to thank Jimmy Flowers personally for taking care of Ricky Ray Ransom's attempt to hijack Roger's phone lines. The proper message was sent. Within forty-eight hours after the murder of Ricky Ray's technology person, the rest of the technology people left San Diego and returned to Philadelphia.

The second visitor was Jack Prickett. He planned to have dinner with Raul and he also wanted to speak with Jimmy Flowers.

Both men walked through the front door of the restaurant at nearly the same time. Roger walked directly to Domenic, Jimmy's sentry at his office door and Jack took a seat at a table in a far corner of the restaurant. The only other people in the restaurant were three men who sat at a table near the entrance to Jimmy's office. Jack continually scanned the room while he awaited the arrival of Raul.

A waiter took Jack's drink order and Raul emerged from the back of the restaurant. As Raul approached him, Jack recognized one of the men sitting at the table. Jack stood to meet Raul.

"That looks like Tony Tri-tip over there," Jack relayed slowly.

Raul looked over at the men.

"Tripeppi. Yeah, that's him."

"He owes me money," Jack told Raul. "Come with me. Let's talk to him."

Tony 'Tri-tip' Tripeppi was a debt collector for Jimmy Flowers. He weighed nearly four hundred pounds and always ordered two meals at a time. He was fifty-one years old and five feet, nine inches tall. He had a fifty-six inch waist and wore shirts with a twenty-two inch neck.

"Hey, Tony," Jack called out to get his attention.

Tony broke his focus on the veal Marsala in front of him to acknowledge Jack.

"Jack Prickett. What are you up to? Put any new notches on your belt?"

"You're a tough guy to get a hold of Tony. I've been calling and leaving messages for over a month. Don't you return calls?"

"I'm busy. Now, let me eat my meal in peace."

"Where's my money?" Jack demanded, dead serious.

"I don't know what you're talkin' about," Tony answered nonchalantly.

"The sixty-two thousand dollars for the work in Ohio."

"Doesn't ring a bell," Tony answered with cavalier style.

Jack pulled out a handgun that he had tucked behind his back. He aimed it at Tony's head.

"Will this jog your memory?"

Tony stared at the gun, but did not blink an eye. One of the men that Tony was with reached into his sport coat and immediately Jack changed the bead of the gun on to the man.

"You better cool your hot nuts."

"Jack, don't disrespect the place," Domenic called to him.

"I'm not," Jack responded.

The man slowly pulled his hand out of his jacket.

Tony Tri-tip was also wearing a sport coat with a black t-shirt under it. He took the napkin off of his chest that he was using as a bib and leaned back in the chair.

"I work for Jimmy. I'm a captain. I can't be touched. If you want to make an asshole move, you're gonna end up as fish food."

Jack perused him as he spoke and then focused on one thing.

"All right," Jack told him and he turned to walk back to his table. He was accompanied by Raul.

"I need to talk to Jimmy. NOW!" he told Raul in a hushed voice.

Raul left Jack's side and proceeded to Jimmy's office door. Tony made a comment as he pointed to Jack.

"Punk. No *stugats*."

Stugats is an Italian slang word for balls or testicles.

Raul knocked at the door to Jimmy's office and he was called to enter. As he did, he saw Roger Legion.

"Hello, Mr. Legion."

"Hello, Raul. How are you?" Roger inquired.

"I'm fine, and you?"

"I'm doing well," Roger told him. "Hey, thanks for taking care of me the other night."

Roger was referring to the killing of Ricky Ray Ransom's technology person.

"No problem." Raul then turned to Jimmy. "Jack Prickett said that he needs to talk to you now. It sounds urgent."

"Go get him," Jimmy commanded.

Within seconds, Raul returned with Jack. Jack shared a handshake with both Jimmy and Roger Legion. He then reached into his coat and retrieved a thick envelope. He placed it on Jimmy's desk.

"I don't know if Raul told you," he said to Jimmy, "there was a little cash bonus with that job the other night. Seventy-five grand. I wanted to give you a little piece. There's also a list of the people who attended. The Judge thinks that is very valuable."

"I appreciate it, Jack," Jimmy told him. "That was a fine piece of work the other night."

"I give the credit to Woody."

"How's he doing?" Jimmy wondered.

"He's hanging on. You know him, he's a tough, old guy."

"You tell him I say 'Hello,'" Jimmy conveyed.

"I will," Jack advised.

"Was this the urgent matter?" Jimmy quizzed.

"No. Tony Tri-tip, out there, is wearing a wire."

Jimmy's visage evolved with serious concern.

"How do you know?" Jimmy queried.

"He owes me money. When I asked him about it, he leaned back in the chair. I could see the outline of a little box in the center of his chest, with leads running off of it on both sides and a long lead running from the bottom of the box down his chest."

Jimmy became pensive for a moment. He turned to Raul.

"Tell Domenic to make sure the guys that he came in with don't leave."

Jack looked at Roger Legion and back to Jimmy.

"Is it okay to speak freely?" Jack requested.

"Yeah. He's my lawyer."

"I'll kill him for nothing, Jimmy. You just give the word."

"How much money does he owe you?"

"Sixty-two thousand dollars."

"All right. But I want to find out how long he's been wearing a wire and what he's told them."

"I should be able to find that out," Roger chimed in. "What's his last name?"

"Tripeppi." Jimmy answered.

"What are you going to do?" Jack inquired.

"Jimmy," Roger spoke up.

Jimmy and Jack turned to Roger. "I have an idea."

Jimmy Flowers and Jack Prickett were about to learn how Roger Legion deals with a liability.

CHAPTER 53

Ruben Herrero and his men had been on somewhat of a murder spree in the last 72 hours. They were checking off names from the list that was provided to Ruben by Judge Cargyle. Under their color of authority, they were easily able to locate individuals and surveil them for the opportunity of a quick kill.

It was dusk and a thick marine layer was rolling in. Ruben was riding in a late model, blue Chevy Malibu that was driven by one of his men, Irving Ordaz. Both men were casually dressed and their small talk was minimal.

"This is going to be a good cash month," Reuben told Irving. "Maybe go on a nice vacation."

"We live in paradise," Irving said. "Why do you have to go anyplace?"

Ruben nodded his head in agreement and his cell phone began to ring. Ruben scoped the Caller ID and saw the call was from John Donzen. John Donzen was a fellow police officer who brought information to Ruben at Starbucks regarding the activities of the Internal Affairs officers in their efforts to follow him.

"Yeah, John."

"That BOLO you put out for the Annabella Romero car, we just got a hit on it."

Ruben had put out a 'Be on the Lookout' for Annabella's car to all San Diego Police officers. They were specifically told not to stop or detain anyone associated with the vehicle.

"Where?"

"On Fifth Avenue in the Gaslamp Quarter near 'F' Street."

"Fifth Avenue near 'F' Street," Ruben told Irving. They drove quickly toward their target.

Inside the Whisky Girl Bar/Restaurant, located at the corner of Fifth Avenue and G, Annabella sat at a booth with her cousin, Itzel Trujillo.

Itzel was in her early twenties, wore rimless glasses, stunning makeup, and a radiant smile. Her clothes were that of a young executive and her laughter was contagious.

Annabella spent the past two hours recollecting stories of their adventures as little girls and Itzel also shared that she was engaged. Her wedding would take place sometime in the next twelve months.

"I want you to be my Maid of Honor," Itzel told Annabella.

"Oh, Itzie," she paused, "I would love to."

"Can I be your Maid of Honor when you get married?" Itzel queried.

"Absolutely, but I don't know if it is ever going to happen."

"Give it time," Itzel expressed. "Everything happens for a reason."

Annabella held up one finger and reached into her Michael Kors bag to retrieve a large envelope. It was yellow and a little larger than a normal envelope. Annabella put it on the table and slid it toward Itzel.

"There are three stacks of money in there," Annabella began. "The largest one is twenty thousand dollars for my mother. The middle one is five thousand dollars for your mother. The smallest one is one thousand dollars for you."

"You don't have to give me anything," Itzel responded.

"No, just take it."

Meanwhile, Ruben Herrero and Irving Ordaz drove north on Fifth Avenue in the Gaslamp Quarter and slowed as they passed 'G' Street heading toward 'F' Street.

"There it is," Ruben exclaimed and pointed to Annabella's dark, graphite, late-model BMW 750. "Park in a red zone, who gives a shit."

Irving pulled into a space at the end of the same block where Annabella's car was located. Ruben gave instruction before they got out of the vehicle.

"Put a tracker on her car. Let's start down at the corner at Whiskey Girl and we'll work our way back."

The Global Positioning Satellite (GPS) tracker was magnetic and was simply placed in a wheel well of Annabella's car. The men walked down to the Whiskey Girl establishment and entered. They began their scan immediately upon entering. Foot traffic in the bar was quite brisk and a series of booths rimmed the perimeter.

Ruben quickly found Annabella. He tugged on Irving's arm.

"Second booth from the end over there. That small girl who's causing big headaches. We won't take her in here. We'll take her out on the sidewalk. We'll cuff her and put her in the back of the car. She's cagey, so be alert."

Annabella and Itzel glided out of the booth and started to walk to their vehicles.

"Go up the block a little ways," Ruben relayed to Irving. "I don't want to make a scene. Keep an eye open in case you have to back me up."

The men exited the restaurant and Irving scurried up the block. Ruben stood outside the bar looking at passing traffic.

The women exited the Whiskey Girl and gave each other a farewell hug. Itzel headed south and Annabella headed north to her car.

Visibility was mitigated by the fog that was cast by the marine layer. Ruben believed that this was an advantage.

"*LA NIÑA!*" Ruben called out in a loud, emphatic voice.

Annabella slowed down, but did not stop.

"Annabella Romero. San Diego Police Department. Stop now! Another officer is waiting right by your car. And a hell of a lot more cops are on their way."

Annabella stopped, but did not turn around. Ruben had his right hand on one of his .45 caliber pistols that he kept behind his back, but he did not draw it out.

Ruben caught up to Annabella and grabbed her right upper arm to swing her around. As she pivoted, she recoiled her left arm and when her fist was within six inches of Ruben, she threw a punch from the Jeet Kune Do style of fighting, made famous by Kung Fu Master, Bruce Lee, referred to as the unstoppable punch. All of her weight, coupled with forward motion and the element of surprise, magnified its power. Her arm moved at the speed of twenty to twenty-five miles per hour.

Ruben took the blow in the center of his chest. More than just the wind was knocked out of him. He took several steps back, but did not fall. Annabella took several steps toward him and delivered a roundhouse slap kick to Ruben's face. Her Doc Marten boot put a gash in the side of his face from below his eye to the bottom of his jaw. Upon impact, his face contorted horrifically from the power of her kick and one of his teeth flew out of his mouth.

Ruben did a one hundred eighty degree turn and face-planted into the sidewalk. His gash would ultimately require thirty-five stitches.

Annabella walked nonchalantly to her car, when she heard a female voice behind her begin to cry out.

"Help. Help. This guy needs help. Somebody call nine-one-one."

Irving left his post and ran down the block to investigate the commotion. Annabella got into her vehicle and drove off.

Ruben was unconscious and his face rested in a pool of his blood. Annabella had lit a fuse that could not be extinguished.

Part 5

CHAPTER 54

Jimmy Flowers emerged from his office in the Bagheria Bedda Restaurant and sauntered over to Tony 'Tri-tip' Tripeppi. Tony and his two friends were the only patrons left in the restaurant. Tony was sopping up the last bits of tomato sauce from his veal Marsala after consuming nearly a loaf of Italian bread.

Jimmy patted Tony on the shoulder to get his attention.

"Tony Tri-tip," Jimmy exclaimed.

"Hey Jimmy, how are you?"

"I'm good. And you?"

"Can't complain," Tony told him.

"You wanted to talk, let's talk."

Tony threw a quick glance to the other two men at the table.

"Tell them to keep my cannolis cold until I come back."

With that Tony lifted his four hundred pound frame off the chair and threw his napkin onto it. He followed Jimmy to the office and Jimmy allowed Tony to enter first.

Inside, Tony saw Raul, Jack and Roger Legion. No one was smiling as Jimmy directed Tony to take a seat in front of his desk.

"Tony," Jimmy began, "Before we have our conversation, I need to ask you a question. Jack tells me that you owe him money. Do you owe him money?"

"Geez, Jimmy, what are you doing, collecting for this piss ant?"

"I'll take that as a 'yes,'" Jimmy responded. "When are you going to pay him?"

"I'll make it right," Tony assured him. "I just need a little time."

"All right. I wanted to introduce you to my lawyer, Roger Legion. We have some legal business to discuss. It involves a property transfer in your area, the East Village, near the Padres ballpark."

"Whatever you need, Jimmy."

Jimmy then pointed to Roger Legion.

"Why don't you start, Roger."

"Tony," Roger commenced, "the information that we discuss is highly confidential and protected by the attorney – client privilege. I would like your assurance that whatever is discussed does not leave this room."

"Sure," Tony coyly uttered.

Just then there was a quick knock on the door.

"Come on in," Jimmy exclaimed.

Domenic, his sentry/bodyguard, entered. He walked up to Jimmy to whisper something in his ear.

"Mickey wanted me to tell you that they stopped listening. He's got the blocker going. They won't be able to re-up the signal."

Mickey handled technology for Jimmy and worked out of a back room in the restaurant.

Jimmy nodded with a brief smile.

"Tony," Jimmy spoke demanding attention, "I hear somebody is wearing a wire. You hear anything like that?"

"No, Jimmy. You know I'd come to you right away."

"What about these two guys out here?" Jimmy asked, pointing to the restaurant area. "You trust them?"

"Yeah. But, these days, who knows?"

"Domenic. Go out there and wand those two guys. If they have guns, take them to hold until we're done. Don't let them leave."

The wand that Jimmy was referring to was a handheld metal detector similar to those used at an airport.

Domenic moved to the door and as he started to open it, Jimmy had another request.

"When you're done out there, come on back in with the wand. I want everyone in this room to be checked."

Domenic left the room and Tony Tri-tip started to get nervous.

"Jimmy, is this necessary? Come on. We've known each other for more than thirty years."

"Unfortunately, it is, Tony Tri-tip. You carrying a piece?" Jimmy's words were calm and muted.

Tony reached into his sport coat and retrieved a .38 caliber revolver. He placed it on Jimmy's desk. Raul walked over and picked it up.

Domenic entered the room with the wand in hand. Tony started to speak with a hurried passion. He leaned forward and held his stomach.

"Jim, do you mind if I just go to the bathroom first, I gotta take a powerful dump."

"Hold on, Tony, this will only take a second."

"No, I gotta go."

Tony tried to rise quickly, but Raul and Jack each placed a hand on one of his shoulders and easily pinned him down to the chair. They both pulled out their semi-automatic handguns and pointed their gun to each side of Tony's head behind his ear, with the hammers on the guns pulled back and their fingers on the trigger.

"Lift your shirt. Take it off." Jimmy ordered, referring to the transmission device. Tony complied.

Jimmy then looked over to Domenic.

"Get rid of it. Put it in the power shredder"

Domenic picked it up and left the room. Jimmy then focused on Tony.

"I want to know who you are talking to, for how long and what are you talking about. You understand me?"

"Jimmy, up in Ohio, they had me on possession and sales of heroin. Based on the quantity, I was looking at sixty years. I had no choice."

"You had no choice. Answer my questions: Who are you talking to at the Attorney General's office?"

"Some low level kid. I don't remember his name."

"Jimmy," Roger Legion interjected, "If you don't mind, I think I can find out the answers to your questions."

"Go ahead," Jimmy told him.

Roger pulled out his cell phone and looked up a number in his contacts list.

"I'm calling the lawyer who's the head of the criminal division at the Attorney General's office.

As Roger did that, Jimmy directed Raul to put a zip tie on Tony's hands, behind his back.

Roger's phone call took less than three minutes and everyone, except Tony Tri-tip, looked to him in anticipation.

"Anthony Tripeppi was arrested approximately two months ago in Ohio. He was unwilling to give up his heroin supplier, but he said that he could give them Jimmy Flowers. The prescription drugs, the murder-for-hire, the gambling, the loan sharking and assorted other things. Today is his first day wearing a wire."

"That's all bullshit!" Tony defiantly declared. "I only told them about money being laundered through the laundromats."

"Raul, grab the duct tape," Jimmy requested. "Shove a napkin in his mouth and tape him up."

Raul proceeded to the task.

"You," he told Raul, "and Jack take him down to the warehouse in National City. Take the panel truck. Make sure the tool box is in there. I'll be there in about thirty minutes."

Raul and Jack escorted him out of the room. Tony's escorts for dinner would also be taking a ride. Before Tony left the room, Jimmy had one last observation to share with Tony.

"If you had paid Jack what you owed him, none of this would have happened."

After they were gone, Jimmy looked over at Roger Legion.

"You didn't call anyone, did you?" Jimmy posed his inquiry.

"No. I find fear to be as powerful as a gun. Both will get you to your desired result."

Roger Legion had once again demonstrated that his value to a criminal enterprise was immeasurable.

CHAPTER 55

It was three o'clock in the morning and Annabella sat on the stoop of Raul's condominium waiting for his return. She rang the doorbell earlier in the evening and a woman's voice answered. It was Linda Green, the lawyer that Raul met at Legion's office, who was also a member of the FOG organization.

As Annabella stared out into the marine layer fog, the sights and sounds of a sleeping city seemed to place her in somewhat of a trance. She began to remember.

It was eight years earlier, she and Raul were madly in love and began living together in an apartment in Chula Vista, a city in southern San Diego County. It was a Sunday morning and they lay naked in their bed with the sound of Raul's faint snoring permeating the air.

Eight months earlier, Raul had commenced his career as a *sicario* after fulfilling a contract to kill his former bosses at the engineering firm. He was developing a reputation for his efficiency coupled with his motto, 'No Footprint.'

Their plan was for Annabella to be a stay-at-home mom and Raul was more than happy to have Annabella take care of him. But

Annabella wanted one thing before she would surrender to that lifestyle.

"Raul," she uttered while shaking him into consciousness. "Raul."

"What?" he answered in a drowsy, nearly drunk-like tone.

"I want you to teach me."

"Teach you what?" he asked while still not completely awake.

"How to be a *sicario*."

"You don't want to be a *sicario*," he replied sheepishly.

"I want to show you that I am able to do it."

"You're able to do it. I believe you," Raul told her with a voice of surrender.

"I also want to prove it to myself."

"I thought you were going to stay home with the babies?" Raul told her.

"How many babies are we going to have?" Annabella quizzed.

"As many as you want."

"What if I want a hundred babies?"

Raul turned from his side to hers and looked at her with comical shock.

"A hundred babies! We better get started."

Raul reached over and grabbed her waist. In one swift motion, he picked her up and placed her on top of him. One of their carnal sessions was beginning.

Whenever Annabella remembered Raul uttering that line about 'getting started,' it always brought a smile to her face.

"Annabella." A voice from the sidewalk re-focused her attention. It was Raul. She stood to greet him and they shared a quick hug.

"Where have you been? Jack has been trying to get ahold of you." Raul quizzed.

"I had to change phones. A cop tried to grab me when I was coming out of a restaurant in the Gaslamp Quarter. He tried to put cuffs on me and I fought back. I really kicked his ass. I might have killed him."

"Do you know who the guy was?" Raul's concern was evident.

"No. But, he called me *La Niña*."

"All right. I'll find out what happened. Let's go inside," he told her.

"I'm not going in. There's another woman in there."

"Call Jack. Use my phone," he said as he handed the phone to her. "He'll make sure you're all right."

"Raul, let me ask you something. When we were in the restaurant, eating the french fries, you asked me if I wanted to try again. You and me. Are you still interested in that?"

"You remember what you told me, Annabella? Too much time. Too much damage. I think you were right."

"I'm sorry." Her refrain echoed disappointment.

"Don't be, *preciosa* (beautiful girl). Call Jack. I know he wants to be with you."

Raul placed his hands on both sides of her head and kissed her forehead.

Annabella had another inquiry to make.

"Do you think you can get me out of the United States?"

Raul thought for a second.

"Where do you want to go? Mexico is just as dangerous as this place. If that cop you tangled with is Herrero, you better hope that you killed him. Because if you didn't, it's going to be all out war."

"Anyplace. You were right. I need a change of scenery."

"If I can't do it, I'm sure Jimmy Flowers or Roger Legion can."

"Roger Legion? How do you know him?"

"Jimmy Flowers is pretty tight with him."

"I think Legion is on one of the hit lists."

"Thanks for the info," Raul advised. "Get your stuff together and get ready to move. As soon as I hear something, I will contact you."

"I've got one more hit to do for the Judge," Annabella conveyed. "Then, I'm totally done."

"Be careful. The Judge was probably the one who put Herrero on to you tonight."

"I will. Thanks, Raul."

Annabella did not want to cry, but she did. She and Raul came together for a long hug. She wondered how she arrived at this place in her life and the cost associated with it.

Linda Green peered out at them through a slightly elevated blind in wonder.

CHAPTER 56

The weather this Monday morning was idyllic; crisp and clear, with temperatures commencing in the mid-sixties and the high temperature this day would reach seventy-two degrees. This was the Chamber of Commerce weather so richly deserved, and associated, with San Diego.

Inside Department Sixty-three of the San Diego County Superior Court, jury selection for the case of *Zantoff Transportation v. Tecton Insurance* was about to go forward. This was one of the largest courtrooms on the third floor of the courthouse located on Broadway in downtown San Diego.

The interior of the courtroom was Spartan, yet efficient. The walls were a crème color and all the chairs, including the jury chairs, had the seats and backs covered in a navy-blue cloth. The wood was Brazilian Cherry with clean lines around the Judge's bench and the court clerk's desk, located directly next to it.

At the plaintiff's table sat Ricky Ray Ransom, Joyce Adler, and Ezra Fillmore. Joyce was an associate attorney from with the Ransom law firm. Ezra was a young, African-American, who was also an associate attorney with the firm. They were awaiting the arrival of their client.

At the defense table sat Roger Legion, Clint Eversol, and Dan Clarkson. The men wore either black or dark blue suits, with white shirts that seemed to almost give off a glare and silk ties. In the pants of each of the three men was a unique item that was a silicone bead placed in the front crease of the pants, courtesy of Roger's tailor. This would cause the pants not to lose their crease.

Ricky Ray Ransom wore a silk white, three-piece suit. His shirt was light blue and his silk tie was yellow. On his lapel was a large pin, in the shape of Texas, with the colors of the Texas flag, and a diamond star in the center. He wore Roper boots, made from ostrich, in a pecan color. On the table was his white, Stetson *El Presidente* felt cowboy hat.

Joyce and Ezra both wore modest clothing that evidenced their pecking order in the firm.

Judge Wendell Proxmire was announced and he entered the courtroom swiftly for a direct trek to his place on the bench.

Judge Proxmire was in his mid-fifties, lean, physically-fit, with a full head of feathered back, brown hair that had not a trace of gray. He had a boyish look that masked a sharp intellect. His welcoming smile could turn deadly in a moment and a wrong answer or bad answer to one of his questions would mete out severe punishment.

If someone were to call Judge Proxmire a prick outside of the courtroom, he would take it as a compliment.

After the case name and number were announced, the Judge began by first, quickly reviewing a few pages of documents that sat in front of him. Then he looked up.

"All right," the Judge began with just a minor hint of an accent from his childhood in Guadalajara, Mexico. "I wanted to get a few housekeeping matters out of the way."

His eyes then locked on Ricky Ray Ransom's hat. He stared at it for more than a moment.

"Mr. Ransom," The Judge declared with stern indignation. Ricky Ray stood.

"Yes, your honor," he responded.

"Get the hat out of here. I want it out of the courtroom. No, out of the building. I don't know how you practice law in Texas, but there is no need for subliminal seduction in my courtroom. Get one of your people to take it out of here. I am going to ask the bailiff to escort them to the front door. You understand?"

"Yes, your Honor," Ray answered with questionable humility.

Judge Proxmire was about to give directions to the bailiff when he had another comment. He returned his focus to Ricky Ray.

"Take the pin off. Your lapel pin. We don't need a billboard for the State of Texas in my courtroom."

"Your Honor," Ricky Ray responded. "May I point out that Mr. Legion is also wearing a lapel pin."

The Judge looked over at Legion. Legion had an American flag pin on his lapel.

"Mr. Legion," the Judge inquired, "how big would you say your pin is?"

"Maybe one inch by a half an inch?"

"Mr. Ransom, if you like, you can wear an American flag pin, the same size as Mr. Legion's pin. You understand me?"

"Yes," Ricky Ray uttered with a tone of defiance. He removed the pin and placed it near the hat.

"Yes, what?" The Judge asked.

"Yes, your Honor."

"You better respect this courtroom and respect me. The reason that I ask people if they understand, is because if they violate any of my orders, they will be sanctioned severely. You understand, Mr. Ransom?"

"Yes, your Honor."

"You understand, Mr. Legion?"

"Yes, your Honor."

The Judge pivoted to the bailiff.

"Bailiff, please escort one of Mr. Ransom's people out of the building with the hat and pin." The bailiff acceded to his command.

Judge Proxmire returned to looking at paperwork. He stopped and looked up.

"Miss," the Judge pointed to Joyce Adler, "would you mind identifying yourself."

Joyce stood to respond.

"I'm Joyce Adler from the plaintiff law firm."

The Judge looked at his paperwork and shook his head in acknowledgement.

"Sir," the Judge inquired, "would you please identify yourself?"

"My name is Ezra Fillmore from the plaintiff law firm.

"Sir, have you made a *pro hac vice* application to this court for this case?"

A *pro hac vice* application is a request by an out-of-state lawyer to appear in court for a particular case even though they are not licensed to practice in the state where the trial is being held.

"No, your Honor. I had no plans on trying the case."

"Then why are you at the plaintiff's table?"

"I, ugh," Ezra stumbled. Ricky Ray had told him to sit there and just smile.

Ricky Ray stood to interject.

"I can answer that, your Honor. Mr. Fillmore is here in a consultant capacity regarding human factors."

"Mr. Legion, is he on the witness list?"

"No, your Honor," Legion quickly responded.

"Mr. Fillmore, I would like you to sit in the gallery, please."

"Your Honor, I wish to lodge an objection," Ricky Ray countered.

"So noted," the Judge acknowledged, "but we are not on the record."

Ricky Ray's composure was being severely tested.

"Mr. Ransom, I am also going to issue a gag order on any and all media discussions outside of this courtroom. Mr. Legion, will you prepare the order?"

"Yes, your Honor," Roger replied.

"Your Honor," Ricky Ray reacted with a bold and indignant tone, "I wish to further object to a gag order."

"We are going to try the case in here. Not out there," the Judge told Ricky Ray, pointing out to the street. "Tell your publicity people that they can take a break."

Ricky Ray slapped his pen down on to the tabletop.

"Don't test me." The Judge warned. "Because I will place you in contempt and you will end up in the county lock-up for thirty days wondering why you are there. Are we communicating?"

"Yes, your Honor," Ricky Ray answered with complete surrender.

"Now, let's pick a jury."

Judge Wendell Proxmire had laid down the law in his courtroom. Both Roger Legion and Ricky Ray Ransom knew that the fireworks were about to begin.

CHAPTER 57

Annabella walked up Third Avenue toward Hawthorn Street, intending to meet Jack at the upcoming corner. It was three-thirty in the morning and both the sidewalk and the street were empty. She walked with her hands inside the pockets of her black, leather jacket. Annabella looked at the ground to avoid eye contact with any police cruiser.

A blue, 1968 Plymouth Fury had been following her for the last three blocks. It contained two, teenage gangbangers, with the monikers of Specs and D-Jazz. Specs was African-American and D-Jazz was Korean. They were both high on cocaine that was mixed with methamphetamine.

"What do you think?" Specs asked with an insidious smile as the car was about to pass Annabella.

"Let's go talk to her," D-Jazz answered and drove up the block and parked near the corner.

They both exited the vehicle and began to walk toward Annabella. Both wore worn-out jeans, jean jackets, and t-shirts with logos from Twisted Sister and Metallica.

As they were bearing down on Annabella, Jack was driving across Hawthorn Street and he spotted the potential confrontation between the men and Annabella. Jack parked in the first available space on the street. He stepped out of the vehicle and removed an aluminum baseball bat from the floor of the backseat of his car.

As they approached Annabella, Specs spoke up.

"Excuse me, you got the time?"

"No," Annabella responded without breaking her gait.

D-Jazz pushed at her shoulder to get her attention. Specs was now holding a knife with a four-inch blade.

"How old are you?" Specs inquired.

"Fourteen," she replied, moving her eyes back and forth between them to constantly evaluate the situation.

"You know what that means?" Specs quizzed D-Jazz.

"That chassis is tight," D-Jazz responded with an evil grin.

"Give us your purse," Specs demanded.

"No!" Annabella conclusively uttered.

D-Jazz went to grab her, and before she could engage in any defensive maneuvers, Jack's bat struck him squarely in the side of the head. The action sent him to the ground, three feet away from where he stood.

Specs had no time to react as Jack struck him in the right kneecap with such fury that Specs' leg inverted backwards for a moment and he dropped to the ground like a dead weight.

Jack looked at Annabella.

"Let's get outta here."

They ran back to Jack's car and proceeded to the 163 freeway.

"You've had a busy evening, Annie," Jack said.

"I didn't plan it," she told him while staring out the window.

"Raul found out that Herrero is still alive, but he's in a coma. That'll buy us a little time."

"Should one of us go over there and finish the job?" she asked.

"There's a lot of heat with killing a cop. Internal Affairs have been chasing the guy for quite a while. Perhaps we can help those guys shag his ass."

"My life has gone to shit, Jack," she told him in a contemplative tone.

"Don't say that. It's a bump in the road. Woody taught me to treat adversity like a pothole. As long as you've got a strong suspension, you can handle it."

Both thought about what Jack had just said.

"You want to go get something to eat?" he asked.

"Can we go to a hotel and order room service?" she wondered.

"Sure. I know a nice place."

They traveled to the Park Hyatt Aviara Resort in Carlsbad. This was a five-star hotel that was completely masked from surface streets. Jack paid cash for two nights, so they would not be bothered the next day.

Annabella had decisions to make.

CHAPTER 58

In Department sixty-three of the San Diego Superior Court, a jury had been selected and Judge Wendell Proxmire advised that opening statements would commence at nine-thirty the following morning.

Ricky Ray Ransom was licking his wounds from the pounding he took from the Judge regarding his cowboy hat, lapel pin, his African-American lawyer's ability to be seen by the jury and a gag order.

Roger Legion spoke to his attorneys regarding preparation of the gag order.

"Do we know who he's going to call first?" Roger asked Clint and Dan referring to Ricky Ray.

"I'll tell you," Ricky Ray injected as he stood less than two feet from the men. "Roger, may I speak to you, please?"

"I'll see you guys back at the office," Roger told his lawyers and turned his attention to Ricky Ray.

"You did quite well, today, counselor, for mostly keeping your mouth shut," Ricky Ray told Legion.

"You're trying too hard, Ricky Ray. And it shows."

"Do you and your people want to talk settlement?" Ricky Ray's inquiry was stern and without emotion. His arms were crossed in front of him.

"You're the one driving that train."

"Twenty-five million. That's a fifty percent discount."

"Still too rich for my blood."

"Well, give me a number then, God damn it!"

"Two million dollars," Roger told him.

Ricky Ray looked at Roger with a blank stare.

"I'll tell you something, Roger. I appreciate that offer. It's a one hundred percent increase from where you were. But it still doesn't move the needle. Do your people know what this will do to them, if I hit it out of the park?"

"They do. But they're counting on me to make you strike out."

"Roger. I like you. You are a true adversary. We got a saying in Texas, 'The worst kind of deception is self-deception.'"

"We have that same saying in San Diego. We just don't brag about it."

"Roger, I'll see you in court tomorrow morning. Oh, by the way, my first witness is going to be the mother, Mae Kaylic."

"Thanks, Ricky Ray."

Roger and Ricky Ray left the courtroom together. Both men knew that, like all jury trials, they were about to roll the dice.

CHAPTER 59

The members of the Face of God or FOG organization assembled for an evening meeting in the living room of Judge Caesar Cargyle. Everyone was casually dressed, including Linda Green and Annabella, who sat as far away from each other as possible. Wine and hors d'ouevres were served and the women engaged in workplace chitchat while they awaited the arrival of their host.

Judge Cargyle wheeled into the room and the women provided him with a round of applause. His pleasure was evident as he beamed a smile and took several bows from the chair. He wheeled to his place at the end of the coffee table.

"Ladies," he began, "as you all know, our success has now been defined. I received word today that Cassie's former boss, Andrew Stansworth, has resigned from the State Bar of California, effective immediately."

He gazed around the room and pointed at Cassie.

"You, young lady, are to be congratulated. You mustered up the strength to slay a monster and your efforts have borne fruit."

"I must thank Leticia. Without her support, I could never do it."

The Judge turned his attention to Leticia.

"A toast to Leticia." They all raised their glasses. "She is a true lawyer. Learn from her, ladies. She is the best."

Leticia smiled and gave a thankful nod.

"Now," the Judge resumed, "we must capitalize on this success and magnify it. Tomorrow, we'll send out demand letters on behalf of all of you remaining women. We are going to increase the dollar amount requested, along with resignation from the State Bar, from $50,000 to $250,000. Leticia will take one third and you ladies will have the rest. Cassie, I am going to personally fund your settlement with an additional $200,000, so it is fair with the other ladies."

"Your Honor, I don't know what to say? Can I give you a hug?"

"Absolutely."

Cassie stood from her place on the couch and walked over to the Judge. She gave him a quick hug and a kiss on the cheek. The Judge felt appreciated.

"Leticia," the Judge proclaimed, "the next settlement meeting on one of your cases is tomorrow with Claudia. If you perform as well as you did with Roger Legion, there will again be cause for celebration."

"What are your plans for Roger Legion?" Linda Green asked.

"They are underway," the Judge advised. "They involve a special skill and keen insight. I will keep you all apprised as necessary."

The butler, Farmington, entered the room. He walked over to the Judge to whisper in his ear.

"One of Mr. Herrero's men is on the phone. He says it's important."

The Judge looked forward with a pensive stare.

"Wheel me into the office," he directed to Farmington. "Ladies, if you would excuse me, I'll only be a moment."

Farmington complied with the Judge's directive. Linda Green looked around at the various girls, but refused to make eye contact with Annabella. Linda turned to the girl next to her, Frida, to pose an inquiry.

"Do you know where the bathroom is?"

"Yeah. Down the hallway, where the Judge just went. It's the last door on the left."

"Thanks," Linda told her and walked out of the living room.

She slowly sauntered down the hallway to admire the Judge's art collection. When she reached the door of his office, the Judge's voice was brazen and resolute.

"It is unfortunate about what happened to Ruben. I cannot give the girl up right now. She has one more assignment to do for me on Thursday. After that, I'll help you to set her up."

Linda was trying to make sense of what she was hearing. Then, she heard another topic of interest.

"What about Legion?" The Judge waited for a response. "I had other plans for him. If he's gotta go, Ruben assured me that he could get a bomb in his office. If you do it around 3:30 in the afternoon, I can make sure that he is on the phone."

A moment passed.

"Okay, so when? This Thursday?" the Judge inquired of the telephone caller. "Let me know for sure. All right."

With that the call ended and Linda scurried to locate and enter the bathroom. Once she did, she turned on the light and locked the door. Linda turned and paused at her reflection in the mirror.

Linda had now overheard the potential assassination plans for Annabella and Roger Legion. She wondered about what her next move would be. Linda would seek advice from the one person who was involved with all these people – Raul.

CHAPTER 60

"Mr. Ransom, you may proceed."

With that proclamation, Judge Wendell Proxmire had commenced, in earnest, the trial of *Zantoff Transportation v. Tecton Insurance*.

Ricky Ray Ransom stood from his chair and walked directly to the podium that was centered in front of the plaintiff and defense tables. Ricky Ray wore a dark-blue, three piece suit, with a white shirt, and a light-blue tie, with a dark-blue star pattern. In his lapel was a small, waving American flag pin.

He began to speak as he walked toward the jury box.

"Ladies and gentlemen of the jury. My name is Ricky Ray Ransom. In the English language, my name would be called an alliteration. Because the beginning syllables all sound the same, it helps you to remember. That is what I am going to ask you to do in this trial – remember.

"I'm a lawyer from Houston, Texas. You're probably wondering why a lawyer from Houston, Texas is trying a case in San Diego, California. I'm going to answer that question before I'm done here this morning. But, for right now, I want to thank you for taking the time out of your schedules to come here today to give," he paused for a moment, "justice to a little, baby girl, named Rebecca Kaylic. Now, Rebecca will not be in the courtroom with us, but I have arranged for you all to take a trip to the hospital, so that you can see her condition, first hand.

"Rebecca was the victim of a horrific accident. She was riding in the back seat of her parent's car and a tractor-trailer, driven by an employee of Zantoff Transportation, who was looking at his cell phone, rammed the rear-end of the Kaylic car. The impact was so extraordinary that that baby flew out of her seat and crashed, head-first, into the front windshield. Rebecca suffered a traumatic brain injury and her spinal cord was damaged.

"Now, those are the facts that give rise to the true reason that we are here. Zantoff Transportation purchased a policy of truck liability insurance from the defendant, Tecton Insurance, with a policy limit of one million dollars. They knew from the first day they received this claim that it was a bad case. I will show you comments in their claim file in which the claim handler is telling management that they should pay the policy limit. But the management of Tecton Insurance refused. Why would they do that?

"Now, please hold on to that question. Contrary to popular belief, most insurance companies don't make money selling insurance. Selling insurance allows them access to vast amounts of money. Insurance companies make money off their investments. They make more than enough money to offset any losses selling insurance. The key is to hang on to money as long as possible and wear down people, like the parents of poor, little, precious baby, Rebecca.

"I will prove that Tecton knowingly violated the insurance law of this state to hold off paying their policy limit as long as possible. Tecton's actions were in bad faith.

"Now, Mr. Legion is going to tell you that they offered to pay the policy limit, way after they should have and the parents refused to take it. They almost did, because they were being forced into a 'take it or leave it' situation.

"Now, I will answer the question that I rhetorically posed earlier. What is a lawyer from Houston doing in San Diego?

"Well, before Mr. and Mrs. Kaylic agreed to anything, Mrs. Kaylic, God bless her, went to her computer and typed 'insurance lawyer bad insurance company.' And guess whose name popped up? Your favorite alliteration – Ricky Ray Ransom.

His last comment brought a smile to the faces of the jurors.

"I came to San Diego and when I saw that precious, little angel, Rebecca, I wept. I have nine children, all under the age of fourteen, and if that were one of my babies, I would have been looking for a rope and a tree with strong branches. Someone had to pay for this.

"So, I come to you today as Rebecca's voice. Asking you to punish those who have contributed to her condition. You must send a message as a group, as a society, that this type of conduct evidenced by Tecton Insurance will not be tolerated. They must be punished. And a slap on the wrist will not be sufficient.

"Let me bring an analogy to your attention. We've all purchased stamps for letters. You put the stamp on a letter, put it in the mailbox, and you forget about it. The cost of the stamp doesn't affect your lifestyle. Because you can easily afford it.

"Mr. Legion is going to tell you that the most Tecton owes is one million dollars. Do you know what one million dollars is to a billion dollar company?

Ricky Ray surveyed the jury.

"It's a postage stamp. They'll cut the check and close the file on Rebecca. As if she never existed. Is that justice?

"Last year the CEO of Tecton, Jesus Loredo, was given sixty-two million dollars in wages, bonuses, and stock options. Why don't you give that amount to Rebecca? There is no other way that you are going to punish those responsible for this travesty. If you let Tecton Insurance get away with paying an amount that is not commensurate with their depravity, then you give them the right to do it again. To your babies. To your grandbabies. And to you.

"The law is the codification of common sense. That is what I am asking you to use to make a determination. When the lawyers are done here, you will become Rebecca's voice. Please don't let that precious, little baby, Rebecca, suffer any more. Give her the justice that she deserves.

"Thank you for listening to me. I know you'll do the right thing."

Ricky Ray returned to his chair and looked at the jury with a somber smile. Tears were welling up in the eyes of at least three of the jurors.

Roger Legion considered Ricky Ray's opening statement to be quite impressive.

Judge Proxmire's voice cut through the courtroom air.

"Mr. Legion, you may proceed."

CHAPTER 61

Roger Legion stood and walked directly to the courtroom podium. He wore one of his trademark, black suits that had a light, yellow thread stripe. His white shirt was accented by a yellow, silk tie. He moved to within two feet of the jury box and moved his eyes to make sure that he had made eye contact with each member of the jury.

"Ladies and Gentlemen of the jury. My name is Roger Legion. I stand in front of you today to represent and defend Tecton Insurance. Mr. Ransom will try to portray my client as a faceless, evil corporation that intentionally goes around wanting to hurt children. But nothing could be farther from the truth. Over the next several days, I will prove that to you.

"Now, the only thing I did agree with, that Mr. Ransom said, is that the law is the codification of common sense. I'll come back to that topic in a moment.

"I want to clarify a few things. First, Tecton Insurance did not cause the accident in which little Rebecca was hurt. Second, Tecton Insurance handled the claim in this matter in compliance with the California Insurance Department regulations. Tecton offered the policy limit of one million dollars, but it was refused by Mr. Ransom, because he wanted more.

"And third, what he didn't tell you is that he made a secret deal with the Tecton insured, Zantoff Transportation, for a settlement of twenty-one million dollars with a covenant or promise not to execute. In exchange, Zantoff Transportation assigned their rights under the policy to the Kaylic family. So, if you were wondering why this case is labeled Zantoff Transportation versus Tecton Insurance, now you know.

"Zantoff Transportation purchased insurance coverage from Tecton Insurance in the amount of one million dollars per accident. Tecton Insurance acknowledged the liability of their insured and offered to pay it. They stand ready, willing, and able to pay it today. But Mr. Ransom would like you to rewrite the contract between Zantoff Transportation and Tecton Insurance because Zantoff does not have the money to pay for the phony judgment they entered into with Mr. Ransom.

"What you are about to witness in this courtroom is a money grab perpetrated by a magician. A magician who is dressed as a lawyer. He will continually try to misdirect you and I will continually get you back on track. I realize that this case may become emotional. When I saw little Rebecca, I became misty-eyed. I have grandchildren about her age and I don't know what I would do if any of them were in a car accident like this.

"The people to blame for the accident is Zantoff Transportation. Tecton Insurance did everything required by law and the law says that the most they owe is one million dollars. They stand ready to cut a check immediately for that amount.

"As I said when I began, the law is the codification of common sense. Please use your common sense when deliberating on this matter. Don't be persuaded by a sleight of hand or a puff of smoke.

"Thank you for listening. I know you'll do the right thing."

Roger returned to his chair and as he did earlier, Judge Proxmire's voice sliced through the air.

"Mr. Ransom, do you have a reply?"

"No, your Honor."

"All right. As I believe everyone is aware, one of the jurors has a doctor's appointment, which was set prior to jury selection. Therefore, Mr. Ransom, I ask that you be prepared to call your first witness tomorrow morning. Do you understand?"

"Yes, your Honor," Ricky Ray stood and advised.

"Very well," the Judge proclaimed. "The Court is in recess until 9:30 tomorrow morning."

Everyone stood and began to exit the room. Ricky Ray walked over to Roger to catch his attention.

"A magician dressed like a lawyer. I like that. I've been called worse."

"So have I," Roger responded.

Roger turned away and Ricky Ray watched him. There were no signs that either was about to fold.

CHAPTER 62

Jack Prickett stepped off the elevator and on to the sixth floor of the Scripps Memorial Hospital in La Jolla. His destination was room 612. He was there to visit his mentor in the art of assassination, Woody Tobag.

As he passed the nurse's station, closest to Woody's room, a voice called out to him.

"Excuse me, sir."

It was one of the nurse's dressed in deep purple medical scrubs. She was forty-six years old, with a mid to large frame. She had brown hair that had some green highlights in it. Her name was Roxy. Roxy had a stethoscope around her neck, along with a communication device that allowed her to respond to internal calls.

Jack stopped and turned toward her as she approached him.

"Are you Mr. Tobag's son?"

"No, but I am his next of kin," Jack answered.

"Yesterday, he had a bad day. We didn't think he was going to make it. We didn't know how to contact you and there are no directives on file as to what he would like in the event of a life-threatening emergency."

"What do you mean?" Jack wondered in dismay.

"Like whether or not you would like him to be resuscitated in the event that's required," Nurse Roxy told him.

"What do you want to do: Take him out back and shoot him?" Jack snapped. His anger was percolating.

"No! We just want to do whatever you want."

"I want you to keep him alive. That's what I'm paying for. If any decisions have to be made, you call me then. All right?"

"Sure," she paused for a moment. "He talks about you all the time. I'm sure he'll be excited to see you. Just stop at the Nurse's Station on the way out."

Jack nodded his head in agreement and continued his trip to Woody's room.

Woody lay in bed with a week's worth of facial hair, just staring at the ceiling with a blank look on his face. As soon as Jack entered the room, a switch turned on within Woody.

"There's my boy!" Woody enthusiastically exclaimed. "You setting them up and knocking them down, boy? Hey, come over here and help me lift up the back of this bed."

Jack located the power control for the bed and lifted the back up, so Woody was in more of a sitting position. They looked at each other and their beaming smiles matched.

"Did you call that girl?"

"What girl?" Jack asked.

"The nurse from over here," Woody told him emphatically.

"No. Not yet."

"Oh," Woody responded in disgust. "What are you waiting for? Where's your phone? I'll call her."

"No, no, no. It's just that I've been doing a lot of running around lately, so I was going to wait till things calmed down."

"You know me: I can't stand a bull-shitter. Actions, not words."

"All right. I swear to you, I'll call her today."

"When?"

Jack knew better than to argue with Woody.

"Let me do it right now."

Jack took the phone and looked through his contacts.

"Next time you're here," Woody said, "you should take her picture, so you remember what she looks like."

Jack had his phone dial the number and it began to ring. After the fourth ring, a mechanical voice answered the call. Jack had a question for Woody.

"It's the answering machine, should I leave a message or call back later?"

"Leave a message. Then, call back later. That's how she'll know you want her."

"I don't know if I want her."

"Jack, my boy, you don't know what you want. That's why you need my guidance and advice.

Jack turned his attention to the phone and the message for Nurse Patricia.

"Hi Patty. This is Jack Prickett. We met at the hospital in Woody Tobag's room. I was wondering if you would like to get a coffee, or maybe even lunch, sometime. Call me when you get a chance. Thanks."

With that the call ended.

"Satisfied?" Jack asked Woody.

"Very," Woody responded.

"They told me you had a bad day yesterday."

"It's just life, Jack. You got bad days and you got good days," Woody paused for a moment. "You wouldn't happen to have that hip flask on ya?"

Jack retrieved the flask from his outer pants pocket and looked around the room.

"Where are the cups?" Jack wondered.

"Just give it to me and I'll take a swig."

Woody took a large gulp from the flask.

"That stuff goes down like velvet. Did I ask you if you had a cigarette?" Woody asked coyly with a mischievous smile.

"NO!"

As he bantered with Woody, Jack could not envision that Woody was so close to death the day before. Jack thought he knew what death looked like. But on that particular topic, he was extremely wrong.

Approximately two hours later, Jack entered the sixth floor elevator and pressed the button for the lobby. As the doors were closing, in room 436 of the hospital, Ruben Herrero's eyes opened.

CHAPTER 63

Judge Caesar Cargyle sat at his kitchen table, enjoying a French vanilla latte, when Annabella Romero entered. She walked to the refrigerator and took out a 12-ounce bottle of water. She removed the cap on the bottle and took a seat on the side of the table, facing the Judge.

As she took her first sip of water, the Judge began to speak.

"Are you ready for tomorrow?"

"As ready as I'll ever be," she responded. "But I've got to ask you, do you think it's necessary?"

"Necessity and liability are two different things. You should understand that in your line of work. Necessity denotes need, while liability denotes responsibility. Do you remember your first assignment? How things went incredibly bad? Raul took care of the loose ends. It wasn't necessary, but there were liabilities. If he didn't step in, you would have to be taken out. But you proved yourself. The Company and I were impressed with your redemption. The only one who never got over it was Raul."

"I think he's over it now" she sullenly responded and took another sip of water.

"Your piece of work for tomorrow has to be done. Just treat it like any of the other ones."

"After tomorrow, I'm done. No more. I am walking away from this life forever," Annabella proclaimed succinctly.

"As you wish. Tomorrow evening, we are having another FOG meeting. I have been advised by Leticia that another lawyer has agreed to a settlement of two hundred fifty thousand dollars and to resign from the State Bar with prejudice. Our plan is proceeding according to our design. So, please join us for a little celebration."

"All right," she answered with a slight smile.

"For tomorrow, we have your credentials and the documentation, so you can move around the building once you're inside. There are cameras everywhere, so I hope you're wearing a good disguise. We'll also have a car, with the necessary identification tags, for you to get into the parking lot. Finally, we have a Glock 17 pistol for you with two extra magazines. Each magazine holds fifteen rounds."

"How long do we maintain radio silence?" Annabella wondered.

"Just a few hours. I'll find out what they know. As soon as I am sure that you are in the clear, I'll get a message to you."

She nodded her head slowly in agreement.

"When this is over," the Judge said, "I will miss you."

"Don't," she replied. "Do yourself a favor and forget me."

Annabella stood from her chair and proceeded to the door of the kitchen.

"Do you want your water?" the Judge called out.

Annabella answered him without stopping.

"No. I'm done with it."

Annabella needed to complete preparations on the last 'hit' of her career.

CHAPTER 64

At three forty-five in the afternoon, Roger Legion was at his desk, reviewing and responding to various emails.

He was of the belief that he was thoroughly prepared for the cross-examination of Mae Kaylic, the mother of the injured child, who was the subject of his trial. Every factual detail, regardless of its significance, would run through his mind. He knew that he had to be careful with her and not come across as a bully. He was hopeful that he would only have to reinforce some of the statements that she will make during direct examination.

Roger's cell phone came to life and the Caller ID indicated that it was Raul Verdugo. Legion answered.

"Hello, Raul."

"Are you available to take a ride?" Raul quizzed.

"Absolutely," was Legion's response.

"I'll be out in front of your building in ten minutes. I'm driving a black Escalade."

"I'll be there."

With that the call ended and Roger hurried out of his office for a rendezvous with Raul.

Raul's black Escalade pulled up in front of the America's Finest City Building, and Roger quickly entered through the front, passenger door. Raul took off as quickly as traffic would allow.

"Where we going?" Legion asked.

"To a warehouse down in National City," Raul told him. "I found her."

"Sharifa?" Roger questioned in astonishment.

"That's the one. I was able to trail her from some of her old contacts in Chicago. It seems that everybody is looking for her. Your friend, Ransom, put a bounty on finding her of one hundred thousand dollars."

"Is she lucid?" Legion quizzed.

"She's coming down off a crack high," Raul told him. "But she understands what you ask her."

"Can you help me protect her?" Legion spoke in a worried tone.

"Absolutely. The warehouse is under armed guard. At night, I'll transport her to this motel, Jimmy owns in El Cajon. I'll have a woman stay in the room with her. The place has bars on the windows and will be under surveillance by our armed guards. And I will personally transport her to wherever she needs to go."

"It sounds good, Raul. Thank you," Legion expressed sincerely.

"Thank me when it's done."

Raul and Roger were heading south on the Interstate Five freeway for a meeting with an elusive witness, who holds the key to one major secret.

CHAPTER 65

Linda Green spent the day catching up on chores around her apartment, like washing clothes, dusting furniture, and vacuuming. She wore gray sweatpants and a gray sweatshirt with white, ankle sport socks.

Her mind continued to race regarding the information that she had obtained at Judge Cargyle's house.

Was Judge Cargyle actually conspiring with someone to kill Roger Legion? Did the same fate await Annabella Romero? Perhaps, she misheard the information. The one person, whose opinion she wanted on the matter, Raul Verdugo, was not answering his phone and not returning any of her text messages.

Linda knew Roger Legion was in trial and did not wish to disturb his focus with a conspiracy theory that may have no real basis. She did not wish to be perceived as a whacked-out lunatic. For now, she would wait for Raul to contact her, then she would make a decision as to her future action on the matter.

As Linda folded her second load of clothes, her cell phone rang. The Caller ID indicated that it was Leticia Harrison, the lawyer who offered Linda a job and was the executive member of the FOG group.

"Hello, this is Linda," she answered.

"Linda, this is Leticia. How are you?

"I'm fine, Leticia. How about you?"

"I'm doing well. Listen, the Judge is going to have a little celebration party at his house tomorrow night for all the FOG ladies."

"What are we celebrating?" Linda inquired.

"Our second settlement," Leticia advised enthusiastically. "Claudia and I had a meeting yesterday with her former employer. When we laid out our case, he agreed to resign from the State Bar and pay us two hundred fifty thousand dollars."

"Wow! Did he even try to negotiate?"

"Not really. He said that he was looking for an excuse to retire. He just wanted a guarantee that everything would remain confidential."

"Can I ask you something, Leticia?"

"Sure," Leticia answered nonchalantly.

"You don't think the Judge would engage in any criminal activity to obtain results?"

"Linda, the Judge sometimes speaks in a brusque manner, but ultimately, he is an officer of the court. He considers that position one of high esteem. I've known him for more than twenty years and I have never seen him engage in any activity that was even remotely illegal."

"Thank you, Leticia. That really calms my concerns."

"Okay, so the van will pick us up in the parking lot of my office at 6:30 tomorrow evening."

"I'll see you then, Leticia."

"Bye, Linda."

With that the call ended. Even though Leticia had provided her assurances, Linda would appreciate Raul's opinion on the matter. Linda remained uncomfortable about the FOG. There was something in it.

CHAPTER 66

On the fourth floor of the Scripps Memorial Hospital, in Room 436, Ruben Herrero continued to get his bearings as to where he was. When he awoke from his coma, Officer Irving Ordaz was in the room. He was dressed in his full police uniform. Irving was the police officer who was with Ruben, when he had his altercation with Annabella.

A large Skin-Flex bandage covered Ruben's left cheek. Half of his face was swollen and the wound inflicted by Annabella required thirty-five stitches. His left eye was encircled in shiny, bright, dark blue and red and evidenced significant swelling.

"How long have I been in here?" Ruben wondered.

"Two days," Irving answered.

"Did you grab her?"

"No," Irving said ashamedly.

"Have you been tracking her? Where's the car?"

"The car's parked in a garage of a house in North Park. That's where our girl's cousin lives. The one who was with her at the bar that night."

"Anything going on since I've been in this coma?" Ruben inquired.

"It's been quiet. I spoke to the Judge. We have the green light to go get Legion. The Judge also said that the girl had one more job to do for him, then he would help us take her out."

"Where are my guns?" Ruben quizzed.

"I got them," Irving advised. "I also have your phone."

"All right. I'll be out of here either today or tomorrow morning. I want you to contact six of our guys."

As Ruben continued to speak, he counted off the men on his fingers.

"Hector, Lyle, Tommy, Strips, Mac and Rondo. Tell them I've got some nice off the clock work. Full tactical. They should be on standby for the next twenty-four to forty-eight hours."

The men that he was assembling were all police officers and members of the San Diego Police SWAT team. They were former Navy SEALs and each was considered an expert marksman,

"Are we going to go after the girl?" Irving inquired.

"We're going to go after all of them. A *blitzkrieg*. Wholesale slaughter."

Blitzkrieg is a German term for 'lightning war.'

The underlying anger in Ruben's voice was evident. His thirst for revenge needed to be quenched.

"How are we going to find her?" Irving queried.

"The Judge will tell us where she is," Ruben surmised. "I think she'll be at his house. That's where his people normally go after a hit until everything calms down. Did he say who she is going after?"

"No," Irving said.

"I hope it's Verdugo. The Executioner. One more that we can take off our list."

Ruben sat up and swung his legs off the bed.

"Help me find my clothes."

Ruben was about to commence an overwhelming, all-out attack on those individuals that were scheduled for death. But his targets were not about to sit by idly without putting up a fight.

CHAPTER 67

National City is located in the South Bay area of San Diego. It consists of 26,000 acres and approximately 60,000 people reside there. It is known for its ship building industry, where it has produced both Navy warships and ships for commercial fleets.

At the corner of 'A' Street and East 20th Avenue sat a large, non-descript warehouse. It had no signage and the interior had approximately 110,000 square feet of space. The building was three stories high with no windows on the first floor. Security cameras covered every inch of the exterior.

The entire property was surrounded by six feet high, black, iron post fencing and a card was needed to operate the gate to allow entrance.

Raul pulled up to the entrance and slid his card into the gate pad. The gate retracted open and the Escalade entered. He parked near one of the smaller service doors. Legion and Raul walked up to the door and Raul produced a key that allowed entrance.

They walked through a small hallway and a light was on in an office at the end of the hallway. The office was filled with ten monitors that continually changed their view of various portions of the interior of the building and the parking lot. A uniformed guard sat at a desk watching the monitors.

Raul tapped on the glass that separated the hallway and office, while pointing to a door at the end of the hallway. The guard acknowledged Raul and then a buzzing sound was heard coming from the door. The buzzing sound indicated that the door was temporarily unlocked.

Raul opened the door and he and Legion entered a large, vacant warehouse area. It was at least 40,000 square feet, well lit, and the ceiling was fifty feet high. There were several overhead doors that would easily allow a tractor-trailer to enter the building.

In the center of the room, a woman sat in an older brown office chair with her hands zip-tied behind her and her legs were zip-tied to the chair's legs. A brown bag covered her head. She wore a thrift store suit and her shoes that were once patent leather, now were scratched up and the soles seem to be coming off the shoes.

"Sharifa," Raul said as he pulled the bag off her head.

Sharifa looked slightly dazed and her eyes took a moment to adjust. Her eyes were bloodshot and her lips were severely chapped. She had a black afro and a small heart tattooed on her left cheek.

"What you want?" she uttered.

"Tell him what you told me?" Raul was referring to Roger Legion.

"Who you?" she asked.

"My name is Roger Legion. I'm a lawyer."

"A law man? Shit, you wearing a pretty nice suit even for a law man. What you want?"

"What's your last name?"

"Monroe. Like Marilyn."

"Do you know Bernie Kaylic?"

"You mean 'Jazzy?' That's what they call him cause he like all da old school jazz guys, like Charlie Parker and John Coltrane."

"How well did you know him?"

"I was his squeeze, you know. He'd call me his little piece of pumpkin pie."

"When was the last time you spoke to him?" Legion wondered.

"Shortly, after he had that accident. You know if he got any money for that. Because I was supposed to get a cut."

"Why was he going to give you a cut?"

"Cause I helped him to set it up. Without me, it woulda never happened."

"Explain it to me," Legion requested.

"I got a cousin whose brother-in-law was running an insurance scam ring. He had doctors, lawyers, and those guys that fix your back."

"Chiropractors," Legion added.

"That's it. He called it swoop and," she paused for a moment "something."

"Squat." Legion shared with her.

"Mr. Law-Man, you are in the zone today. Swoop and squat. That's the one."

A swoop and squat insurance scam involves a lead car suddenly stopping in oncoming traffic, while the victim car is forced to stop suddenly, while a third vehicle, that is also in on the scam, crashes into the rear-end of the innocent vehicle.

"My relation said the cars didn't have big enough insurance policies. He said the big trucks had policies of at least seven hundred fifty thousand dollars. He was having trouble finding people to be victims because they were afraid they might get creamed by a tractor-trailer. But I told Jazzy about it and he was all in."

"Did they have an inside guy at Zantoff Transportation?"

"That relation of mine got a job working there driving tractor trailers. He was the driver of the truck on the day of the accident."

"What was Jazzy going to do about his wife?"

"He had a plan all worked out. She liked to go places and look at nature. He said that he was going to take her to the Grand Canyon and push her off a cliff. Then, him and me were gonna set up house."

Legion looked at her for a moment as he was digesting what she said.

"Can I get some water?" Sharifa asked.

Legion looked toward Raul.

"I'll get you some," Raul told her and walked back to the office.

Sharifa and Roger looked at each other for a moment.

"I'm twenty-eight years old," she told Roger. "I got four kids. I know that I can't get'em back legally, but I would like to see them. Can you help me do that?"

Roger thought before answering.

"Yes."

"You're the first person who ever said they would help me with anything."

Tears began to roll down Sharifa's cheeks.

"Can you ask your friend to cut these ties off me?" she asked. "I won't run or do anything stupid."

Raul returned with the water and Legion told him to cut her restraints.

The truth had emerged in the case of *Zantoff Transportation v. Tecton Insurance*. Roger now wanted to deliver the message to Ricky Ray Ransom.

CHAPTER 68

A blue, late model Cadillac CTS left the parking lot of the Del Frisco Double Eagle Steakhouse located on Bayfront Court in Downtown San Diego. Ricky Ray Ransom had just enjoyed a bone-in filet mignon, with a side of creamed corn and Château mashed potatoes.

He wore the same clothes that he had on when he gave the opening statement, earlier in the day, in the _Zantoff_ case. He had removed his tie and it sat on the passenger seat of the car.

Ricky Ray met two friends for dinner from Houston: an investment banker and an oil wildcatter, who made his fortune off speculating off oil reserves in the desolate areas surrounding Houston in Harris County.

It was approximately 8:15 pm and the marine layer rolled in with its accompanying fog blanket.

Ricky Ray was listening to voice mail messages when he heard a short blast of a siren from behind him. In his rearview mirror, he saw the red and blue lights of a police cruiser attempting to get his attention and pull over to the side of the road. He complied.

Officer Wendell Grammar stepped out of the police car and walked up the driver's side of the Cadillac. He touched his thumb on the red taillight of the car as he passed it.

"Can I see your driver's license, registration and proof of insurance?" the officer asked Ricky Ray.

"Sure," Ricky Ray responded as he pulled out his billfold. "What's the problem, officer?"

"You were weaving in and out of the lane. You were also talking on your phone."

Ricky Ray handed his driver's license to the officer.

"This car is a rental," Ricky Ray advised. "I wasn't talking on the phone. I was just listening to some music."

"It appeared to me as if you were talking. Where were you coming from?"

"Del Frisco's."

"How many drinks did you have?"

"Two," Ricky Ray answered.

"What's that smell?"

"One of my friends had a Cuban cigar."

"All right sir, please wait a minute."

The officer walked back to his car and Ricky took his cell phone and held it below the officer's line of sight from the police car. Using only his peripheral vision, Ricky Ray attempted to delete the phone history on the phone without success. The officer reappeared at his door.

"Sir, your license is suspended."

"That's impossible!" Ricky Ray responded with a raised voice and incredulous tone.

"Texas DMV says it's for failure to pay renewal fees."

"There has to be some sort of clerical error. Let me call someone at my office and I'll get this whole thing straightened out."

"No. Keep your hands on the wheel. Don't move," Officer Grammar told him with a no-nonsense tone.

The police officer could see the telephone on the passenger seat of the car and he could read the display: CLEAR ALL RECENTS.

"You weren't tampering with evidence, were you?"

"No," Ricky Ray's anger was beginning to be evidenced. "I want to talk to your supervisor."

"Sir, would you please step out of the vehicle?"

"I want to talk to your supervisor," Ricky Ray again issued his demand.

Officer Grammar looked at him and requested a supervisor and a K-9 unit over his police radio.

"All you're doing is racking up charges," the Officer told Ricky Ray. "Now, you got failure to comply."

"Do you know who I am?"

"Richard Ransom?"

Ricky Ray was disgusted with his answer and looked into the rearview mirror to see two additional police cars arrive. One police officer exited each of the vehicles and a German Shepard police dog also exited the second vehicle. They all walked along the driver's side of the vehicles.

Both men and the dog arrived and looked in the car before speaking to Officer Grammar.

"Watch him," he said to the officer holding the K-9 dog. "He's trying to erase the call history on his phone."

The officer focused on Ricky Ray while holding back the dog. Officer Grammar stepped back to his car with the other officer, who was his supervisor, Sergeant Jerry Leos.

"What do we have here?" the Sergeant inquired.

"He was not maintaining his lane and he was talking on his phone. He said he had only two drinks and he was listening to music, not talking on the phone. His license is out of Texas and it's suspended for failure to register. There's a smell inside the car that he claims is from a Cuban cigar. He was trying to clear the call history on the phone and he refuses to get out of the car."

The Sergeant looked over and the K-9 was appearing to be slightly more aggressive than normal, but was not barking. He walked to the driver's side window.

"Mr. Ransom, I'm Sergeant Leos of the San Diego Police. I'm a supervisor from the Traffic Division. You wanted to speak to me."

"Yes, I did. It's regarding the tactics of this patrol officer."

"Step out of the car and we'll talk," the Sergeant told him.

Ricky Ray complied. He and the Sergeant walked to the front of the first police car. The Sergeant gave a nod to the police officer who was holding the dog.

"*Gaan*!" the officer said in a raised voice and the dog began sniffing the perimeter of the vehicle. *Gaan* is the Dutch word for 'go.'

"Listen," Ricky began as he spoke to the Sergeant, "I'm a tourist, from out-of-town, who just spent five hundred dollars in one of your restaurants. I'm also a lawyer, so I know my rights. Look at the weather out here. The fog is so thick, there's zero visibility and he claims I can't stay in my lane."

Ricky Ray was suddenly interrupted.

"Sergeant, we got a hit."

Ricky Ray's face showed concern as to what the officer was talking about. The German Shepard was sitting and staring at the trunk of the car.

"Open it," the sergeant told him.

Officer Grammar opened the trunk from inside the driver's door. All the police officers began to survey the contents. There were two banker boxes of files and a green duffel bag.

Officer Grammar slowly undid the tie at the end of the duffel bag and retrieved, what appear to be, a MAC-9 machine gun. He showed it to the other two officers, then removed the magazine on the gun, which showed it was fully loaded.

The Sergeant then began to look through one of the banker's boxes. Underneath the files, at the bottom of the box, in heavy-duty, shrink wrap plastic, was, what appeared to be a kilo of cocaine.

The Sergeant then moved to the other box. Under the files, he found a dozen magazines. All of them were pornographic in nature and all dealt with children under the age of ten years old.

The Sergeant turned and walked back to Ricky Ray. Ricky Ray knew it wasn't good.

"Who else has access to your vehicle, Mr. Ransom?"

"I'm the only one with a key. Why? What was in there?"

"A machine gun, a kilo of cocaine, and child pornography."

"It's not mine. I swear to you. I'm being set up," Ricky Ray spoke urgently with nervous energy. "And I know who's setting me up. He's a lawyer named Roger Legion."

"All right. We're going to have to let the detectives sort this out."

"Can I get my phone?" Ricky Ray asked.

"No," the Sergeant told him. "It's evidence."

The Sergeant then walked over to Officer Grammar.

"Hook him up. Toss the car. Field test the dope. I'll call the detectives."

Ricky Ray was placed into handcuffs, read his *Miranda* rights, and placed in the back seat of Officer Grammar's police cruiser.

Ricky Ray was concerned that, if this was all being done at the behest of Roger Legion, what else did he have planned for him?

CHAPTER 69

Three hours later, at the San Diego County Sheriff's Department Central Jail, located on Front Street, Ricky Ray Ransom sat in an attorney conference room, awaiting his opportunity to call someone. The room was sterile with half walls of Plexiglas.

The furniture consisted of a stainless steel table and two stainless steel chairs on each side of the table that look like bar stools. All the furniture was bolted to the floor. On the side of the table farthest from the door, an iron ring was welded to it. Ricky Ray wore a handcuff on his left wrist and the other side of the handcuffs connected to the table ring.

He sat in total frustration and gazed without focus. Suddenly, from out of the darkness of the hallway, emerged Roger Legion. He entered the room and stood, looking down at Ricky Ray.

Legion thought Ricky Ray was going to explode at him and Ricky Ray also thought he would explode at Legion if given the chance. But he did not.

"You've got a hell of a nerve coming down here to gloat. I swear to God I am going to make sure that you lose your law license."

"I didn't come to gloat. I spoke to Sharifa."

Ricky Ray looked at him quizzically.

"Bullshit," he replied.

"I found her. I've got her under armed guard."

"What did she say?"

"The accident was a set-up," Legion said. "It was part of a swoop and squat insurance scam that your client, Bernard Kaylic, was in on."

"My client told me she was a crackhead. Do you believe her?"

"I do. She's not on crack now and she's very knowledgeable about the details. And the police believe her. They plan on arresting your client tomorrow morning when he shows up for court. They're going to charge him with insurance fraud, perjury, and conspiracy to commit murder."

"What's the deal with the conspiracy?" Ricky Ray wondered.

"He planned on killing his wife after a settlement or verdict was reached."

Ricky let out an exasperated sigh.

"You know, Roger, something about the *Zantoff* case never smelled right. What did the insurance company say?"

"They don't know and I'm not going to tell them. Because you and I are going to settle this case right now. My client is going to pay the little girl five million dollars. She shouldn't be punished because her father is an asshole. You are going to waive any claims to your attorney fees and your costs."

"I must have three hundred thousand dollars into this case," Ricky Ray flared.

"Write it off as the cost of doing business. I'll set up a trust for the girl and her mother and a local bank will be trustees. We are going to pay the mother two hundred fifty thousand dollars and the father gets nothing."

Ricky Ray looked at him with a dour expression. Roger held out his hand to shake with him. Ricky Ray accepted the handshake.

"One final thing:" Roger added. "I'm going to make all this adventure that you've gone through tonight disappear. Without a trace. But you and your people have to be out of here within twenty-four hours."

Ricky Ray fixed a stare on Roger.

"By sundown?"

"Yeah," Roger responded.

Both appreciated the Old West reference.

"Roger, who put that stuff in the trunk of my car?"

"I don't know, but I'm going to find out."

Roger had a suspicion about who may have planted the items. Now, he needed to prove it.

CHAPTER 70

The next morning, Ruben Herrero sat alone on a park bench in Poinsettia Park, located in the southwestern corner of Carlsbad. Carlsbad was approximately thirty-five miles north of downtown San Diego. It was a few minutes before 8:00 am and the fog from the marine layer cut visibility down to less than half a mile.

The park was empty with the exception of three dog walkers and the sound of lawn mowers could be heard in the distance. Ruben gazed out into the emptiness of the fog and suddenly, he saw the outline of a man.

The man was tall, lanky, and his stride was slow and deliberate. He wore a black, double-breasted, trench coat, tortoise-rimmed sunglasses, and a black fedora.

He emerged from the fog and began to speak.

"Hello, Ruben."

"Hello, Mr. Seesay."

Ozy Seesay was a mysterious, shadowy figure, who provided the assignments for assassination to Judge Caesar Cargyle. Most people did not know his first name and he only dealt with people over the phone. But his phone conversations would only take place after he received assurance that the phone line was secure.

"Too bad about this," he told Ruben as he fanned near his left cheek to mimic the location of Ruben's injury.

Ruben wore a large bandage that covered nearly all of his cheek from below his eye to his chin. His black eye was purplish red and shiny. The left side of his face was so swollen, it distorted his facial features.

"It keeps me focused. When I look in the mirror, it forces me to remember."

"Thank you for meeting me out here. Less eyes. Less questions," Seesay advised.

"No problem."

"Ruben, I am quite disappointed with the Judge. He continues to come up with excuses as to why those three mercenaries are not dead. I think he's protecting them. Particularly, the girl."

"I think he just wants to make as much money off them as possible before he finally gets rid of them."

"It makes no difference. The Company has decided to close Cargyle's shop." Seesay reached into his coat and pulled out a piece of paper. "Here's the final list. Take a look at it. I want you to sunset them all."

The Company was Seesay's employer. Nothing was known about it other than it was the financier of a murder-for-hire operation run out of the Rancho Santa Fe home of Judge Caesar Cargyle.

Ruben perused the list.

"All right. I'll take care of it."

"You note that the Judge is on the list and the butler, Farmington. The butler was in the Royal Air Force. He ran covert ops for the CIA."

"Impressive," Ruben commented.

"What about Verdugo?" Seesay wondered.

"The executioner? What about him?"

"Any concerns?"

"Don't worry about him. I'll take care of him."

"The last three men who gave me that assurance have wound up dead. Are you giving me the same assurance?"

"I'll let my actions speak for themselves," Ruben told Seesay.

"If the list isn't cleared within seventy-two hours, men will come from out-of-town to clear it. They'll show no mercy. And you'll be on the next list."

Ruben rose from the bench and placed the list in his pocket.

"Mr. Seesay, it was a pleasure to see you."

"Mine, also."

Both men walked away in different directions and disappeared into the fog.

Less than an hour later, Mr. Seesay was entering the Bagheria Bedda Restaurant in Little Italy to discuss a topic with Jimmy Flowers that had nothing to do with his conversation with Ruben.

CHAPTER 71

In Department sixty-three of the San Diego Superior Court, Roger Legion, Dan Clarkson and Clint Eversol sat at the defense table, while Ricky Ray Ransom's associate attorney, Joyce Adler, sat alone at the plaintiff's table. They were awaiting the arrival of Judge Wendell Proxmire. The jury was not present.

The only items on the table were drinking glasses and a water pitcher. Dan poured a glass of water for himself and offered to pour a glass for Roger and Clint. Both declined.

The court clerk was typing and the bailiff was surveying the courtroom and the door to the hallway that led to the Judge's chambers. The bailiff was in her mid-30s, approximately 5 feet tall and appeared to weigh one hundred sixty pounds. She had blonde, curly hair and wore glasses.

Judge Proxmire appeared in the doorway and signaled to the bailiff.

"All rise," the bailiff commanded. "Department sixty-three of the San Diego County Superior Court is now in session. Judge Wendell Proxmire presiding."

The Judge regained his perch on the bench and began immediately.

"Good morning, everyone. Let's go on the record."

The Court stenographer acknowledged his request.

"All right," the Judge commenced, "Miss Adler, Mr. Legion, my understanding is that a settlement has been reached in this matter. Is that correct?"

The attorneys all stood.

"Yes, your Honor," Joyce Adler replied.

"Where's Mr. Ransom?" the Judge wondered.

"He had to return to Houston on urgent business."

"Please send him my regards," the Judge told her.

"I will."

"Mr. Legion?" the Judge inquired.

"Yes, your Honor, the matter is settled," Roger said.

"Who is going to read the terms of the settlement into the record?" the Judge once again inquired.

"I will," Legion answered. He put on his reading glasses and looked down at his yellow notepad.

"Defendant, Tecton Insurance, agrees to pay in trust to the minor child . . ."

Roger suddenly stopped when he heard a gasping sound. Dan was struggling for breath and was foaming at the mouth. He began to tremble uncontrollably and Roger and Clint each grabbed one of his arms. Dan's legs buckled under and Roger and Clint lowered him to the floor. Roger loosened his necktie and unfastened the top button of his shirt. Roger spoke as he stepped into action.

"CALL NINE-ONE-ONE! CALL THE PARAMEDICS!"

Dan was tightly grasping Roger's arm and wanted to say something to him. Dan telegraphed his words with a loss of energy.

"Roger . . . I would never disappoint you." Dan paused. "I have seen the Face of God." Dan again paused. "They are coming for all of us."

Dan's trembling became seizure-like and suddenly stopped and his eyes rolled back in his head.

"WHERE ARE THE GODDAMN MEDICS?" Roger screamed as emergency medical technicians burst through the doorway.

Roger allowed them to take over, but he continually stared at Dan in anguish. Roger's breathing was heavy. He was in a slight state of shock.

Dan was still alive, but barely. Roger followed Dan's gurney into the hallway of the courthouse, followed closely by Clint. Roger stopped to speak with Clint.

"I'm going to ride with him to the hospital. Go back to the office and tell them what happened. Then come to the hospital and pick me up."

"Roger, I heard what he said to you. I gave him a ride to work today. He said that under the windshield wiper of his car, he found two index cards, he showed them to me. One said, 'YOU HAVE SEEN THE FACE OF GOD.' The other said, 'NO ONE SEES THE FACE OF GOD AND LIVES.' He said that he didn't know what it meant." Clint paused. "Do you know?"

Roger's face had a look of despair.

"I think I do."

Roger recalled Linda Green's comment that the Female Optimization Group or FOG had changed its name to the Face of God.

Now, there was another question that needed to be answered. But this one would be given priority.

CHAPTER 72

Jack's gray, late-model Challenger pulled up to the corner of Third Avenue and Ivy Street, where Annabella was waiting. She was holding a large gym bag. Jack popped open the trunk and she placed her bag within it. Annabella then got into the car and they sped off.

"Done?" Jack asked.

"Done," Annabella answered.

"Clean?"

"I think so. No problems. I had to ditch the car at the lot right over here. Now, I have to kill a couple of hours before I can go back to get my stuff at the Judge's place."

"We can go together. I have to get my stuff over there too," Jack told her.

"You know I'm done, right?" Annabella relayed. "With this life."

"Good for you. I might be, also. I haven't decided."

"Do you have a place to go, for tonight?" she inquired.

"No. Do you?" he responded.

"No," she told him while looking out the window. "You want to be roomies?"

"Sure. That sounds good," Jack acknowledged.

"I'll start looking. Any part of town in particular that you like?"

"I don't care. Maybe something near the hospital, so I can go visit Woody."

Annabella looked at Jack and smiled. She nodded her head in agreement.

"You hungry? You want to get something to eat?" Jack inquired with renewed energy.

"You know what I could go for?" she relayed. "A hot-fudge sundae. I know this place in Carlsbad where they are excellent. But if you want regular food, we can go do that."

"No," Jack announced. "Let's go get hot-fudge sundaes."

Less than thirty minutes later, Jack and Annabella were sitting at a small, round table in front of Handel's Ice Cream & Yogurt, located on State Street, each enjoying a hot-fudge sundae. She turned her focus from the ice cream to Jack. She stared at him, but he didn't notice.

"Can I ask you for a favor?"

"Sure," Jack answered.

"Can I get a hug?"

Jack nodded and stood up. He stepped away from the chair toward her. Annabella came at him with a big smile and leaped up onto him. Her legs wrapped around his legs near his butt. Both clenched each other tightly. She gave him a kiss on the cheek and a quick peck on the lips. Jack let her down.

"I received bad information about you," Annabella told Jack.

"What was that?" Jack wondered.

"That you didn't like to be touched."

"It depends on who's touching me." Jack stated with a smile.

Annabella and Jack returned to their ice cream treat. Annabella thought about her request to Raul for assistance to get her out of the country. Perhaps, now, that would not be necessary.

CHAPTER 73

Roger Legion and Clint Eversol returned to the firm at approximately 1:30 that afternoon. Dan Clarkson was still in intensive care where doctors were extremely concerned about damage to his internal organs. The doctor-in-charge of the emergency room was certain that Dan had ingested some type of poison. They would know for certain when the toxicology report was prepared.

Roger returned to his office and sat at his desk chair. He swiveled to gaze out at the landscape of the sea. Its tranquility was unable to assuage his concerns. If Dan was poisoned, perhaps he was the real target. What further added to his internal conflict was Dan's comment about seeing the Face of God. Did the comment have anything to do with the organization that Linda Green referenced earlier in the week when she visited Legion?

On the desk in front of him was a pile of phone call messages from the receptionist, Nina. His plan was to review them and return calls that he deemed to be urgent.

As Legion was instituting his plan, the elevator doors opened and a non-descript gentlemen stepped out and walked directly to Nina's counter. He was nearly 6 feet tall, medium-build, clean shaven and he wore gray trousers, and a blue sport coat. The red and blue striped tie around his neck was loosened and the top button of his shirt was unfastened.

He started to speak as he almost reached the counter.

"I'm here to see Roger Legion," he said quickly.

"Do you have an appointment?" she inquired.

"Nah, don't worry about it," he relayed and took off down the hallway to Legion's office at an accelerated gait.

Nina stood from her seat to run after him.

"Stop. STOP!" she screamed.

Nina almost caught him when Roger stepped out of the doorway to his office. Both the man and Nina slowed down their pace.

"Mr. Legion, this man doesn't have an appointment and he took off before I could announce him. Do you want me to call security?"

"Yeah, Roger. Do you want her to call security?"

Legion looked at both of them.

"Nina, this is Detective David Anderson of the San Diego Police."

"It's a pleasure to meet you, Nina."

"Next time, let me announce you," she replied with a tone of resentment and returned to her chair.

"Come on in, Dave," Roger told him and they both proceeded into Roger's office.

Neither of the men sat down. Both stared at the ocean for a moment. Detective Anderson began their conversation.

"Sorry about what happened to your boy, today."

"I don't know how it could have happened," Roger spoke in a somber voice.

"The doctors at the hospital are convinced he was poisoned," the Detective said. "My concern is that you and the other attorney could have also been targets. Let me ask you this: In my experience, poison is the murder weapon of a woman. It's kinder and gentler, but it still achieves the desired result. Do you know if your boy had any female problems?"

"Not that I'm aware of. I met his wife, she was deeply concerned and there didn't seem to be any problems," Roger relayed.

"If someone was trying to murder you or one of your attorneys, we think we know who it is."

Roger looked at the Detective craving the name of the individual.

"Who?"

"The bailiff. We have her on video taking the glass and the pitcher off the table during the commotion." Dave reached into the breast pocket of his sport coat. "Here's a still that we got off the video feed."

Dave handed a picture to Roger of the short, heavyset bailiff with blonde, curly hair and glasses removing a glass and a pitcher.

"Do you recognize her?" Dave asked.

"No," Roger said as he nodded his head negatively, while in deep pensive thought. "Can I keep this?"

"Yeah. I can always burn another one. You want to show it to your guys over here and see if anyone can ID her?"

"Yeah," Roger told him with one hundred percent focus.

"If you hear anything, you call me," Dave conveyed as he extended his hand to Roger for a handshake.

"All right. You do the same," Roger acknowledged as they shared a strong grip.

Dave Anderson left the room and Roger could not take his eyes off the picture. He did not know the name of the individual, but he knew someone who did. It was time to call Raul.

CHAPTER 74

It was 3:15 pm and Raul had just finished visiting a variety of drug store locations, at the request of Jimmy Flowers, to determine if there was any activity taking place in and around the pharmacies that may impede Jimmy's cash flow at that particular location.

If Raul saw anyone trying to sell drugs in the neighborhood, or casing the pharmacy for possible robbery, he would defuse the situation.

Raul wore his trademark black suit with a white shirt and a black and gray striped tie. His shoes were brown, leather, lace-up dress oxfords.

Raul was heading home to his condominium in Little Italy. When he reached his block, he pulled his Cadillac Escalade into a parking space within one hundred feet of his front door.

As he walked to his home, he heard a familiar voice.

"Raul," Linda Green called out to get his attention.

Linda had been sitting in her silver Acura that was located two cars ahead of Raul's car. He turned and walked toward her with a smile.

"Where have you been? Why don't you answer my calls? Or my text messages?" Linda's voice echoed more concern than anger.

"I've been working," Raul responded. "Plus I got a new phone."

"Why did you get a new phone?"

"I just do that every once in a while."

"Don't you keep the same number?"

"Not always."

As Raul uttered his last sentence, his cell phone came to life. He looked at the Caller ID. It was Roger Legion.

"Yes, Mr. Legion," Raul answered. A moment passed as he listened. "All right, I'm on my way."

The call ended and Raul turned his attention back to Linda.

"I've got to go see Legion," he told her.

"That's one of the reasons that I'm here. I was at the Judge's house the other night for a FOG meeting. I overheard a telephone call that he had. Now, I only heard his side of it, but it involved Roger Legion and that girl you know, Anna."

"What did you hear?" Raul wondered.

"The Judge said Ruben told him that he could get a bomb into Legion's office. It sounded like they were going to set it to go off at 3:30 today."

A look of worry enveloped Raul's face.

"What was said about Annabella?" Raul demanded.

"That she had an assignment to do for the Judge today and then the Judge would help them set her up."

Raul quickly assessed the situation and put a plan into action. He looked at his wristwatch, then back to Linda.

"Call Legion, tell him to get out of his office, now! If you can't get ahold of him, call the receptionist there, Nina, and tell her to get him out of there and they should probably evacuate the whole floor. I'll call Annabella."

Raul turned to race back to his car.

"Raul," Linda called out to him in a raised voice. He stopped. "Is she your girlfriend?"

"No. She's just a friend. About eight to ten years ago, we were really close. But not now. Now, we just occasionally work together."

"You know what she told us that she did for work at the FOG meeting? She kills people."

"She does." Raul paused for a moment. "So do I."

Linda looked at him with her mouth slightly open and a stared focus.

"You kill people?" she asked with disbelief.

"I do. I'm an assassin. I kill people all over the world."

"I am shocked and fascinated at the same time," Linda expressed.

"Call Legion now. We can discuss it later."

Raul ran off and Linda re-focused on her mission to alert Roger Legion that his life was in grave danger.

CHAPTER 75

Roger Legion was awaiting the arrival of Raul Verdugo to show him the photograph of the alleged assassin in the courtroom from earlier in the day. One of the Legion attorneys, Dan Clarkson, lay in a coma after ingesting some type of poison from a water pitcher that was set on the defense table.

Legion's landline phone rang and he answered it.

"Yes?" he inquired of Nina, the firm's receptionist.

"Tabitha Winslow. She says that she is the clerk in Department 73. It's regarding the *Mezalone* case."

"Put her through," he requested. The phone again rang and he pushed a single button.

"This is Roger Legion."

As his conversation began, his cell phone started to ring. The Caller ID indicated it was Linda Green. He thought about sending the call to voice mail. Roger decided to halt his landline conversation for a moment.

"Would you excuse me one moment?" he asked. "I'll be right back."

Roger pushed the 'answer' button on his phone.

"Linda, I can't talk. . ."

She immediately cut him off.

"Roger, get out of your office right now. Right now, DO IT! PLEASE DO IT!"

Linda's voice was beyond emphatic. She was screaming demands.

Roger launched himself out of his chair moving at breakneck speed. Just as he crossed the threshold of the door to his office, the bomb exploded.

The immense, concussive power of the blast hit the back of Roger with a fireball that lifted him off his feet and propelled him twenty feet down the hallway. He slammed into the floor with the back of his suit coat on fire and the back of his pants were singed.

From outside, the peace and serenity of the air surrounding the twenty-fourth floor was, within a second, destroyed. When the high-powered explosive device in Legion's office detonated, it shook the building, and could be heard on the ground. The explosion expelled two hellacious fireballs like rockets that smashed out the windows and continued for at least seventy feet out of the building. Burning debris rained down, including Legion's desk, which continued to burn after it smashed into the ground with ferocious intensity like a runaway train. A mannequin that Roger used for his new suit fittings also flew out the window. To the naked eye, it looked like a person went out the window.

Legion's office continued to burn. The sprinklers for his office had been turned off.

Every lawyer in the office raced back to Legion's office to see what happened. One of the first attorneys to reach him was Luke Cordel. He happened to be wearing his suit coat and immediately took it off to slap it on Roger's back to smother the flames. Another attorney appeared with two, large bottles of water and then poured them over Roger's back and the back of his legs.

"NINA, CALL NINE-ONE-ONE!" a voice screamed down the hallway.

The water that poured on Roger served to awaken him. He had a trickle of blood running out of one of his nostrils and some blood was running down from the right side of his forehead, where it crashed into the floor.

From the open windows, caused by the explosion, the wind was fiercely blowing into the hallway and the sound level elevated to a position where it was necessary to blare your voice to be heard.

Roger tried to get up, but Luke warned against it.

"Roger, stay down," Luke advised. "Get him some water," he asked one of the other attorneys.

"No, help me up," Legion commanded. Luke and another attorney helped Roger to his feet but held on to him as his shakiness was evident. He spoke with gasps between his sentences.

"Luke, make sure everybody else is okay. Tell Louise on the twenty-third floor what happened. I want everybody to go home right now. Both floors. No one is to come back until I say so."

"I'll stay to make sure it all happens," Luke told him.

Nina was in shock, sitting at the reception desk, not knowing what to do. The first elevator doors opened and Raul stepped off, racing to Roger's office. The second set of elevator doors opened and four paramedics with a gurney exited. Nina pointed them in the direction of Legion's office.

The third set of elevator doors opened and off stepped Detective Dave Anderson, who visited Roger earlier in the day. He also raced back to Legion's office.

As Legion tried to shake off his pain, he wanted to know who was the architect of the plan to murder him. When he saw Raul racing down the hallway toward him, Roger knew that the answer was on its way.

Part 6

CHAPTER 76

Judge Caesar Cargyle sat in his wheelchair looking out on the natural beauty of his backyard and Rancho Santa Fe. The high temperature of the day had reached seventy-four degrees and a mild breeze was simply a flavoring to the perfect weather. Judge Cargyle still hoped to enjoy it one day without the albatross of a wheelchair hanging around his neck.

His KryptAll cellular ringtone went off and his review of the Caller ID indicated that it was Ruben Herrero.

"Ruben," the Judge began, "it's good to hear from you."

"It's done. Legion."

"Are you sure?"

"He was on his landline when it went off."

"Get me some proof. What about the girl?"

"That's what I was calling you about. Where can I find *La Niña*?" Ruben wondered.

"She'll be here tonight. I'm having a meeting of my FOG organization and she'll be there."

"When is the meeting over?"

"I suspect 8:30," the Judge answered.

"Keep her there. I'll come with my guys to grab her."

"Jack Prickett may be with her," the Judge cautioned.

"Two off the list at once. I love it."

"I want no bloodshed in my house."

"As I have told you many times, don't worry. Just keep both of them there until I get there."

"All right. I'll put it in your good hands," the Judge relayed.

The call ended and the Judge felt an uneasiness about his conversation with Ruben. Ruben's voice had a calmness that did not sound like he usually did. He usually echoed a bloodlust for killing with some sort of visceral response.

The Judge was unaware of Ruben's true intentions. In the annals of hitman lore, this night would come to be known for the Battle at Rancho Santa Fe.

CHAPTER 77

Roger Legion sat in a desk chair from one of the empty offices as Raul reached him. He was surrounded by Legion lawyers and Nina was staring at him with evident concern. The blown out windows were causing a wind tunnel near his office. It was also causing voices to be raised in order to communicate.

"I want everybody except Luke to go home, now," Roger said as he gasped for breath. "I want one of you guys to escort Nina to her car."

"I'll be fine," she piped up.

He then repeated himself more emphatically.

"*I want one of you guys to escort Nina to her car.*"

"Let's go," one of the attorneys said and gently took her arm. Before she left, she gave Roger a kiss on the cheek.

Legion refused any assistance from the paramedics and the Fire Department was arriving on the scene. The police and members of the San Diego Metro Arson Strike Team or MAST also appeared. Additionally, Roger spoke to the building security and maintenance to discuss temporary repairs.

The entire floor would be red-tagged for at least three days or longer, depending on the fire and police investigation. Red tagging means that the floor would not be habitable.

"Let's go down in the conference room," he told Raul and Detective Dave Anderson. "Luke, you check the twenty-third floor. Make sure they're all gone."

Luke acknowledged his request and moved directly to the stairwell.

In the conference room, Roger once again sat and looked at Raul. Raul wanted to say something, but did not want to speak in front of a police officer.

"It's all right," Roger told him. "He's a friend of Jimmy's."

"I know who did it," Raul pronounced, referring to the explosion. "It was the Judge."

Roger looked at him and reached into the breast pocket of his suitcoat. He pulled out a photocopy of a picture. Roger handed it to Raul.

"Do you recognize this girl?" Roger inquired with deadpan seriousness.

Raul gazed at the picture and raised his eyes slowly. His expression displayed concern. Roger knew the answer to his question.

"Where is she?" Legion demanded.

"She's at the Judge's house," Raul told him.

"I want to go talk to her. Now."

"All right," Raul advised. "I'll drive."

"You should let me take care of it," the Detective, Dave Anderson, spoke up for Raul's attention. "I know what he wants," referring to Legion. "I can handle it."

Raul looked at the Detective.

"I'm too invested in it."

Dave Anderson acknowledged Raul's comment.

Roger stood and put on his burned suitcoat.

It was now closing in on 7:30 in the evening, and the fog from the marine layer reduced visibility to zero miles. All traffic was moving quite slowly.

There was no conversation between Roger and Raul. Roger looked out the window, with dried blood on his forehead and under one of his nostrils. Raul broke the silence.

"Mr. Legion, I'd like to ask you to give her a pass."

Roger did not move his head from his window stare.

"I want to talk to her, first. Then I'll decide."

The ride to the Judge's home was longer than usual this evening due to the fog. Raul had at least one decision to make.

CHAPTER 78

Legion and Raul pulled into the driveway of Judge Caesar Cargyle and stopped just as the driver's door lined up with keypad/intercom. Raul knew the access code from years earlier, which he punched in, and the gate began to slowly recede. When it opened far enough, the Escalade proceeded toward the house.

Inside, all the women from the FOG organization were enjoying champagne, cocktails, and assorted finger food served by Farmington, the house butler. The Female Optimization Group or FACE of God was reveling in their second settlement which, in addition to a cash component, included the resignation of one of their targets from the practice of law.

Annabella was in attendance. She wore a simple, red bohemian top with blue jeans that had slices in them, cut horizontally at the knees. Her Doc Marten shoes were on her feet.

She quietly chatted with Leticia Harrison, the African-American woman, a lawyer who was also the executive member of the FOG. Cassie, the girl who obtained a settlement from her boss, represented by Roger Legion, rounded out their conversation circle.

Linda Green wore a blue dress with a floral pattern. She spoke with Daniela and Frida. The Judge wore a white, golf shirt with black trousers. He was speaking with Claudia and Alexandra.

Raul parked his vehicle not far from the entrance doors to the house and he and Legion proceeded inside.

Laughter inside the room was causing voice levels to escalate and Raul and Legion followed the voices into the living room. When they entered, it was as if a drape of silence had fallen.

Roger Legion surveyed the faces of the women and the Judge decided to speak.

"Roger Legion. I don't recall seeing your name on the invitation list. Come. Join us. This is a celebration."

When Roger saw Annabella, he locked eyes with her. He wondered for a slight moment if she was the person in the photograph, but her facial features made it conclusive.

"You're much thinner in person. That was a good disguise."

Annabella did not say a word, but rose from her seat on the couch.

Jack Pricket entered the room wearing a white t-shirt, blue jeans and a jean jacket. He stood within two feet of Legion and Raul, looking out at the women.

"Were you trying to kill me today or just one of my lawyers?" Legion posed his inquiry.

Annabella did not respond.

"I want to know who hired you to try and kill me and my lawyers."

Annabella kept her green eyes locked on Legion's ice, blue eyes.

"Roger," the Judge interjected, "this is neither the time nor place to discuss this."

"No," Roger said emphatically. "Where should we discuss it, my office?"

"Save the theatrics for the courtroom," the Judge said. "I am not going to make any admissions. And I am not going to allow any of these ladies to make any admissions. But, *what if*, they hired someone to kill you. What was your plan? To walk in here, with this Ricky Ricardo knock-off, and kill everyone in this room. Wholesale slaughter? Not that you don't have any experience with that."

All the women, except Annabella were becoming nervous. Legion shifted his focus to the Judge.

"I thought I taught you better than that, Roger. You have to look at the far end of the runway, if you're going to land properly. If you just look at the point of touchdown, you will crash."

"Why, Caesar?"

"I realized that it was time for you and others to atone for the perversion that you call the practice of law. I'll agree that I was your accomplice and helped facilitate it, but no more. These women provided the perfect vehicle to achieve that end."

"You planted that stuff in Ricky Ray's car, didn't you?" Roger asked.

Roger was referring to the machine gun, kilo of cocaine, and child pornography found in the trunk of Ricky Ray Ransom's Cadillac.

"Roger, I believe you're having a problem with your memory. You called me, remember? You said you were worried because the *Zantoff* case was a loser. I said I'd take care of it. And I did. But serendipity intervened. YOU are a great lawyer. You never needed it, but you wanted to guarantee it!"

Roger stared at the Judge in disbelief.

"Oh," the Judge continued, "and as for the bomb in your office, how did it get there – Raul?"

An audible gasp was heard.

"He's lying!" Raul proclaimed to defend himself.

"He trusts me, you said. I can get close to him, you said," the Judge proselytized.

"You stink of desperation, Caesar," Raul admonished.

"Roger, you can't trust a *sicario*," Caesar advised. "They're treacherous. Because they're mercenaries. They can be bought for a price. Now, if you were duped into thinking you could walk in here and kill Annabella, well, I don't think Raul will allow it. And I don't think Jack will allow it. Your name has been on the last three assassination lists that I have received. All three of the *sicarios* in this room would make money if they killed you. Even Jimmy Flowers blesses it."

"What if I just kill you?" Legion insinuated.

The Judge stood from his chair and a gasp of awe was sounded. He was not shaky at all. Even Legion was impressed by this feat.

"If I disappear or show up dead, my lawyer has specific instructions to send detailed records and recordings that I have prepared detailing your nefarious activity to the *San Diego Union-Tribune*, the *New York Times*, and the *Washington Post*. It includes your involvement in the event of July 18, 1984, the date of the worst mass shooting up until that time in the history of the United States. McDonalds. San Ysidro. Twenty-one people dead. Nineteen others wounded. You could have stopped it."

"You're crazy," Legion told him with percolating anger.

"Am I? I tell you now as a colleague and a friend. Just walk away from the practice of law. You do that and your life will be spared."

"I don't trust you."

"I don't believe that you have many options."

Suddenly, Farmington entered the room and began to speak quickly with a sense of urgency.

"Someone's trying to breach the gate."

Raul, Jack, Legion, and the Judge, walking under his own power, followed Farmington into the Judge's office. On one of three monitors, Ruben Herrero was looping a length of cable through the iron gate. When he finished, he stepped back as the cable tightened, drawn backwards by the panel van. Then the cable began to tear the gate off its track.

Behind Herrero's twenty foot box truck was a GMC Denali that contained six SWAT officers, all former Navy Seals that Ruben had recruited specifically for this job.

Raul looked at the monitor, then turned to look at Jack, then Legion. There was no time to ponder his next move. Survival mode was about to kick in.

CHAPTER 79

As Ruben and his men proceeded up the driveway, Raul took command. He began with a simple question.

"Farmington, do you have a panic room in this house?"

"In the library," he told him.

"Let's get the women in there," urged Raul.

Raul immediately ran back to the living room to address the ladies.

"We are going to put you girls in a safe room until we get this situation under control."

Suddenly, all the lights and the power went out in the house.

"They've cut the power," Farmington advised. "We've got a backup generator."

"There is no cell signal," Frida exclaimed in distress.

"Everybody stay calm," Farmington demanded.

He went into a walk-in closet down the hallway and immediately returned. All of a sudden, the power returned.

"I want to go home," Cassie initially spoke up. "I'm not part of this foolishness and you people are all crazy."

"It's not possible to send you home right now," Raul said. "If you stay out here, there may be trouble. And I really don't have time to discuss it."

Annabella stood from her seat and stared at Linda Green in disgust. She walked over to Raul and tugged on his lapel. Raul thought Annabella had something to tell him.

"Give me a kiss on the lips," she demanded.

"What?" he wondered incredulously?

She reiterated her demand more emphatically.

"Give…me…a…kiss…on the lips!"

Raul complied. Initially, he thought it would be a quick peck, but Annabella jumped up into his arms and planted a heavy duty smooch-cake right on his lips.

Annabella jumped off him and shot Linda an evil glance.

"He's mine, bitch!" Annabella told her. Then turned to Raul. "I'm going to go get some gear."

Jack was stunned to see Annabella make her choice; it wasn't him!

"Ladies, please, you've got to go into this safe room," Farmington demanded.

All the ladies followed Farmington into the library. Once inside, Farmington pressed a button on one of the wall sections and it slowly sprang open like a door. Behind it was a metal door that contained a large, circular handle, similar to a bank vault. There was also a keypad and a pad for biometric entry.

"Leticia," Farmington called to her. He punched a code on the keypad and a small light on the biometric pad went from red to green.

"Put your hand on here," he told her.

Leticia complied. She placed her entire palm on the pad and a two-bell sound was heard.

"Your handprint will get you out," Farmington told her.

Leticia placed her hand on the biometric and a click sound was heard. Farmington pulled the door open with noticeable effort, which was approximately eighteen inches thick. The inside of the room was fifteen feet by fifteen feet with a bench around the perimeter, three cases of bottled water and a case of M-R-E (Meals Ready to Eat) meals. In the far corner, there was also a toilet and a sink.

The ladies began to enter the room and Cassie refused.

"No. I'll take my chances out here. That place is like going into a tomb," she told them all, referring to the room.

Raul turned to Roger Legion.

"You go in there with them," Raul commanded.

"No," Legion shot back. "I'm staying out here. If I went with them, they would probably accuse me of something."

All the women went into the panic room except Cassie and Annabella. Raul and Farmington's eyes met.

"Do you have any weapons in here?" Raul quizzed.

"There's a gun cage in the office."

"Let's go," Raul directed. "Jack, come on."

They proceeded to the office and Farmington located a hidden button on one of the walls that popped open a portion of the wall. Behind the wall was a small wired caged area. Within it, on one wall were four tactical rifles: two Windsor Arms AR-10 machine guns, chambered in 5.56 caliber and each with a short barrel, a muzzle brake and a heat shield on the barrel area of the guns. These guns had the ability to fire at a rate of 800 rounds per minute.

The third rifle was an M-16 rifle. This automatic machine gun was also 5.56 caliber. It was able to fire at a rate of 700 rounds per minute.

The fourth rifle was a Heckler & Koch MP-5K submachine gun. This gun was short, approximately thirteen inches overall, and fired 9mm ammunition at a rate of 900 rounds per minute.

All of the rifles had magazines that contained fifty rounds of ammo, except for the M-16, which held thirty rounds.

Farmington began to hand out weaponry.

Raul and Jack were each given an AR-10 rifle and two additional loaded magazines. Roger Legion took the M-16, with two extra magazines, and Farmington was going to handle the MP-5K.

"I want a weapon," Judge Cargyle insisted.

On the wall, opposite the handgun rack, hung four handguns. Farmington handed the Judge a Colt .45 caliber 1911 semi-automatic pistol.

"It's loaded," he told him. "Ready to fire."

Raul looked at the handguns and was intrigued by one of them.

"Is that a Desert Eagle? Can I see it?"

Farmington held out the gun, grip first to Raul.

"Fifty caliber. Extremely powerful and it has an extraordinary kick."

"I've fired one before," Raul told him. "Anything else?"

"We have video surveillance on the entire exterior perimeter of the building. We also have a light flooding system. We can light up the yard like it's daylight. We might be able to blind them to give us a little advantage."

"Get it ready to turn on, but don't do it yet," Raul advised.

Just then, Annabella entered the room. She wore Dragon Skin body armor that covered her chest and shoulders. The armor consisted of two-inch wide circular discs that overlap like scale armor to allow maximum flexibility.

She carried an UZI Pro 9 mm submachine gun. What was unique about the gun was that it had a 100 round twin drum magazine.

Now, everyone was armed. They were awaiting Ruben's next move. Farmington moved frenetically at the office computer terminal in an attempt to determine what was . . . in the fog.

CHAPTER 80

Ruben pulled the 20-foot box truck parallel to the entrance doors to Judge Cargyle's home. The truck was approximately seventy feet from the doors. The thickness of the fog made it impossible to see the doors from the truck and vice-versa.

Irving got out of the truck and immediately proceeded to the rear to open the overhead door on it. Irving entered the box of the truck and the GMC Denali pulled up within ten feet of the truck. The six men exited the Denali and walked to the back of the truck. The men all wore white t-shirts, green, bullet-proof vests, a utility vest on top of the bullet-proof vests, cargo pants, and tactical boots.

Ruben exited the truck and walked to the back of it. He would not be using a rifle, but rather his .45 caliber Smith & Wesson semiautomatic handguns.

Irving passed out a Sig Sauer SIG 516 AR-15 tactical assault rifle. This rifle was chambered for 5.56 mm ammunition and could fire at a rate of 300 rounds per minute. Each man was also provided with four additional 30-round magazines.

Finally, they were each given a walkie-talkie for communication.

The house had the shape of a pentagon, so four of the men each took one of the sides, then one man took the Denali to the end of the driveway to fend off any potential looky-loos. The sixth man, Hector, would assist Ruben and Irving at the truck as needed.

Ruben was waiting until he received word that all of his men were in position. He gave a final instruction over the walkie-talkie.

"The visibility may cramp our style. Initially, I just want to strafe the house. Just lay down a line of fire right through the center. That should rattle them to come out. Wait for my command."

Ruben then turned to Irving.

"Get the bullhorn."

Irving grabbed a bullhorn megaphone from a utility box and handed it to Ruben.

"INSIDE THE HOUSE," his voice blared. "I'M GOING TO COUNT TO TEN. IF YOU DON'T COME OUT BY THE TIME I FINISH, EVERYONE IN THE HOUSE IS GOING TO DIE. ONE, TWO, THREE...."

Inside the house, as Ruben counted, Raul gave final instructions.

"Mr. Legion, go upstairs and take one of the sides. If you see any movement when we flood the lights, take them out. Headshot. Don't take any chances."

Roger headed to the staircase at a jackrabbit pace.

"Somebody go with him!"

Before anyone in the room could respond, the Judge spoke up.

"Raul, let me see if I can put a stop to this."

The Judge moved at a quick clip to the entrance doors and opened both of them wide. A cool breeze entered the building. The Judge spoke from the threshold of the doors.

"RUBEN," he screamed out, "this is Judge Cargyle. Come in here and we can discuss this. You don't want to kill any innocent people."

"Sorry, Caesar," Ruben responded. "The time for talk is over. I've got marching orders. And you're on my list. Are you coming out?"

"Let me talk to the people inside. I'll see if I can get them to come out."

"You better do it quick."

The Judge went back inside and looked around the room.

"What do you want to do?"

"Go upstairs and help Legion," Raul told him. "We got the downstairs covered."

The other people in the room, except Cassie, looked at the Judge telegraphing that they were in agreement with Raul. The Judge sullenly ascended the staircase.

"CAESAR, LET'S GET GOING!" Ruben yelled.

Raul and Jack took position on each side of the entrance doors on the west side of the house. Annabella covered the center window on the south side of the house. Farmington was going to cover the east side. Legion was covering the southeast corner side. The Judge continued to slowly ascend the stairs.

Cassie looked around at all of them with their guns up, ready to fire. She took off, like a sprinter hearing a starter pistol, and raced out the entrance doors, right past Raul and Jack.

"NO!" Raul hollered.

"I'M COMING OUT! I'M COMING OUT!" Cassie screeched.

Two shots rang out and Cassie was silenced.

Jack and Raul looked at each other.

"What do you say?" Raul asked.

"Let's go," Jack answered.

"Farmie, turn on the lights," he called over to Farmington, who was sitting at the desk in the Judge's office. Farmington pressed several keys on the Judge's computer and the lights came on. The illumination flooded the yard.

Jack and Raul both pivoted into the doorway and opened fire. They strafed the truck and the glass on the passenger side door and the windshield blew out. The bullets would be powerful enough to penetrate the box of the truck, but the inside walls of the truck were lined with one-inch steel plates. The back tires on the passenger side were also blown out. But neither Ruben, nor any of his men, were in sight. When Jack and Raul had both fired through their fifty-round magazines, they pivoted back to the side of the entrance way.

"Cut the lights," Raul yelled to Farmington.

Both Annabella and Legion commenced fire as soon as they heard Jack and Raul's gun. Legion had a slight advantage because of his second floor view. He could see the fire coming out of the muzzle of the rifle being fired by Tommy, one of Ruben's men. Legion moved an adjustment nob on the gun from 'full automatic' to 'single fire.' He lined up a shot and took it.

Ruben's man, Tommy, was struck just above the right temple with the bullet in a downward direction. The back of his skull blew off and he went to the ground, still pulling the trigger before he hit it.

Ruben, Irving and one of his SWAT team members, Hector, were cowering behind Raul's Escalade. Cassie's body was on the ground between the truck and the entrance to the house.

"I thought you said this was going to be easy," Hector vented to Ruben. "That this guy was a cripple and he wouldn't put up a fight."

"How the hell was I supposed to know?" Ruben flared.

"Well, Jesus Christ, I thought you would've had better intel on the place in advance."

A voice then came over the walkie-talkie.

"Ruben, Tommy's down."

"What do you mean, 'down?' Ruben wanted to know.

"They took him out with a headshot."

"God damn it!" Ruben paused for a moment. "Everybody fall back. Come back to the truck."

CHAPTER 81

Inside the house, the walls were a hodgepodge of holes that looked like an abstract painting, created by the fusillade of machine gun bullets which shredded the paintings and tore open the furniture.

Raul and Jack changed out the magazines on their guns. Both of the men realized that after they finished the current magazine, there was only one left. Jack sat down against the open door.

"Is everybody all right?" Raul inquired while looking around the room. Farmington appeared from the office.

"We got one of their guys. Legion got him with a headshot."

"That's probably why we've got a little pause in the action," Raul surmised.

The Judge had reached the top of the stairs. Legion was in the process of changing the magazine on his gun. Even though his current magazine was not empty, he wanted to make sure that he was utilizing a full magazine in the event the gunfight restarted. Roger continued to gaze out the window in search of movement.

The Judge was out of breath and he slowly approached Legion.

"You brought this pox upon my house," the Judge declared.

Caesar raised his .45 caliber semi-automatic pistol to shoot Legion. As he leveled the gun, a 3-shot burst could be heard. All 3 bullets struck the Judge and rattled his body as he was struck. His body fell to the floor like a bag of rocks.

Legion looked to the doorway and he could see that it was Annabella who saved him. They locked eyes and Legion nodded his head in thanks. Annabella turned to proceed down the staircase.

Once downstairs, she saw Jack sitting at the base of the door. She walked over to speak to him."

"You okay?" she wondered.

"Yeah. How about you?" Jack asked.

"I'm surviving. The Judge is dead upstairs. He was going to kill Legion and I took him out."

Jack simply nodded.

"I'm sorry about all this, Jack. I think I just lost my mind at one point. Thinking about where I am and where I want to be."

"You'll get there Annie," he told her.

"Do you pray?" she asked.

"No."

"If you ever do, pray for me, okay?"

"Deal."

Jack extended his hand to shake Annabella's when the sound of two rifle shots were heard in rapid succession. Hector saw a glint off her body armor and fired the shots. This first one struck Annabella directly in the center of the chest. The power of the bullet pushed her back and off her feet as she was struck by a second bullet in the lower left side of her abdomen.

She smashed like a ragdoll against a wall that was located on the left side of the hallway to the living room. She dropped to the floor in a sitting position with her lips parted slightly and her eyes wide open in shock.

The bullets did not penetrate her bullet-proof vest, but both bullets did cause a penetration into her chest cavity of nearly one inch.

Both Jack and Raul watched her fly through the air. Jack stood and immediately commenced firing out the door. He accompanied it with a primordial scream.

"Aaaaaaaaaaaaaaaaaaah!

Jack had fired another fifty rounds of ammunition. Raul raced over to Annabella and knelt beside her. He loosened the Velcro straps on her vest.

"Annabella, *cariña* (sweetheart)! Come on, you're going to be all right."

Jack stood over them and watched.

"No, Raul, I'm busted up inside. Save these people in here. No footprint. Right?"

As Annabella spoke, a trickle of blood started to run down the corner of her mouth.

"*¡Por favor, nena, espera!* (Please, baby, hold on!)" Raul begged as he felt her weakened pulse.

"Raul, remember when we used to lie in bed and talk about our future. Did you ever think it would end this way?"

"Annabella, *preciosa* (beautiful girl), I'm going to get you help."

"Remember when I would ask you 'How many babies are we going to have?' and you said 'As many as you want.' And I said 'What if I want a hundred babies? Remember what you would say?"

Raul thought for a moment. He answered her through a cracked voice.

"A hundred babies? I guess we better get started."

Annabella smiled, closed her eyes, and her head tilted to the side. A *sicaria* was gone.

Raul kissed her on one cheek and Jack kissed her on the other. A tear rolled down Jack's face.

Both men turned from Annabella and looked out the entrance door. The battle was not over.

CHAPTER 82

Outside, Ruben's men assembled on the far side of Raul's Escalade, near the engine. The engine block was considered to provide the most protection in the event that bullets started to fly from inside the house.

"We're gonna end this, now," Ruben told them.

"How?" one of the men, Rondo, asked. "We go to walk back there now and that second story man is going to pick us off one by one."

"I'll distract them."

Ruben pulled a ring of keys out of his pocket and handed them to Irving.

"Open the side overhead door on the truck."

Irving sped to the truck and found the key to unlock a lock that kept the gate handle closed. This door was three feet wide and ran the entire height of the box of the truck.

Once the door was fully opened, it revealed a weapon mounted on a tripod. It was an XM556 Microgun. This was a defensive suppression weapon chambered in 5.56 mm caliber. It featured a six-barrel rotary machine with a high-sustained rate of fire. This gun could fire between two thousand to six thousand rounds per minute. The bullets were belt-fed into the gun and Ruben had five thousand rounds of ammunition available to fire through the weapon.

Ruben then grabbed a crowbar from a toolbox on the floor.

"Open these crates," he commanded Irving.

There were two wooden crates, each approximately four feet long, three feet wide, and one foot high. On the side of the crates, it read 'PROPERTY OF U.S. MARINE CORPS.'

Irving pried open the first crate and pushed it to the end of the truck for the other men to examine. Mac was the first man to see the contents.

"Hoe-lee shit!" he responded in amazement.

Inside each crate were two Shoulder-Launched Multi-purpose Assault Weapons (SMAW). Each contained a .85 mm rocket powered projectile. This round of ammunition contained an airburst explosive that would add to the damage caused by the shell itself.

The three remaining house shooters were each handed one of the shoulder-firing weapons. Ruben called down to Lyle, who was waiting at the end of the driveway with the Denali, over the walkie-talkie.

"Lyle, get up here, we need you. Bring the car."

Within moments, the Denali was behind the truck. Lyle got out of the truck and was immediately handed one of the SMAW weapons.

One of the men, Strips, seized an opportunity to pose an inquiry.

"If you had all this heavy duty artillery, what are we doing pinging the place?"

"I never thought they would put up a fight. I'll lay down some fire with this puppy," Ruben patted the gun as he spoke. "You guys head back to your positions. Lyle, you're going to have to take Tommy's position. You let us know when you're all in place and ready to fire."

Ruben surveyed his men. They were battle-worn.

"Let's do this." Ruben turned to Hector. "Keep an eye on the belt feed of the gun. It's got to go in there straight or it's going to jam."

The men moved to the tree-lined entrance.

Inside, depression loomed over Raul and Jack with the death of Annabella.

"Come on," Raul told Jack and they each picked up their rifles. Jack changed out his final magazine into the gun. Raul yelled up the staircase.

"Mr. Legion, how you doing?"

"I'm okay," Roger replied.

"Farmie, you ready to go?"

There was no reply. Raul walked back to the office.

Farmington was on the floor just inside the threshold of the door. He had been struck three times in various parts of the chest, including his heart. Raul let out a sigh and proceeded to the Judge's computer where the lights were operated.

Raul assessed what needed to be done to operate the lights and scanned the video monitors.

"HERE WE GO!" he screamed.

Suddenly, the yard, including the driveway was illuminated. Ruben's XM556 Microgun with its six rotary barrels came to life. The vicious power of the gun tore into the building. The hinges on the entrance doors were blown off and whole areas of plaster were falling off the building.

Jack saw the gun as soon as the lights went on and he ducked for cover. Jack was struck in the right shoulder and the bullet went all the way through him. He was also grazed by a bullet at the top of his hairline.

Raul turned off the lights. The shooting from outside the building had stopped. He raced out of the office not realizing that Ruben was quickly changing the belt in his microgun. The gun's violent rage came to life and Raul was ambushed in the hallway, being struck three times.

He was hit in the pelvis, left forearm and lower right-side of his abdomen. Raul slammed to the floor on his back.

Outside, all of Ruben's men, around the perimeter of the house, acknowledged that they were in place.

"Light it up!" Ruben commanded.

Right before Ruben gave that order, Roger Legion was able to identify the position of one of the shooters. He took the shot just as the order was being given. The target, Rondo, fell backwards, pulling the trigger on the weapon as he fell. The missile struck the ground approximately ten feet in front of him, blasting a crater into the front yard.

Ruben's three other men fired their rockets as ordered. The missiles struck the house simultaneously from the three different angles. Their destructive energy, coupled with a ginormous, concussive, explosive force, tore the building to shreds. The explosion blew through the roof, which pancaked onto the second floor, which then pancaked onto the first floor.

The accompanying fire was surprisingly minimal. The house was framed out of steel and not wood. The only thing burning was any organic material in the house, such as the furniture and wall hangings. The Judge's wheelchair was mangled and crushed like a piece of aluminum foil.

"Anything on the police or fire bands?" Ruben inquired of Irving to determine if any police or fire department was being dispatched.

"Get everybody back, including Tommy. Something must have happened to Rondo, I hope they didn't get him."

Irving called out to the men and shared Ruben's commands with them.

Ruben jumped out of the truck and began to stare at the entranceway to the house. He drew one of his .45 caliber pistols and pointed it forward as he approached the house.

"You guys come with me," he called out to Irving and Hector.

Hector still carried his AR-15 rifle and Irving carried a Glock 17 pistol. All three men were ready to fire. As they approached the entrance, it began to come into focus. Acrid smoke from gunpowder filled the air.

Surprisingly, the entryway was not damaged as much as the remainder of the building. Ruben looked in and could see a portion of the hallway remained. The way the second floor had collapsed, it cause a teepee like positioning of the rafters that protected it from total collapse.

As Ruben slowly walked into the building, they saw Raul, Annabella, and Jack sitting against a wall, near the hallway. Raul reached for the .50 caliber Desert Eagle semi-automatic handgun that he thought was being held in his waist band behind him. It was not there.

Both Raul and Jack looked Ruben directly in his eyes with stoic faces. Both men were resigned to their destinies.

EPILOGUE

7 Years Later

At an upscale home in the Carmel Del Mar section of San Diego, four children, two boys and two girls, all under the age of six, played peacefully, while their mother washed and folded clothes on the second floor. The three older children were engaged in a game of tag, while the youngest played with a stuffed bear and a plastic dinosaur.

"Daddy's home!" the eldest said, as he heard the garage door open. "Mom, Mommy, Mom! Daddy's here."

"I'll be right down," she called out.

The four children raced to the kitchen, eagerly awaiting the return of their father from work.

The kitchen door to the garage opened and in walked Jack Prickett, who greeted his troops with a big smile. He looked the same, except for one or two strands of gray hair and his hair was combed across the top. He wore a button-down shirt, with a blue, box pattern and gray slacks.

There was a rounding chorus of "Daddy, Daddy," as they all vied for his attention.

"Okay, one at a time, ladies first."

"Daddy, can we get ice cream?" the smallest child asked.

"Sure," he answered her quickly and moved on the next.

"Daddy, can we go to Legoland?"

"We have to ask Momma?"

"She said to ask you."

"Okay, we can't go today. But we'll find a day to go soon."

"Daddy, can we get pizza?"

"Sure, let's ask Momma now."

Then, the youngest one asked the final question.

"Daddy, can we get a dog?"

"We have to ask Momma, then we'll go looking."

Jack's wife entered the room. It was Patricia Chatsworth, the nurse who cared for Woody in the hospital and was introduced to Jack by Woody. She still radiated beauty and she was everything Woody said that she would be. They were married less than a year after the Battle at Rancho Santa Fe.

"How was your day?" she asked and shared a quick peck on the lips.

"It was good. How was yours?" he asked.

"Very good. We all went for a nice long walk and I was able to wash clothes. I'm almost done."

"Were you going to cook something?" Jack wondered.

"The kids wanted pizza."

"Okay. Call for it and I'll go get it."

As Jack finished his sentence, the doorbell rang. The sound level from the children was continuing to elevate and Jack stopped before opening the door.

"KIDS!" Jack's elevated voice would always bring them to a freeze position. "Please lower your voices."

Jack opened the door and there stood Raul Verdugo. He was another man who aged well, with slight gray hair around his temples, but the same goatee facial hair, and his hair was cut the same way, tight on one side and combed over the top to the other.

Raul wore a blue suit, with a light, blue shirt and a yellow tie.

"¡Mi amigo! (My friend!)," Raul exclaimed and they met each other with a tight hug. They then backed-up and perused each other up and down.

"Look at you," Raul told him, "Mr. Business man."

"Look at you, still trying to be a Ricky Ricardo knockoff." Jack's comment made them both chuckle.

"C'mon in. I want you to meet my family," Jack told him.

Raul entered and Patty had walked over to them while they spoke.

"This is my wife, Patty. Patty, this is an old friend of mine, Raul."

"It's nice to meet you, Jack has mentioned you in the past."

"It's a pleasure to meet you, Mrs. Prickett."

"Call me Patty."

"Kids," Jack called out. "Come and meet a friend of mine."

The children assembled in a straight line. Jack introduced them.

"This is Woody. This is Annabella. This is John. And this is Elaine."

"It's nice to meet you all."

They all smiled and nodded at Raul. Jack turned to Raul.

"Stay for dinner. We're having pizza."

"That sounds good," Raul answered.

"Let's take a ride. We'll pick it up."

The drive to Bronx Pizza in the University Heights section of San Diego would take about twenty minutes. Raul started to speak as soon as the doors closed on Jack's late model Lexus GX sport utility vehicle.

"How you been, Jack?"

"Good. You?"

"Good, also. I recuperated south of the border after our gunfight and up until now I've been doing some freelance cartel work. What about you? What are you doing?"

"I work for an insurance company," Jack told him.

"What do you do there?"

"I handle bodily injury claims involving trucks. Like tractor-trailers."

"Do you enjoy it?"

"I think I'm pretty good at it."

"What's the name of the company?" Raul wondered.

"Qualitas Insurance."

"Very popular down in Mexico."

A moment passed.

"I got a job and I need some help. You interested?" Raul inquired.

"No. You see, I got the wife, the kids, and thanks to the Judge, the Swiss bank account with tens of millions of dollars."

"I should walk away too," Raul said.

"What brings you here now?"

"Jimmy Flowers and Roger Legion. You know I can't say 'no,' because of everything that happened."

"I totally understand," Jack told him.

"I don't even remember all the details," Raul shared.

Jack did. And he began to remember.

After Raul was struck with three bullets, he dragged his body, using his right arm, to the location of Jack and Annabella. His body left a blood trail on the floor.

When Jack saw Raul, he moved into action. He could not use his right arm, because of his shoulder injury. Using his left arm, he was able to lift Raul to his feet. Jack held him up with his left arm.

"Come on," Jack told him. "There's one more secret to this house."

They trudged into the kitchen. Raul was unable to use his left leg, so he dragged it along. He began to feel woozy from the blood loss. In one corner of the kitchen there was a door to a pantry. Jack dragged Raul into it and closed the door.

Once inside, Jack pressed a button on one of the walls that would have been at the Judge's height from his wheelchair.

A metal door slid across the opening followed by the sound of a locking mechanism.

It was then that Ruben yelled "Light it up!"

The massive explosion shook the room and items fell from the shelves. The integrity of the structure stayed intact.

"The Judge was one of those doomsday guys. A prepper. I came in here looking for something one day. He told me about it. This was his bunker. To survive a nuclear blast."

Jack opened the door and they proceeded out while holding up Raul. Jack grabbed some kitchen towels that he saw for Raul to hold against his wounds. They both wanted to see Annabella.

The men were writhing in pain as they hobbled back toward the hallway and Annabella's body was sitting exactly where they left her, untouched by the colossal explosion and the accompanying devastation.

"Put me down next to her," Raul told Jack.

Jack complied and then he sat on the other side of her. Each man held one of her hands and stared forward.

Ruben entered the building, accompanied by Irving and Hector. Each man had a weapon out that was leveled and ready to fire.

An evil grin came over Ruben as he recognized both Raul and Annabella. He saw Jack's Yankees tattoo and his identity was revealed.

"Well, well, well," Ruben gloated. "The mighty executioner. Today's the day, he gets pushed off the mountaintop. And I will gladly take your place. What's it like to. ."

Before he could finish the sentence, a shot rang out. Ruben's forehead exploded. In rapid succession, Irving and Hector were both the recipient of headshots. The three bullets were fired within two seconds. Then, a voice was heard.

"I can't stand a bullshitter."

It was Woody, Jack's mentor, who had been in the hospital because he was dying from lung cancer. He wore baggy, gray sweat pants, a flannel shirt, a windbreaker that went down to his hips, and a worn, Yankees baseball cap. He also wore a holster for his gun.

Woody surveyed the wreckage that was once a mansion. He holstered his gun. In one partially-surviving wall, bullet holes were copious.

"There're guys on the perimeter," Raul advised in a weakened voice.

"Not anymore," Woody said. "I took'em all out."

Jack nodded his head in relief.

"Jack, what did I tell you to do when bullets start coming through the wall?"

"Get on the floor. What are you supposed to do when a missile comes through the wall?"

Woody gave a slight chuckle.

"Kiss your ass goodbye," he said. "Come on, boy, we gotta get you and Raul to a doctor."

Woody helped Jack to his feet and the shadows of three men appeared in the entranceway. As they came in from the fog, their identities were revealed.

There was Jimmy Flowers, Ozy Seesay and Dave Anderson, the Detective from Roger Legion's office. The men surveyed the war zone in disbelief.

"Hello, Jimmy, Seesay," Woody said. "I don't think I know you, young man."

"Dave Anderson, San Diego Police."

"How've you been, Woody?" Jimmy asked.

"I been better. It was a good thing that I come to check on my boy. What do you think of this craziness?"

"Craziness is a good word for it," Jimmy agreed.

"Any a you guys got a cigarette?" Woody asked.

The three men nodded negatively.

Now, a fourth man was in the entryway. He walked in and they all recognized Roger Legion, still carrying his M-16 rifle.

"How did you escape this, Roger?" Jimmy wondered.

"When I saw they had missiles, I was able to take one of them out with a headshot. Then I raced downstairs and out the door into the fog. I was able to get behind the garage and stayed there while the explosion went off."

"Raul, we've got to get you to a hospital," Jimmy told him.

"I know a veterinarian place up in Carlsbad," Roger suggested. "Everything is state of the art. It's as good as any hospital."

Roger put his gun down and helped Raul to his feet.

"What are you going to do about this place?" Woody inquired.

"I don't think we can get a helicopter in here. I'll call for a tractor trailer," Jimmy answered.

"Do you want me to call Internal Affairs and just say Herrero went rogue?" Dave Anderson, the Detective, asked.

"There are too many cops here. The Chief would have a stroke. We'll take the bodies out of here, except for the Judge and the butler. I'll call a guy that I know, he can make it look like a propane explosion."

"Joe Cheech?" Woody asked.

"Yeah," Jimmy responded.

"Best torch in the County. Maybe the State," Woody proclaimed.

"There were five women in the back panic room," Raul spoke up. "We don't know their conditions."

"We'll get them out of there. Roger, can you take these guys to the doctor?" Jimmy asked.

Roger and Raul and Jack and Woody lumbered to Raul's Escalade. The clothing of both Jack and Raul were soaked in blood. Roger and Woody also had blood on themselves from providing their assistance.

"Hang on, gentlemen," Roger said as he raced to the Kisses and Tummy Rubs Veterinarian Clinic, located in Carlsbad.

Back in the car, on the way to Bronx Pizza, Raul had a question.

"Is Woody still with us?"

"No," Jack said. "He lasted about five years after the gunfight; he lived with Patty and me for the last two years of his life. He was a great guy. How about you? Did you settle down or what?"

"I did," Raul relayed. "With somebody you know. Do you remember Linda Green?"

"Yeah. She was there on that day? Right?"

"She was. We are coming up on our fourth anniversary."

"You got any little ones?"

"A three-year-old girl, Julieta," Raul stated.

"We should get our kids together," Jack told him. "How did you know she was the one?"

Before answering, Raul began to remember.

About eleven months after the Battle at Rancho Santa Fe, Montgomery 'Monty' Lindstrom of the law firm of Rayne, Lindstrom & Avici finished work on a non-eventful Tuesday and left the office at 6:15 pm to head home.

Monty Lindstrom was the attorney who verbally berated Linda Green and caused her to quit or be fired from his law firm.

As Monty approached his late-model Mercedes E300, in the distance, he saw Linda looking at him and talking on a cell phone. She got his attention and gave a short, quick wave.

He gave a half of a nod, but hardly acknowledged her. Monty placed his suit coat and briefcase into the trunk of the car and moved to enter the cavity section. Once inside, the seat seemed to be back farther than usual. He began to adjust with the automatic controls on the door and Raul popped up from the back seat. He was on the floor of the backseat under a blanket that matched the carpet of the car.

As he sprung up, he placed a heavy duty plastic bag over the startled Monty's head and held it with one hand. Monty was pushing the horn on the car, but it did not work unless the car was turned on. Raul held the bag with one hand and with the other hand, he pulled a disposable scalpel, made of German steel, from his pocket.

As Monty grappled to remove the bag, Raul pulled the scalpel across his throat, from left to right and he made sure that Monty's carotid artery was severed.

Blood gushed from Monty's throat with every beat of his heart. The last thing he saw was Linda Green in front of his car, giving him a slight wave by holding up her hand and flexing her fingers, at the knuckles to form a ninety degree angle. The smile on her face was that of satisfaction.

Monty stopped fighting and Raul left him there to bleed out.

"How did I know she was the one?" Raul repeated Jack's inquiry. "Sometimes you just know."

Jack and Raul continued their conversation to Bronx Pizza and back.

The women in the panic room survived the explosion, but not without some personal injuries. The walls collapsed on them and the ceiling pancaked down, but there were also air pockets that saved them.

Leticia Harrison broke both of her legs. Claudia Hernandez and Daniela Castro each broke an arm. Alexandra Velasco broke three ribs. Only Linda Green and Frida Carranza were unscathed by the explosion.

Roger Legion negotiated a settlement with the Estate of Judge Caesar Cargyle to pay each of the women two million dollars. This was for their injuries and their silence. Roger Legion did not accept any payment for this service.

Roger also arranged for Sharifa Monroe to visit with her children on a monthly basis through the San Diego Health and Human Services Agency. She moved into a halfway house and successfully completed a residency there. After that, Roger Legion gave her a job at Legion & Associates.

Ricky Ray Ransom would contact Roger from time-to-time seeking advice when dealing with difficult defense counsel. Whenever Ricky Ray came to San Diego, he would invite Roger to dinner. Both men admired the legal talent of the other.

A final question is what, or who, was 'The Company?' It was a cabal of rich, powerful men that included some Fortune 500 CEOs, tenured politicians, and billionaires, who all wanted their power to include murder, if necessary.

Jimmy Flowers was a member of their Board of Directors. When he found out what was going on with the murder list in the final days from Mr. Seesay, he stepped in and put a stop to any action against Raul, Jack, or Roger Legion.

Ozy Seesay was found murdered approximately thirty days after the Battle at Rancho Santa Fe. His killer has never been found.

Raul and Jack thought about Annabella often. The good times and the bad. The men realized that the synergy they had with her was so powerful that it could not be stopped.

In his final days, to anyone who would listen, Woody Tobag had a story to tell: about three *sicarios*, a mansion in Rancho Santa Fe, and a lawyer, named Roger Legion.

About the Author

Vince Aiello grew up in upstate New York before moving to Southern California where he attended California Western School of Law. He is admitted to practice law in both New York and California. *Lawyers in the Fog* is his seventh novel. His earlier novels, *Legal Detriment, The Litigation Guy, Legion's Lawyers, Faith Full, Lethal Equity,* and *3 Days till Dawn* were all acclaimed bestsellers. Visit his website at www.vinceaiello.com.

ACKNOWLEDGEMENTS

I would like to thank the following individuals for providing support and, in some instances, the use of their name for a fictional character in *Lawyers in the Fog*:

Ethan P. Aiello
Sarah Rose Aiello
Valerie R. Aiello, RPh
David Anderson
Frida Carranza
Daniela Castro
Glenn Edgarian
Nina Eiffert
Claudia Hernandez
Mark Jurecki
Michael Lim
Alejandro Lopez
Jesus Loredo
Irving Ordaz
Eduardo Pedrero
Jack Prickett
Itzel Trujillo
Alexandra Velasco

www.ingramcontent.com/pod-product-compliance
Lightning Source LLC
Chambersburg PA
CBHW071534260626
47170CB00002B/632